I0670367

The XLs

By
Gerhard Plenert

Outer Banks Publishing Group
Raleigh/Outer Banks

The XLs. Copyright © 2022 by Gerhard Plenert. All rights reserved. Published in the United States of America by Outer Banks Publishing Group – Outer Banks/Raleigh.

https://www.outerbankspublishing.com

No part of this book may be reproduced in any manner whatsoever without written permission except in the case of brief quotations embodied in critical articles and reviews.

For information contact Outer Banks Publishing Group at

info@outerbankspublishing.com

This book is a work of fiction. All the characters and events in this book are not real, and any resemblance to actual events, places, organizations, or actual persons living or dead, is unintentional.

Cover photo by Peter Fischer – Germany

FIRST EDITION – June 2022

Library of Congress Control Number: 2021948075

ISBN 13 - 978-1-7367218-3-4
eISBN – 978-1-0053803-7-3

Dedication

This Book is dedicated to Renee
And the 8 Kids and the Yet to be Numbered Grandkids
Who Work Hard to Keep Life Interesting

About the XLs

"It's a science fiction novel that breaks free from traditional sci-fi themes and explores new worlds while attempting to maintain some level of scientific integrity. It mixes drama and suspense with a scientific twist. It introduces thought-provoking themes that leave the readers emotionally involved as they weave through a tangled web of intrigue both on earth and in space."

- Author Gerhard Plenert

Table of Names / Key Actors

The XLs -
Stephan Torres - the first XL from Vacaville, CA
Chong Cheng - the XL from Malaysia
Frida Zsigmond - the XL from Hungary

XLs Doctors -
Dr. Clawson - the doctor who created the first XL
Dr. Wagton - attempted to recreate Dr. Clawson's surgery

Various individuals -
Rogan - USA President
Blake - Nevada citizen
Butch - Puerto Rico Radio Telescope Operator

Center Earth Citizens -
Abigail - Stephan's girlfriend
Chaviva - Prophet and Senior High Priest for the Tribe of Asher
Abbott - representative of the Senior High Priest
Barak - representative of the Senior High Priest

Aliens -
Gartig-847-X2R-b - The alien that Stephan met at the first encounter

Chapter One

A New Day is Dawning

April, 2020 AD, Vacaville, California

Today wasn't a normal day. Everything seemed like it should be normal. But Stephan Torres wasn't feeling normal. Something was wrong and he couldn't place his finger on it. Waking up in the morning he was feeling a little dizzy and became slowly worse as the day went on.

His normal day started around 10:00 AM. He would get out of bed and the lights would automatically come on. Homes were computer regulated. They were called "smart homes" but Stephan felt they should be called "lazy homes". The technology made it possible to minimize thinking and moving, which, in Stephan's opinion made people vegetables. When he sat up in bed his movement told the computer that it was time to turn on the bedroom lights. As Stephan walked to the bathroom, the bathroom light came on and the bedroom light shut off. Sometimes, just for fun, he would walk back and forth between the two rooms just to watch the lights go on and off in each room. He didn't care if it wore out the electronics faster. Once in the bathroom, drawers would start to open and supplies would appear based on the time of day. This morning it was his toothbrush with new toothpaste already applied, his hairbrush and hair jell, and his shaver that moved to the counter for him to use. The first thing he worked on was his hair. He would spend about an hour working on his hair. It had to be perfect. He greased it up to make it stand about 5 inches above his head. Then he swooped it forward toward the front of his head in a point. It was a work of art which took careful effort and time. And besides, he wanted everything to look just right for the girl at work that he had been eying.

Stephan was 5 foot 4 inches, not abnormal for his Filipino heritage. He was 20 years of age and had just recently moved away from the home of his parents and into his own apartment. He was considered cute by the girls and was generally in demand. But he was oblivious to their interest. His attention to his work took priority over his personal and social life. He enjoyed his work. He enjoyed being the "expert" at the Fette tablet press that he ran. Everyone at the plant recognized him as the expert.

After working on his hair and the remainder of his morning preparations, it was close to noon. He headed for the small living room – dining room – kitchen combination that made up his studio apartment. As he walked into the room the lights went on and the television, which was wallpapered on the wall, automatically came on and switched to all four of the channels that he watched in the morning. The television automatically broke the display into four quadrants so he could see what was happening in each quadrant. He commanded the TV, "upper right," which told the unit which show he wanted to watch. It flipped to show to full screen and the sound came on. He headed for the kitchen and commanded, "Tuna sandwich." Within 5 seconds, a plate containing a tuna sandwich appeared on the counter. The computer knew exactly how to make the sandwich the way he liked it. For example, Stephan had previously instructed it on how much pickle to put into the sandwich. Every sandwich was perfect. He wished that sometime the computer would make a mistake so he could have something to complain about, or to just give him some variety. In any home, the AFDU (Automatic Food Dispensation Unit) was no longer a luxury. It was in every house and was considered to be a standard feature. Sometimes it was so precise that it became boring. It was like the microwave oven. First it was a luxury, then it was desirable, then it became a necessity and was always expected, even more so than a regular oven. The entire transition took less than ten years.

He sat down at the small two-person dining room table and had lunch as he watched the news. An airliner had mysteriously disappeared in spite of all the tracking mechanisms and satellites. No one had any idea what had happened to the plane. It was driving all the experts crazy. It had become world headline news. The frustrating part was that it was difficult to separate the news from the opinions. You couldn't just get a news report anymore. There was always a barrage of experts that spent hours and hours expressing their views on any piece of news that came up. Today was no different. The news report was less than a minute, but the opinions and discussion went on for hours.

Computers and their software systems regulated everything. They controlled your house. They drove your car. They prepared your food. They communicated messages. They watched your every move and knew exactly where you were and what you were doing. They drove Stephan nuts. His favorite thing to do was to travel to the country and go out into the middle of nowhere and shut everything off. Unfortunately, that didn't happen often enough. He wished he could just pull the big plug in the sky and disconnect Technosoft's mother ship software systems which controlled everything through the electronic grids that came into each home via the electrical outlets that the mass of the world's computers were connected to.

A second news report came on reporting that someone, whose power had been cut off because they didn't pay their electricity bill, was found dead in their apartment after two months. Apparently, they weren't able to get out of their unit because the computer had locked up everything prior to the power shutdown and none of the windows or doors could be opened. The AFDU wasn't operational without the computer so there was nothing to eat. And the water didn't flow because it also was regulated and controlled by the computer which had now been shut off. His cellular phone was discovered sitting in the charging unit. Apparently, it was dead as well. So there was no way to communicate and cry out for help. The person literally starved to death, in the middle of his own apartment, at the center of a large city. It was tragic. A debate was going on between the politicians on what should be done about it. They were discussing the merits of creating a new law that would prevent this type of tragedy. But, in Stephan's mind, the real tragedy was that everyone was so dependent on electricity and on computers that they had lost all ability to control their own lives. Sometimes he wished for the "good old days" when life was simpler; when people used computers to make their lives easier. Now it seemed like these roles had been reversed. Now it seemed as though it was the computer that controlled people rather than people controlling the computers.

With lunch completed it was time to get ready to head out to the Johnson and Johnson plant just north of Vacaville off Interstate 505 on the Vaca Valley Parkway. His work schedule was swing shift which started at 02:00 PM and ran to 10:00 PM. He always arrived just in the nick of time.

As he approached the door of his apartment, the door swung open and all the lights in the house shut off. The television shut off as well. The house went into an energy saving rest mode. As he left the apartment the front door closed itself and locked. Only Stephan's voice print would be able to open the door when he returned from work.

After arriving at the plant Stephan had to work his way through the elaborate security system. To work at the Johnson and Johnson pharmaceutical factory in Vacaville required several stages of security. This place was a security marathon. The first swipe of his ID card gave him entrance into the parking lot. The second swipe allowed him through the front door. The third swipe helped him get past the security barriers just inside the front door. The fourth allowed him into the secured production access area. From there he had to go to the men's dressing room where he opened his locker and changed into his GMP (good manufacturing practice - the buzzword for clean-room apparel) approved shoes. The next step was to enter the gowning area where he put on a hair net, and beard cover, a surgeon's mask, and safety goggles. His head was completely covered. Next, he put on coveralls which covered all his clothing from the neck down to the shoes including his arms to the wrist. This was the standard GMP clothing requirement for the food and pharmaceutical industry. Everyone had to go through this procedure if they wanted to go out on the production floor.

The next step was to sit down on a bench divider which separated the "dirty" side of the room from the "clean" side of the room. He pulled off his shoe coverings which were required when his "clean" shoes entered the "dirty" side. Now, with the exception of his hands, he was covered from head to toe with "clean" clothing. His hands came next. He had to wash them with warm soapy water. Then he had to use hand cleaner to disinfect his hands. And last of all he had to put on rubber gloves.

Everyone in the factory had to go through this dressing ritual several times per day. If you left the floor for any reason, you had to repeat the process. Every time you left the production area, for example to go to the bathroom, or to take a break, or to go to lunch, you had to undress to leave the production area, and then you had to completely redress in the GMP clothing to get back into the production area.

Security and cleanliness were incredibly high in this facility because it used controlled substances to create prescription required medications like pills and pain or nicotine patches that would later be sold in drug stores. Sometimes it seemed like every grain of dust from the production process had to be accounted for. Sadly, in spite of all the security, there had been numerous occasions when chemicals and drugs had been stolen from the facility. The result was that accountability for all the chemical and drug ingredients became a priority.

Unfortunately, today Stephan wouldn't make it all the way on to the production floor. He had just made it through the third security swipe of his card, and he was still in the lobby of the J&J facility, when he collapsed to the floor and stopped breathing. Several individuals quickly rushed to his aid. The plant was strong on first aid training and there was no shortage of individuals who knew what to do. The security personnel at the front desk immediately called for an ambulance. While they waited for the arrival of the EMT team, employees performed CPR and successfully resuscitated Stephan. At least they were successful in reviving him to where he was breathing again. But he remained unconscious.

The ambulance team quickly swooped him away and rushed him off to the closest hospital, which was the Kaiser hospital next to the Interstate 80 freeway. The emergency room took him in and immediately started running tests to see if they could determine the source of the problem. Nothing seemed to fit. All the tests came up negative. The next step was to run a Cat scan (correctly called a CT scan – Computerized Tomography). The scan was ordered, and Stephan was rushed off to perform the procedure.

A couple hours later the verdict came in and it wasn't good. Stephan had a tumor in his brain which was about the size of a softball. What made the news even direr was that the tumor was in the center of his brain, immediately between the two lobes of the brain. Surgery to remove this tumor would be extremely dangerous and delicate. The potential existed that his brain could be severely damaged. He could lose both his mental and physical functionality. It was so risky that there weren't many doctors who would be willing to engage in this intricate surgery, especially since the tumor appeared to be attached to both lobes of the brain.

Stephan's immediate family was brought in and consulted. But there really wasn't much of a choice. If they didn't perform the surgery, Stephan would probably never recover. He would be in a coma for the rest of his life until the tumor eventually destroyed his brain. And if they did perform the surgery, he could end up becoming a living vegetable.

The surgery was ordered. Next came the problem of identifying a doctor who had both the skills and the willingness to take on such a high risk surgery. It had never been performed successfully the few times it was attempted. Each time the patient ended up with severe brain damage and, in a few severe cases, ended up being brain dead.

The family was conflicted and in grief. How could this happen to someone so young and with such a promising future? Why did it happen to him? But in the end there really wasn't any choice. All they could do was to go to the hospital chapel to pour out their hearts to God, hoping that he may see fit to rescue Stephan from the disaster that the doctors were predicting.

Chapter Two

Surgery

April, 2020 AD, Vacaville, California

A rash of phone calls was made to doctor's offices all over the world. Fortunately, a doctor was found at the nearby hospital in the UC Davis Medical Center in Davis, California. Dr. Clawson was extremely familiar with brain surgery and had performed numerous brain tumor operations, but never one as critical and as difficult as Stephan's. This would be a challenge for him. This would be risky. But he felt more concern for the boy than for his own reputation. He felt that if he wasn't willing to perform this surgery, then Stephan would be left stranded and untreated. And that just wasn't right. So he agreed to give it a try and to do his best.

Dr. Clawson was in his mid-fifties, six feet tall, balding on the top with a little gray around the edges. He had a dominating and authoritative personality. That was the type of personality that would be needed to accomplish this tricky and delicate surgery. He was married for the second time, his first wife having passed away from cancer five years earlier. He lived alone with his wife in a private and exclusive gated community and enjoyed his privacy. He enjoyed studying and learning, and this type of case fascinated him because it presented a learning challenge. He knew he would learn by doing this surgery. Even if he wasn't successful in helping this patient, what he learned would be helpful for future patients.

Dr. Clawson started by examining all the diagnostic information about Stephan. He also met with the family. He wanted to learn as much about Stephan's history as possible. He wanted to have a thorough understanding of every element that could come into play as a part in this surgery. He asked questions about previous tumors in the family. He asked about abnormalities in the physical conditions in family members. He researched similar cases of other patients with tumors in this part of the brain. He repeated many of the diagnostic procedures, including the CT scan, so he could have the most current data. He also knew that sometimes tests were processed incorrectly and that it was always good to double-check the results, especially in a case as critical as this one.

After several days of research, Dr. Clawson felt he was ready to attempt the surgery. He requested the assistance of a very specific team of doctors and nurses to help him in the procedure. He knew who he could trust, and he wanted to work with the best team possible.

The surgery was scheduled to occur immediately. There was the fear that any delays would allow further damage to the brain and that it eventually would be unrecoverable, no matter how well the surgery went.

Emergency surgeries were a nightmare for hospital scheduling. There was a limited number of Operating

Rooms (ORs) and they were normally booked solid. So when an emergency of this type occurred, schedules were adjusted and shifted. Lots of phone calls were made to doctors, patients, and OR teams. But there wasn't any choice. This surgery was critical.

Stephan was prepped for what was anticipated to be a lengthy surgery. It would take at least six and maybe as much as twelve hours to complete. Computers would be used to scan, visualize, and monitor the surgery. But, even with all the computer sophistication in the world, this type of cutting-edge surgery still required the scalpel and a surgeon's steady hand. As always, there would be surprises as he went through the surgery which required his experience, not the computers, in order to make the correct split-second decisions.

The time arrived. Stephan was prepped, ready, and in the OR room laying on the table. Dr. Clawson had done as much preparation as possible to understand all the potential hazards of the surgery he was about to engage in. He had held a conference call with other doctors from around the world. He felt there wasn't much more that could be done but to proceed. One of the doctors from Amsterdam would even be on call during the surgery and the internet would be used to transmit pictures of the surgical procedure as it progressed. But Dr. Clawson knew that in the end, it would be up to him to get the job done.

The tension in the OR room was so thick it felt like you could cut it with a knife. Dr. Clawson tried to soften the mood by cracking a joke, "Well you're a somber looking group today. Can someone sing us a song to cheer us up a bit?"

"Not sure my singing would cheer anyone up," one of the nurses said.

"We're all just extremely concerned for Stephan," was the assisting doctor's response. "I would hate to be in your shoes. This is almost a no-win situation."

"Well, you're a delight," answered Dr. Clawson. "I wanted a little more cheer. But I see that's not going to happen. So let's get to work."

Part of the prep procedure for Stephan was to shave his head. Dr. Clawson was standing above Stephan's head looking down at the bald head in front of him. He picked up a scalpel and started to make an incision from the forehead all the way to the back of his head. The incision was made in a zig-zag pattern rather than one straight cut. The doctor explained, "I know how Stephan loves his hair. His family told me all about how much time he spends doing his hair. So, I'm going to use this zig-zag so that a scar won't be as noticeable after he recovers and his hair grows back."

"That's about as optimistic as you can get," interjected one of the nurses.

The surgical team had seen this methodology used before and they were familiar with how a straight-line cut would keep the hair from growing back and would be visible for the rest of his life. What impressed them the most was that Dr. Clawson was optimistic that Stephan would one day again be fixing his hair, pasted upward, and pointed toward the front. They all hoped that the optimism would become reality.

With the head scalp cut open the doctor was able to peel the skin over to each side of Stephan's head. Next came the even more delicate process of cutting away the skull bone. This would require cutting a large oval into the skull. It was a delicate process since cutting too deep would damage the lining of the brain and possibly the brain itself. Not cutting deep enough would leave portions of the skull connected.

The tool for cutting the skull bone was a vibrating saw. The idea was that if the saw vibrated rather than stroked it would still cut through the hard skull bone, but the brain membrane and the brain itself wouldn't get cut because it would vibrate back and forth with the saw. It didn't always work out that way, but that was the principle behind using the vibrating saw and usually it worked. There wasn't any other tool that could be used. This saw was the safest.

It was a delicate process and took over an hour just to cut the skull open as the doctor inched his way in a circle around the top of Stephan's head. Eventually the job was completed. Dr. Clawson successfully plucked the skull cap off the top of Stephan's head, exposing the brain underneath. He hoped that he would be able to see the tumor at least partially exposed once the skull cap was removed, but he was disappointed to see that the two lobes of the brain closed in and surrounded the tumor making it impossible to see. The doctor would have to separate the two brain lobes in order to open access to the tumor.

Dr. Clawson delicately cut the membrane separating the skull from the brain and peeled it over to the two sides of Stephan's head. Then he reached in with his two hands and gently pulled the two brain lobes apart. The lobes started to separate, but then there was a tug. The tumor was attached to the brain lobes in several spots.

Using the scalpel, the doctor started to cut the lobe from the tumor. At times the two separated easily, but at other times it seemed that there was a direct welding between the two and as the doctor cut he would cut into the tumor or into the brain tissue to create the separation. If he cut into the brain tissue, he could possibly damage the brain. But if he cut into the tumor, then there was the risk of leaving some tumor cells behind which would continue to reproduce and possibly grow into a new tumor. Neither was desirable, but it couldn't be avoided. The tumor had to be removed.

Dr. Clawson continued pulling, cutting, and separating the brain from the tumor. This process took about three hours. Finally, the two were separated and the tumor needed to be pulled out of the center of the brain. Then the clean-up began. Little bits of stray tumor needed to be cleaned out of the brain cavity. Having completed the cleaning, the doctor folded the two lobes of the brain together. It was then that something strange and unexpected occurred. The portions of the brain that had been sliced into when it was cut away from the tumor, sealed itself with the opposite lobe of the brain. The two lobes seemed to seal together at various points. They moved rapidly toward each other as if they were magnetized. They connected themselves together.

The doctor pulled his hands out of the brain area and stepped back in amazement. He had never experienced anything like that before. It was as if the two lobes were meant to be joined together and now that there was membrane removed that had previously separated them, they were able to join.

The doctor reached into the brain and tried again to separate the lobes, but they would have no part of it. They were joined together and that's the way they were going to stay. Rather than force the separation, the doctor decided that it would be better to leave the lobes together rather than potentially cause more damage to the brain.

Dr. Clawson contacted the on-call doctor in Amsterdam and asked him if he had ever experienced anything like that. The European doctor watched the videos of how the two brain lobes joined and claimed he had never seen anything like it before in his life. This was definitely a first.

Dr. Clawson took numerous pictures to make sure he could document what had occurred, and then he went to work restoring Stephan's head to its original form. The brain was together. The brain's membrane was returned back from its stretched position and laid over the brain. The skull bone was laid back into its former position and the scalp was positioned back over the skull and stitched together.

Now came the wait. Would Stephan regain consciousness? And what would he be like if and when that occurred? Would he be a vegetable? Or would he return to full consciousness with no defects from the tumor and the surgery? There was no way to predict the outcome of this delicate and lengthy procedure. In spite of all the lessons and research performed by science, the workings of the brain still remained a fog and a mystery.

Chapter Three

And So It Begins

April, 2020 AD, Vacaville, California

Days one, two, and three after the surgery passed with no change in Stephan's condition. He lay on the bed in a coma making no motions and no sounds. His family and the medical staff had high hopes that they would see some type of progress. But they saw nothing. Dr. Clawson wasn't surprised. From the research he had seen with other patients it could be weeks before they experienced any progress in Stephan.

Day four came as a complete surprise. When the day nurse entered the room to check on him Stephan was alert, sitting up in his bed, and feeling the stiches on his head. She was so surprised that she forgot to say good morning. Instead, she ran out of the room and placed an immediate call to Dr. Clawson to come visit his patient.

Running back into the room the nurse exclaimed, "Hello Stephan. How are you feeling?"

"I'm feeling strange," was Stephan's curt response. "What has happened to me?"

"The doctor is on his way," explained the nurse. "He'll explain everything to you. I really don't know all the answers so it would be good to hear it directly from him. In the meantime, can I get you anything?"

"I'm starving," replied Stephan, "and I'd like to get my hair back? That was my pride and joy. What happened to my hair?"

"He'll be here any minute," was all the nurse would say. It wasn't her place to tell him any more than that and if she made any mistakes she could get fired. Then she left the room.

Minutes became an hour, but the doctor finally arrived. Upon entering the room Dr. Clawson asked the same question, "How are you feeling?"

Stephan gave the same answer, "I feel strange. What happened to me?"

The doctor went over to Stephan's bed and checked the monitors for his vital signs. He found everything to be in order. Then he sat on the side of the bed and started to explain, "You had a massive tumor in your brain which caused you to pass out at work. You've been unconscious for over a week. We had to operate on you and cut out the tumor, which was an extremely delicate operation and, quite frankly, you seem to be the first successful operation of its type."

"What happened the other times?" asked Stephan.

"For the most part they never regained consciousness, or their brains were so damaged that they became human vegetables," explained the doctor.

"That's horrible," came back Stephan. "Then why would you operate if the survival rate was so bad?"

"Because you wouldn't have ever come out of the coma," Dr. Clawson replied. "There really wasn't any choice."

"Well I'm glad it worked," commented Stephan thoughtfully. "But I don't feel totally the same either. I feel strange. I don't know how to describe it. I feel different but I haven't been able to put my finger on it exactly."

"Different?" asked the doctor. "How is it different?"

"Right now, when I'm talking to you, I'm thinking about something else too," replied Stephan. "In fact, I can be thinking about several things at once. It's weird. I don't know how to describe it, but I can consciously do multiple things at the same time. It's kind of like I'm multiprogramming. One of the programs is the conversation I'm having with you, but another program is thinking about my morning before I went unconscious, and another is worried about how they're going to run the Fette press without me. I'm completely in control of each of these trains of thought at the same time."

"Wow," was all the doctor could say.

Stephan continued, "It's not like a computer which switches back and forth between different programs, sharing the computer's capacity. I'm actually working each of the thought streams simultaneously, like if I had multiple brains. It's the strangest feeling I've ever had."

The doctor was dumbfounded. He had never heard about anything like that before, a multi-processing brain. Science had always thought of the brain as one-dimensional; that it could only run one track at a time. But Stephan demonstrated that the one-dimensionality was a physical constraint. The brain was actually capable of much more than that.

"Another thing that's really strange is that I've been able to access a part of my brain which basically gives me photographic memory recall of everything I've ever experienced," explained Stephan. "I didn't know my brain had enough room to photographically remember everything in my life. But apparently it was all stored up and I just never had access to it until now. This is really cool. I can see every word of every book I've ever read."

Then Stephan suddenly stopped and sat up, as if something strange had just happened to him. "What is it?" asked the doctor.

"I can feel the emotions of every person I've ever come into contact with," responded Stephan. "I don't just see them, I feel them. Like right now I can feel your confusion and slight disbelief." Then Stephan stopped talking, however his words continued to travel into Dr. Clawson's brain, *"I think I can communicate with you without verbalizing what I'm saying. Do you understand what I'm saying?"*

The doctor nodded his head "yes" in total disbelief. Just then the nurse entered the room and she suddenly stopped in her tracks. Stephan had started communicating with her as well, but in a completely separate train of thought from the conversation with the doctor. Stephan was able to send messages to each individual separately and independently. He looked at the nurse and out loud asked, "Did you understand me?"

"Yes," the nurse responded, still in shock and awe.

Then Stephan looked at the doctor and asked, "Did you understand what I was saying to the nurse?"

"No," replied the doctor, also in stunned confusion.

Stephan continued, "Then I can actually communicate to several people at the same time. Try to send a message to me."

The doctor and the nurse both attempted to generate a mental message that they hoped would transmit to Stephan, but nothing happened. Stephan explained, "It looks like I can only send messages out telepathically. But I can't receive them. How curious. I suppose that if you had the same metal abilities that I now have you would probably be able to send messages to me too."

This comment made the doctor wonder to himself, *"Could this surgery be repeated? Was there something that I did that could actually be duplicated so that more individuals had this ability?"* He decided then and there that he was going to research the videos of the operation to see if he could identify what had happened. But, in the meantime, he would keep a close eye on Stephan to see if there were any additional unusual developments.

He was happy to learn that Stephan couldn't read his mind. That would have been even more disconcerting. But he wanted to explore what Stephan was able to feel. "What do you mean by saying that you can feel the emotions of people? Are you saying that you can feel the emotions of someone that you talked to ten years ago, and you can feel what they felt at that time?"

"Exactly," replied Stephan.

"Is that part of what's imprinted into your photographic memory?" asked the doctor.

"Yes," answered Stephan.

"So you have some form of expanded photographic memory, and you have the ability to multi process," summarized the doctor. "Is there anything else that you have? Are there any other abilities that you now have that you didn't have before?"

Stephan decided to send messages to the doctor's mind. Communication by voice seemed extremely slow now that he had this mind-to-mind communication ability. He sent the message, *"Nothing for now. But I'll keep searching and I'll let you know if I discover anything new."* He was able to transmit the message in a fraction of the time that it would have taken to say the words out loud. And now he realized that he could be sending messages to several persons at exactly the same time, whereas voice communication limited him to one conversation at a time. Stephan was starting to get extremely comfortable with his new abilities. He liked being special and different. He liked having his own version of superpowers.

"Is there anything we can get you?" asked the nurse.

"You can get me out of here," suggested Stephan.

"We can't do that just yet," replied the doctor. "We need to check that your recovery is going the way it should. We need to observe you and run some tests for a few more days. Then you can get out of here." But the doctor was also hoping to get a chance to observe these new powers in more detail. He wanted to see if this process was sustainable and if it was repeatable. Would Stephan keep these powers or was this just a short term fluke. And how does he document these abilities. If he's going to share this information with the medical community, he needs some evidence and some tests that the community would find believable.

"Can I see my family?" asked Stephan.

"Of course," agreed the doctor. "But I'd be slow to share your new abilities with them. It may scare them.

They may become afraid of you. I'd be very selective who you share this information with."

"OK," said Stephan, somewhat disappointed. He could see the logic of what the doctor was saying, he could feel some of the same confusion and fear emanating from both the doctor and the nurse. But he was also excited to share the things he could now do.

"I'll get a message to your family that you are awake and that they can come and visit you," responded the nurse.

The nurse left the room and brought Stephan some magazines to read. Then she left and made phone calls to Stephan's family. The doctor also left but before he left, he suggested to both Stephan and the nurse, "Let's not broadcast these new abilities just yet. We need to be careful about how others will react. Let's think this through so we don't have any regrets."

"Agreed," said both the nurse and Stephan.

"I'll be back in a little while," commented the doctor to Stephan. "I want to do some research to see if anything like this has ever occurred in the past. I can't believe this is the first occurrence. But maybe it is. Anyway, let me do some research and then I'll get back to you and we can think through how we should share your new abilities with the public."

"I think you're right," responded Stephan. "I've been thinking this through as we've been talking, and I agree. We don't want to move too fast and make any mistakes."

The doctor departed and Stephan picked up one of the magazines. He looked at the first few pages and then realized that he didn't have to read anything one page at a time. He could go through the pages taking photographic images of them and then recall them and read them later. In fact he could be reading several magazines at the same time using his multiprocessing capabilities. He was excited and decided to test out the idea. He viewed every page of a couple of different magazines, and then, using his multiprogramming capabilities, he started reading each of the magazines at the same time, while he continued doing other things in the world outside of his brain. He decided that he needed to allow his inside world to continue reading, studying, and analyzing. He would use his outside world for communicating. The two worlds could co-exist but still function completely independently. He could have several mental programs learning and studying various topics from multiple books simultaneously. He suddenly realized that his ability to acquire knowledge had become unlimited. And that the knowledge could be recalled at will. He suddenly felt like he could accomplish anything.

Chapter Four

New Found Abilities

April, 2020 AD, Davis, California

Dr. Clawson had difficulty controlling his excitement. The entire reason he wanted to do this surgery was in the hopes that some new knowledge could be attained. But this was above and beyond all expectation. Apparently, he had tapped into an ability that made the brain more powerful than a super computer. The human brain was capable of analysis beyond anything ever imagined. Its ability to learn, process, and recall was more than anyone could have fantasized in their wildest science fiction novel.

The doctor searched the internet. He searched the medical research libraries. He even searched the extraordinary and fantastical fringes of the unexplained. But he couldn't find anything about a multi-processing brain anywhere. It was just too fantastical.

He would continue researching the subject, hoping to find some trace of evidence that something similar had been experienced by someone else. But after an exhaustive search he gave up.

The other aspect of this new discovery that he became obsessed with was the need to identify what had

Gerhard Plenert

happened during the surgery. What might have caused Stephan's transformation? The only part of the procedure that was unusual was the way the two lobes of the brain rejoined themselves together at the end of the surgery. The doctor had scraped portions of the brain when he was separating the lobe from the tumor. Originally, he was convinced that cutting into the brain would have damaged that particular portion of the brain. But now he wondered if that scraping wasn't the thing that allowed the lobes to mysteriously bond together. Was this bonding the secret behind the creation of the superpowers that Stephan now possessed? There were more questions and no were answers. The doctor became convinced that the only way to get any answers was to repeat the surgical process on someone else. But how was he going to find someone else with the same type of tumor in the center of the brain? That would be nearly impossible. And how would he explain to them what he was trying to accomplish? It was all too fantastical.

He decided to advertise a search for similar patients within the medical network. He explained that he had developed a radical new procedure for removing center brain tumors and that he had the grant funding to perform more of these experimental operations. He made the claim about the funding so that third world opportunities would present themselves. He would worry about the funding later. For now he wanted to get his name out there to see if there was anyone who was willing to allow him to perform these radical and dangerous surgeries. He was sure he would get takers. In general, the medical community was afraid of this surgery. And since he was willing to try, he was sure he would find patients and soon have the opportunity to repeat the surgery he had previously performed on Stephan.

Stephan was excited to see his family. His mom and dad were the first to arrive along with a couple of his sisters. Again, the conversation started with his mother asking the same question that everyone else asked, "How are you feeling?"

Stephan was getting tired of the question, so he answered it differently this time, "Feeling like I want to get out of here."

His mother wasn't satisfied with the answer and asked her question differently, "Do you feel affected by the brain surgery that you went through?"

This time Stephan answered the question with, "I feel a little strange, but I think I'm OK. I won't really know until I try to return to normal life. Then there might be some surprises. But for now, I feel great!"

For Stephan the experience was somewhat surreal. With his new abilities he not only heard their verbal communications, but he felt them as well. He knew the intent behind the questions and comments and was often tempted to address the intent rather than the actual question.

"What do you mean by 'strange'," questioned his father. Stephan could sense that his father felt a deep concern for Stephan's well-being. He could sense that his father took pride in Stephan's success. He could sense his love for him. On the surface the question that his father asked would have seemed like he was just prying and could possibly even be interpreted as a little rude. But with Stephan's insight to the intent behind the question he was now able to interpret the question differently.

"I feel slightly queasy," answered Stephan. "That's all. It may just be related to the healing process. Apparently, the injury to my brain was quite dramatic."

"Dramatic is putting it mildly," answered Stephan's sister. "They cut your brain open and then put it back together. There's nothing minor about that. Now there's literally a big hole in your head where the tumor used to be. I always knew there was a hole in your head, but now I have evidence that I was always right."

Stephan was able to sense that behind the smart-alecky-ness of his sister's comment, she was truly concerned for him and wanted desperately for him to be OK. His normal response would have been to say something rude back to her but being able to see her concern completely changed his response. "Hole or no hole, I'll be out of here soon enough and you'll have to put up with me being around again."

"We were thinking that you should come back home and live with us for a while during your recovery," recommended his mother. Stephan could sense that she was feeling the need to be a mother hen who took care of her baby chick. He could sense that complying with her suggestion was more about her feeling fulfilled and useful than it was specifically about his care and well-being. Feeling her love for him he was reluctant to do anything but accept.

"But where am I going to stay?" Stephan asked, knowing that his room had been taken over by his youngest sister.

"You can move back into your old room for a while during your recovery," suggested his mother. Stephan looked at his little sister to see her reaction. She acted pouty about the idea, but he could feel that she would gladly give up her room to have her big brother back in the house. She wanted to take care of him and help him recover as well. So how could he resist.

"OK," he replied. "But only for as long as it takes for me to recover. Then I need to get back to my own life again." Stephan struggled to keep his new powers secret. He hinted at the possibility that things might not be the same, but he was never able to fully and completely explain why. He now realized that, with his insight into their feelings, his relationship with his family had been changed forever.

A short time later his brother arrived as well. He was also extremely excited to see that Stephan had magically recovered. His whole family was concerned that they would never again see the Stephan they used to know. Yet here he was, acting as if nothing out of the ordinary had happened.

Stephan sensed an entirely new feeling from his brother, one he never before would have expected. His relationship with his brother had always been competitive and sometimes even tense, but now he sensed his brother feeling enormous relief. Stephan sensed a happiness from his brother that he didn't expect.

This was when he found himself in trouble. Stephan's multi programming capability was processing his brother's reaction in one train of thought while another train of thought was experiencing the feelings of his little sister. All of these emotions were being processed at the same time that he was talking to his mother and telling her that he would appreciate her taking care of him. What happened next came as a total surprise to his brother, his sister, and himself. His brain sent a mental message to his sister saying, *"It would be cool to have you help me through this recovery,"* while he simultaneously sent a mental message to his brother, *"thanks for visiting me. I was missing our relationship,"* all at the same time when he was verbally telling his mother, "Thanks for helping me out."

His sister was immediately freaked out and took a step backward. Her face had a shocked expression on it, and she said, "What just happened?"

His brother looked at the sister and said, "Did you hear that too?"

The sister said, "What did you hear?"

The brother explained, "Stephan told me that he missed me, but he said it directly to my mind."

The sister explained, "That's different than what he told me. He told me he would like to have me take care of him."

The brother and sister turned to Stephan with questioning looks, expecting some type of explanation. Stephan didn't know what to do. He didn't know how he should react. His confusion caused him to ignore their comments and continue his conversation with his mother, discussing when he would be getting out of the hospital.

"What just happened?" the brother asked Stephan again, insisting on an answer.

"What are you talking about?" asked Stephan, attempting to down-play the entire event.

"You just sent us a message directly to our minds," said the brother. "How did that happen?"

"I don't know what you're talking about," was all Stephan could think of saying. He knew he had to deny the event, or it would just generate a lot more questions that he didn't have any answers for.

"That was freaky," explained the sister. Then she looked at the brother who had the similar experience and said, "I'm not sure what to make of that." They both decided to leave it alone for now. Stephan's denial made it difficult to dig any deeper into what had happened. They would do a watch-and-see to discover if it happened again.

Stephan realized that he needed to control his new ability to send out messages directly to someone else. He needed to keep his communication as a verbal communication and no communication in any other way. Otherwise, he was going to end up in trouble. He knew there was no way he could explain his abilities and he didn't know how long they would last. Perhaps the whole thing was temporary. For now, it would have to remain a secret between himself and Dr. Clawson.

Chapter Five

Now There Are More

April, 2020 AD, Davis, California

Dr. Clawson received a couple responses almost immediately, from two different parts of the world: one from Malaysia and one from Hungary. The one from Malaysia, Chong Cheng, was described as a patient who had a brain center tumor which was only about half the size of Stephan's. This tumor was identified when the patient kept getting seizures. He had been carrying the tumor for about four months since the diagnosis. The patient was lucid except for the epileptic-like attacks that he occasionally experienced. The medical community at the University of Malaya Hospital had no idea how to treat this tumor and had told the patient that he would simply have to live with it for the rest of his life. But, when they received Dr. Clawson's message, they immediately responded.

Dr. Clawson requested the patient to be urgently transferred to his home hospital at the University of California, Davis Medical Center. He agreed to pay for the travel expenses out of his budget. The patient was immediately put on a plane for the 30-hour journey from the Kuala Lumpur, Malaysia airport to the Sacramento, California airport.

The second patient was from Hungry and was in a more dire circumstance. This patient, Frida Zsigmond, had been in a coma for over six months. During that time the tumor had steadily increased and was now occupying two-thirds of the skull cavity. Her brain was slowly getting smashed out of existence. Dr. Clawson was less optimistic about her as a patient for this surgery. He was concerned that it may already be too late for her to recover and that she may be too close to being brain dead. But he also felt that there were lessons to be learned and so he agreed to also have her transported to Davis.

Chong Cheng would be arriving in the Sacramento airport in a couple days. He would be able to travel on a commercial airline flight. However, Frida wouldn't be arriving for about a week. Dr. Clawson had to negotiate special transport for her using an Air Force flight that would eventually land her at Travis Air Force Base just 30 minutes west of Davis. The Air Force transport was outfitted for medical evacuations from Iraq or Afghanistan and was therefore better equipped to handle an individual in a coma. The transport would stop over in Budapest just long enough to load Frida before continuing on to California.

During the wait for these patients, Dr. Clawson carefully reviewed the videos of the previous surgery. He took special notice of each time the brain was scraped or cut in any way. He wanted to exactly replicate the process, if at all possible, with these two new patients to see if Stephan's experience was repeatable or if it was just a fluke.

The doctor also visited Stephan several times a day for the next couple days and spent a couple hours with him each time, experimenting with his new capabilities. He ran several CT scans to see if there was any identifiable change to the brain itself. Nothing new was identified from the CT scans. However, there was a noticeable change in Stephan's knowledge and ability. Stephan was scanning books and studying new languages, advanced science and math, and a variety of other topics. Stephan was able to run sophisticated computations that would rival the abilities of any computer. He seemed to have an unlimited ability to store and process information. At one point the doctor attempted to test the number of parallel processes that Stephan could do simultaneously. He had arranged a test of 30 different distinct and unique activities and asked Stephan to perform as many as possible simultaneously. Some of these tasks involved complex math and physics problems. Some involved the translation of text from one language into several other languages simultaneously. Some involved research into historical topics. Some involved writing or outlining books and articles. Some involved creating presentations on specific topics.

Stephan was asked to spend exactly 30 minutes on each of the individual 30 parallel efforts. The doctor wanted to see how closely each of these 30 items was completed. He wanted to see if there was any sharing of mental capacity which gave priority to one task over another.

Stephan loaded each of the tasks into his memory and waited for the doctor to give him the signal to go ahead before beginning the tasks. At the doctor's mark, Stephan began the parallel processing exercise. Exactly 30 minutes later Stephan informed the doctor that all 30 tasks had been fully engaged in the 30 minutes of effort. The doctor was flabbergasted. How was it possible for one brain to execute 30 parallel activities simultaneously? No computer in the world could do that. Yet here, in the human brain, it was entirely possible.

The doctor asked for the results of each of the 30 exercises. Stephan immediately transmitted the results of each of the 30 activities to the doctor's brain. It was a mental overload and the doctor's brain didn't know how to deal with all of it. The result was that Stephan had to retransmit the information several times to the doctor before he was able to capture all of it. It was just too much for a simple, traditional functioning human brain to handle.

The doctor was dumbfounded. He didn't know what to do with Stephan's abilities.

After four days in the hospital, there was very little excuse for keeping Stephan in the hospital any longer. His head wound was healing perfectly. His CT scans gave no indication of an infection or of any other abnormality. The doctor decided he would release Stephan to the care of his family, but he would insist that he come in for regular visits. He discouraged him from returning to work too soon and recommended another month of rest.

On the day of Stephan's release, while the doctor was still in his office at Davis, he received a message into his brain directly from Stephan who was sitting in the hospital in Vacaville. Stephan said, "We need to talk. I'm ready to go home. Come by for a visit so you can release me." The doctor was dumbfounded. Apparently, Stephan no longer needed a cell phone. It seemed as though he was able to transmit and communicate directly to anyone in the world he wanted to. Did this mean that people with Stephan's ability would be able to hold conversations from anywhere to anywhere without the aid of electronics.

The doctor immediately took the 20-minute drive to the Vacaville Kaiser hospital where Stephan was convalescing and went directly to Stephan's room. As he entered the room he asked, "Did you know that you were sending me a message all the way to Davis?"

"I wasn't sure if it would work but I thought I should try. It's so cool that it worked," explained an excited Stephan. "There isn't anyone else I can transmit to because I'll freak them out, like I did when I accidentally transmitted to my family. Anyway, I want to see how strong this ability really is."

"I'd be curious to see if there is a distance limit," responded the doctor. "Next time one of us travels, we're going to have to try some experiments. I'm also curious if there is any type of time delay in the transmission. Maybe you can text me at the same time that you send the message, and we'll see if there are any time gaps."

"Cool," replied Stephan. "Let's try it. So what's your answer to my question? Can I go home?"

"I'm going to send you home," instructed Dr. Clawson, "but I need you to call me immediately if anything unusual occurs. And that includes both the healing of your skull as well as a change in your abilities. I would still like you to come in for a couple hours every couple days just so we can stay in touch. I think you know that sharing any knowledge of your abilities with anyone other than myself would end up with you getting labelled as a freak. It would cause more stress and confusion."

"But at some point, I won't be able to keep this a secret any longer," responded Stephan.

"You're right," explained Dr. Clawson. "But I think that after we have several people that have this same ability it won't seem so much like an amusement park trick. If we can show that this is a capability that anyone can acquire, we'll have a more believable message. I have two patients coming to me from other parts of the world and I am going to try to repeat the procedure that I did on you. If the process repeats with the same result, then we'll know we have a gold mine here. If the process does not repeat, then we're going to have to have a conversation of how we keep you from becoming a spectator sport."

"I understand," replied Stephan. Then, using his ability to transmit directly to the doctor's brain he said, *"Please keep me informed about these two operations. They'll obviously have an enormous impact on my personal future."*

"Of course," responded the doctor verbally since he didn't have the ability to transmit thoughts. "For now, I'll instruct the day nurse to release you. You can go ahead and let your family know that they should pick you up," explained the doctor as he left the room.

"Thanks," was Stephan's mentally transmitted response to the exiting doctor.

Chapter Six

More Surgeries

April, 2020 AD, Davis, California

The day after Stephan's release from the hospital Dr. Clawson learned about the pending arrival of Chong Cheng from Malaysia. The doctor made arrangements for him to be picked up from the airport and driven 20 minutes directly the UC Davis campus where he would be staying at the UC Davis Hyatt Place Hotel immediately adjacent to the campus. He also received most of the charts and medical history electronically, so he immediately went to work studying Cheng's case, trying to familiarize himself with the dangers.

The doctor was surprised to find that, although the tumor was smaller, it had more connections with the brain than in Stephan's case. This would make Cheng's operation even more delicate. Additionally, the separation of the brain lobes would be more complex since the tumor was more completely encased by the brain than previously in Stephan's case.

The doctor scheduled a CT scan and various tests for the day after Cheng's arrival. He wanted to make sure the patient would be able to survive the surgery. He also scheduled the OR room and the required staff for two days after Cheng's arrival, which would result in a lot of additional schedule shuffling. Dr. Clawson wanted to get to work on the patient's brain as soon as possible. He was excited to see if he could replicate the results.

April, 2020 AD, Davis, California

Stephan came for his regularly scheduled visits to the office of Dr. Clawson in Davis. The doctor had his nurse run the normal set of tests, like blood pressure, temperature, weight, and several blood and urine tests. He didn't expect to find anything out of the ordinary, but he also didn't want to miss anything. If there were any changes it would be critical to know about them as soon as possible.

The tests were completed, and Stephan was waiting as Dr. Clawson opened the door, entered the room, and shut the door behind him before speaking. "So how are you feeling? Has anything changed?"

"Nothing has changed," replied the patient.

"Have you discovered any new capabilities?" asked the doctor.

"Only that my abilities seem to be unlimited," replied Stephan. "I have scanned dozens of books, including textbooks and language training books, and then I'll start various parts of my brain working on each of them independently yet simultaneously. I can keep track of exactly what is happening at each of the parallel processes in my brain. I have yet to encounter a situation where my abilities are tapped out. I can always load more. I can always do more. There simply doesn't seem to be a limit. It's truly incredible. I can now speak several languages and I have completed over a dozen college courses in just a few days. It's completely amazing."

"I can tell by your language that your vocabulary is getting larger," commented the doctor. "How about your ability to sense people's feelings?"

"That's downright scary," replied Stephan. "It's amazing how I can see that people are feeling things that are completely different than what they are saying. I can't read their minds, so I don't know what's behind their deceptions. Maybe they're scared about being honest. Or maybe they have some ulterior motive behind their deception. I can't tell that. But I'm just amazed by the level of deception."

"Interesting," commented the doctor. "Sometimes I mentally try to compare your abilities with those of a computer. You seem to be able to process information more completely and more thoroughly than any computer. And, because of your photographic memory, input seems to be easier for you than for a computer. But what seems to be lacking is output. You don't have a built in printer or display screen. I was wondering if there is some capability that we haven't explored or encountered yet."

"Actually, I think we have to rethink computer output and even the use of cell phones," replied Stephan. "For example, if everyone had my capabilities, why would I need a cell phone? I could directly communicate to their brains, and they could directly communicate back to mine. In fact, I could have a hundred of these communications going on simultaneously. There is basically no limit, and no need for a cell phone. And as for a printer, again assuming that everyone has the same abilities that I have, who needs paper? I can send them my images, my analysis, my thoughts, and we can mentally look at them simultaneously. Who needs power point or a word processor, or even a spreadsheet? I can do all of that mentally and share it with anyone, even if they don't have my abilities. But I can't get anything back from them unless they have the ability to send messages as well. And, unlike electronics systems like computers, my memory seems to be unlimited. Bottom line is that if everyone had the abilities I have then we wouldn't need computers or cell phones or lots of other technologies that we've become so dependent on. Communications would be faster than even the internet can provide. How cool is that!"

"Unbelievable," replied the doctor as he tried to process what Stephan was telling him. "Can you send entire books?"

"Probably, but you would have to have the photographic memory capabilities to be able to recall what I send out or you wouldn't be able to look at it," suggested Stephan. "I'm not sure it would work unless we have the same abilities."

"Well," continued the doctor, "I have another patient from Malaysia that has a similar tumor and I'm going to try to do the same operation on him that I did to you. I'm going to try to duplicate it exactly. If it works, we may have two people with your abilities. Then we'll be able to test out a lot of the ideas that we've been talking about."

"That's really cool," replied Stephan. "I'd love to have someone I can talk to about this ability other than just you. Especially someone else who has the same abilities. You'll have to keep me updated on how the surgery goes."

"I plan to," responded the doctor. "I'll be curious to see how the two of you interact. I'll let you know how it goes. So, I guess that's it for now. See you again in a couple days."

The doctor walked him to the exit, and they said their good byes.

April, 2020 AD, Davis, California

It was the day of Chong Cheng's operation, and everything was prepared. Cheng was scared but at the same time excited. Dr. Clawson was more nervous than Cheng, mostly because right now Cheng was lucid. He was able to communicate and other than his surging headaches he could live a normal life. But this surgery could leave him in a coma, brain dead, or worse. In Stephan's case there was nothing to lose. But in the case of Cheng there was the risk of stealing away years of an active life.

Cheng was of Chinese descent and lived in Malaysia, a Muslim country where 60 percent of the population was Malay and Muslim, 30 percent were Chinese and Buddhist, and 10 percent were Indian and Hindu. The Chinese and Indian population dominated the business leadership, and the Malay population dominated the government positions. Cheng was in his late fifties, about 5 foot 6 inches. He had recently lost his wife to cancer, and he didn't want to succumb to the same fate. He had three children, two daughters and a son. The daughters were married and living in the United States, and the son was attending college in Hawaii. He didn't feel the pressure of family obligations since his children were well on their way into their own lives.

Cheng wanted to proceed. He understood the risks. He knew that the tumor was steadily getting worse, and he knew that the risk of his mind being completely destroyed was extremely high. He felt that the risk of dying versus living a long and prosperous life free from the migraines and the threat of an imminent coma was worthwhile.

Cheng was dressed down and laid out on the surgical table. His head had been shaved. He was waiting for the anesthesiologist to come and do his magic. The wait wasn't long and within a few minutes Cheng was completely unconscious. The orchestra of doctors and nurses were in position and ready to go. Everyone was thinking they were working on a tumor removal except for Dr. Clawson. For him this surgery was a scientific experiment. He wanted to see if Stephan's experience was repeatable.

The surgery proceeded in much the same manner as Stephan's had earlier. There was the additional challenge of dealing with a smaller tumor that was completely encased in the brain cavity.

The skull was opened, the lobes were separated, and the tumor was discovered. Dr. Clawson carefully separated the tumor from the brain lobes. As he

Gerhard Plenert

performed the separation, he made sure to scrape open the same sections of the brain that needed to be opened during Stephan's surgery.

It had been six hours since the start of the surgery and the team was now ready to start putting the brain and skull back together. Dr. Clawson hoped he had accurately reproduced the previous operation, in spite of the differences in the tumor. He was pleasantly surprised when the two lobes of the brain became attracted to each other, similar to what had occurred in Stephan's case. He became excited at the thought that maybe the attraction represented a successful reproduction of Stephan's experience.

The skull was reassembled. The scalp was replaced, and Chong Cheng was moved out into a holding area to be monitored. After four hours of relative stability, he was moved back to his hospital room where he would be monitored by the nursing staff. From here on it was just a waiting game. In the best case, Stephan's abilities had been reproduced. And in the worst case he would never recover consciousness.

Chapter Seven

Cheng

April, 2020 AD, Davis, California

It was one of his regular status checks and Stephan was sitting in Dr. Clawson's office waiting for him to arrive. Suddenly and unexpectedly, he received a surge of energy. It felt like a door had been opened, giving him access to a new world, one that he had never before encountered. He wasn't sure how to react. He mentally sent out a message to the source of this open door asking the question, "Who is this?"

The message came back to him, "Cheng. Who are you? What is happening here?"

Stephan jumped up from his seat and started heading to the door of the office just as the doctor entered. Stephan barked out, "Cheng is awake!"

"How do you know that?" asked the doctor, looking for a phone.

"He just sent me a message and he's confused about what is happening to him," replied Stephan.

The doctor was hyped. Was this a sign that the entire experimental operation had been a success? "We need to hurry and see him," was the doctor's urgent comment. He and Stephan headed out of the office and worked their way across the departments of the hospital toward the section of the hospital where Cheng was located. As they walked Dr. Clawson received a message on his phone which read, "Cheng is out of the coma and is asking for you."

After arriving at Cheng's room, the doctor spoke first, "How exciting to see you back among the living. How are you feeling?"

"Strange," was the reply, causing the doctor and Stephan to exchange smiling glances. Stephan snickered at the response.

"What's so funny?" asked the patient.

"You gave the same answer that Stephan gave when he came out of his coma," replied the doctor.

"Explain what that means?" asked Cheng. "What has happened to me?'

"I think it would be a good idea for Stephan to spend the rest of the day with you and explain what he went through," recommended the doctor. "You have some new abilities and Stephan should compare notes to see if you have exactly the same thing that he has, or if you have something different. And as you go through this exercise you'll learn about your new capabilities. However, let me stress that the world is not ready for what you've accomplished. So, keep it between the two of you for now. Eventually we'll hold a press conference and share your abilities with the world."

"Agreed," replied Stephan. Cheng looked confused so Stephan continued, "I'll explain it to him so he understands what we're talking about."

"Thanks for your help," the doctor replied. Then to both of them he said, "Call me immediately if you have any questions."

The doctor left the room and Stephan explained his story to Cheng. He explained his coma, the surgery, and the discovery of his new capabilities. He explained that the doctor wanted to know if Cheng had also received similar capabilities. He wanted to know if this capability was repeatable, or if it was unique.

After talking for a while, Stephan shifted the explanation to one of his separate trains of thoughts and sent the messages directly to Cheng's brain. The explanation continued in a second partition of both of their brains. Then, leaving that discussion running, Stephan asked Cheng verbally, "Are you able to receive my message separate from the conversation we're having?"

"Yes," replied Cheng. "This is incredible. How is it possible that I can be doing two activities at the same time and be fully in control of both?"

"You can do a lot more than two at a time," replied Stephan. "Using another partition of your brain, start sending me a message as well. I can have dozens of simultaneous trains of thought. I'm guessing you can too." Within seconds Stephan started receiving messages from Cheng. The two of them had successfully become capable of working together in three partitions.

Next Stephan explained how he had photographic memory. He explained his ability to record books into his memory and then go through the books separately, learning from or simply reading the books. He asked

Cheng to try to do the same, and they soon discovered that he also had the same capabilities.

"What if we tried to work together?" asked Stephan. Then he explained, "What if I give you the books that I have already scanned in, and you send me the books that you scan in. The scanning process is the slowest part of the process. That way we can scan twice as much material in the same amount of time. I'm going to try to send you a book and let's see if it comes across OK." With that Stephan began sending the book images of one of his books to Cheng's brain and in a matter of seconds the entire book was received.

"That was really cool," replied Cheng. "Send me all your books and I'll make sure I only scan in ones that you haven't already recorded. I love this. I love reading anyway, but I never dreamed I'd be able to read multiple books at the same time. This is really incredible."

The two of them were like small children with a new toy. They played and shared. They read and scanned. They had no need for any verbal conversation. They even discovered that they could have multiple conversations about different topics simultaneously. In a short amount of time, they were able to share more information than traditional communication could have shared in years.

Frida Zsigmond, from Hungary, arrived at Travis AFB the same afternoon that Cheng came out of his coma. A military ambulance transferred her the short drive to the UC Davis hospital that evening. Dr. Clawson immediately forgot about Cheng, leaving him to Stephan, and made

Frida his priority. He scheduled the medical tests and CT scan for the next day. He scheduled the OR room for the following day. Frida's case was urgent, even more so than in the case of Stephan. She was on the verge of the tumor destroying her brain. It might be too late. He wished he could put her on the operating table immediately, but that would be too dangerous without a better understanding of the patient.

The doctor was no longer worried about Stephan and Cheng. They were successful and off and running. They were spending the entire day together every day. Their intelligence gathering had gained a level of momentum that seemed out of control. While they were busy in their effort to share and learn, the doctor had time to focus his attention on Frida.

The scan came out worse than expected. The tumor was even larger than the previous images had shown. The surgery, scheduled for the next day, would be extremely dangerous. The danger of losing Frida was very high.

The morning of the operation. Frida was prepared. Her tests indicated that her vital signs had attained acceptable levels to proceed. Her head was shaved. The initial cuts were made. With her skull opened the tumor was readily visible and easy to identify. Dr. Clawson went to work immediately cutting the tumor out. During the process he made sure to scar the areas of the brain where Stephan and Cheng had been scarred. He wasn't sure she was going to recover from the damage that had already occurred to her brain because of the enlarged tumor, but he was going to try.

The doctor was coming to the end of his surgical procedure. He was at the stage where he pushed the two brain lobes together. Then, quite unexpectedly because he had become so engrossed in the surgery that he had forgotten the desired reaction, Frida's brain lobes fused together. It was as if the two lobes were excited to see each other and were giving each other a big hug.

After eight hours of surgery, Frida was finally finished and moved to the intensive care unit (ICU). She was now in recovery and in wait mode. Her vital signs would be closely monitored because of the additional complication that her long-term coma presented. It was now a wait-and-see game for the doctor and the rest of the surgical team.

Cheng and Stephan spent three solid days together in the hospital, playing with and practicing their new capabilities. Learning had become so easy for them that they wanted to learn everything. And, since they were the only two in the whole world with their capabilities, they naturally bonded together. Who else would understand what they could now do? No one. They realized that if they went public with their knowledge, they would be deemed a freak show. And they didn't want that to happen. So, they waited until Dr. Clawson was ready to go public.

On the fourth day, the day after Frida's surgery, Dr. Clawson came for a visit to his two patients. He started the conversation with, "As you know, I have tried to replicate the procedure on another patient. She is still in a recovery coma, but I suspect that if the surgery worked, you'll know about it before I do."

"We're excited to see if this keeps replicating," commented Stephan. "One of the big benefits of our new powers is the ability to share. We can learn together, and we can communicate telepathically without the limitations of distance. It's really fun. We look forward to Frida's recovery."

"I also have a surprise for you," continued the doctor. "I arranged for a three-bedroom apartment for you here in Davis. I want to keep you close by so I can continue monitoring your progress. I'd like both of you to move in there right away and spend time together. The third bedroom will be for Frida if she comes around with her capabilities."

"Excellent," responded Cheng. "I'm tired of this hospital bed anyway. It will be nice to get into a real bed."

"The nurse will help make all the arrangements for you to get out of here and get into your new home," commented Dr. Clawson. "Get in touch with me if you need anything. I'll come visit you in your new home tomorrow. I'm going to leave you now, unless you need anything, and go see how Frida is doing."

"Excellent," responded Stephan. "We'll see you tomorrow." Then, after the doctor left the room, Stephan said to Cheng, "What if we turn out to be the only individuals that have this capability. It's sure going to get lonely."

"I was wondering about that too," commented Cheng. "I hope the doctor is successful with replicating his surgery. It would be nice to have a larger group of people with our capabilities."

Then, jumping to an entirely different topic, Cheng continued, "I've always been interested in Science Fiction, and I wonder if there are alien worlds out there somewhere with more sophisticated capabilities, like the ones we're working with. I wonder if it would be worth a try to see if anyone is out there."

"How are we supposed to do that?" questioned Stephan. "There have been transmissions out into space for decades, and we still don't know anything. What makes you think that we can do any better?"

"We know more," responded Cheng. "We already know more. I'm going to spend some time reading what has been done to find ETs out there. I'm curious to see if our ability to integrate all the available research and experiments can lead to any new approaches."

"Go for it," suggested Stephan. "What can it hurt? At the very least you'll learn something that you don't know before. And maybe, if you find something unique that hasn't been tried before, we can move forward and try it out."

"I think I will," replied Cheng. "I'll start with the internet and then, when I'm up to it, I'll go visit the university library. Maybe I'll get a chance to test out my ability to process multiple books simultaneously."

"I'd love to read them too," explained Stephan. "You do the scanning and I'll do the reading. Maybe, if both of us work at it, we'll be able to compare notes. But I'm OK with you doing all the leg work if you insist." He had a joking smile on his face.

Chapter Eight

Frida

April, 2020 AD, Davis, California

It was a week after Frida's surgery. She was still in the coma but her vital signs were stable. Stephan and Cheng were busy with their project of defining a way to transmit messages to other solar systems. They were sitting, visiting in their new apartment, when Cheng rushed out of his bedroom and into the living area where Stephan was seated, mentally shouting, *"I have it! I've found the missing piece that hasn't been tried. I think I know how to transmit a message to another solar system."*

Excitedly Stephan mentally asked, *"What do you think we should do?"* Verbal communication between the two had ceased days earlier. All their conversations were now mental transmissions. The place where they lived had become very quiet.

"The speed of light is not the limit," replied Cheng. *"There are dozens of examples of how particles moving separately will respond simultaneously. For example, if one changes direction, the other also changes direction in a similar way. How do they communicate? They obviously don't communicate in any traditional way*

that we think of. They aren't affected by light. The change in movement could happen just as easily in the dark as in the light. So how do they communicate?"

Going on he explained, *"There are lots of stories of one person sensing a family member's injury or death, and the member is on the other side of the world. But the knowledge of it was instantaneous. There has to be another level or layer of communication that we don't know about."*

"So what are you suggesting?" asked Stephan. *"Are we going to think a message to the aliens?"* was Stephan somewhat sarcastic comment.

"Exactly," replied Cheng to Stephan's surprise. *"We're going to use our new superpowers to blast a message about our world and see if anyone responds."*

"That's a little on the crazy side, don't you think?" asked Stephan.

"What have we got to lose?" replied Cheng.

"How do we do this?" questioned Stephan. *"I've only been able to send messages to specific individuals. How do we send a specific message to some unknown receiver?"*

Cheng explained, *"Astronomers have been busy identifying solar systems and planets that have the potential of life. They have ranked these planets by their potential. I think we send out a message to each of the specific planets that have already been identified with the highest probability of possessing life. Then, on the receiving end, if no one receives the message we can assume they don't have our capabilities. But, if they do receive the message, if they're able to catch it somehow, then we'll know that their intelligence is at least equal and probably greater than ours."*

Stephan wanted more explanation, *"So you're saying we pick a specific planet even though all we know is its name. We can't see it or pinpoint its location. Then we send out a random message in English, which they probably can't understand. We can only hope that someone picks up that message at the other end. Which is highly unlikely, but we have to try."*

"Again, what have we got to lose?" stressed Cheng. *"You're wrong in saying that we only know its name. We can use astrological charts to pinpoint its location and thereby focus our message to a specific target. I already have a list of these planets.   Of course, astronomers are finding more all the time, but we can at least send out to the ones we know about."*

"OK," agreed a skeptical Stephan. *"Like you said, 'What have we got to lose?'"*

With that Cheng transmitted the list to Stephan and suggested, *"Let's both send out messages to all the high potential planets on the astrology list. We can send to all these locations at the same time using different partitions of our brain."*

"Got it," replied Stephan.

Cheng decided that his message would be the same message that had been sent out by the SETI (Search for Extraterrestrial Intelligence) organization during its Arecibo messaging. The message consisting of 1,679 binary digits was chosen because it was the product of two prime numbers which can only be arranged rectangular as 73 rows by 23 columns. It was a well-crafted message teaching lessons about humanity, our planetary system, our number system, and our DNA structure. It made sense to use this message since binary mathematics was assumed to be the only universal language.

It was slow and tedious to send out 1,679 bits of data to each of the over 20 planets that had been declared by astronomers as "potentially sustaining life." But Cheng's ability to mentally transmit the same information on parallel tracks, doing all the plants simultaneously, made it less of a burden.

Stephan decided to send his message in English and several other languages. His message was also sent simultaneously to all the locations. He hoped that the parallel transmissions would somehow make the message translatable. The message was, *"We are looking for life on other planets. If you can receive this message, please respond and we can share information about our locations. Pictures and images would be helpful. And I will respond similarly."*

Neither Stephan nor Cheng had high expectations about how their communication might be received. But they thought this might be faster than trying to transmit the message the SETI way, which was expected to take 25,000 light years to arrive at its destination. Maybe Stephan and Cheng's new abilities would open doors that had never before been considered.

"Now that we've pretty much reached a dead end on that line of research, how about we use our mental abilities to take on some of the mysteries of science?" asked Stephan. That was a personal interest of his and he wanted to experiment with solving larger and more realistic issues.

"*What kinds of things are you talking about?*" asked Cheng.

"*There is no end to the mysteries that need solving,*" explained Stephan. "*For example, we could work on cold energy fusion, or anti-gravity tools like the ability to move large stone structures without fancy equipment or solving Einstein's problem of creating a formula that explains everything, or anti-aging, or we could explore some fun and controversial topics like the hollow earth theory, or we could delve into some more abstract ideas like the existence of God. I don't have anything specific in mind. But we could have some fun stretching our abilities a little.*"

"*I like it,*" responded Cheng. "*We don't necessarily need to work on the same topics. Where do you want to start? I think I'd like to spend some time studying some of the big issues in the area of medicine, like a cure for cancer. What do you want to explore first?*"

"*I've always been fascinated with the concept of a hollow earth,*" suggested Stephan. "*There are lots of places in the world that claim to have experienced people from the center of the earth. There are even people that claim they know where there are some center earth access points. For example, the Bermuda Triangle, or the North Sea close to Greenland, or even in the South Pole. It probably won't get me anywhere, but it would be fun to explore anyway.*"

"*Well, I like it,*" replied Cheng. "*I like having a mission and a direction for applying our talents. I don't like wandering around aimlessly not knowing what to do with these new capabilities.*"

"I'm going over to the library to scan all the books that were ever written on the hollow earth theory and then I'm going to hit the internet too," suggested Stephan. *"Are you game to go with me?"*

"Sure," answered Cheng. *"This is exciting. It's a new adventure."*

"I need to do that as well," responded Stephan. *"I'm concerned that we need to be careful about letting them know exactly where we are. For now, if we're going to meet with them, let's arrange to see them at some neutral location, like a park or something."*

"That seems reasonable enough. I know that the doctor has some concerns about our safety and so that is probably a good suggestion for you, but I don't think my family will be able to afford travel from Malaysia anytime soon."

The two proceeded to send telepathic messages to their family members. It was a lot easier than using the phone. And then, as they sensed questions or concerns in their family's minds, they would send their responses. Using their telepathic tools, and their abilities to sense the feelings and emotions of their family members, they were able to respond much quicker than if they conversed verbally. The entire communication took seconds, rather than minutes or even hours using any other communications tool like the telephone or the internet social media tools.

The nurse was checking Frida's vital signs. It had been nearly two weeks since her surgery. There hadn't been any indication of a change since the surgery. It began to feel like the surgery had been a failure, at least for Dr. Clawson's expectations. As the nurse checked the IV drip lines Frida suddenly jerked. Her legs and arms swung out over the sides of the bed. Her left arm smacked the nurses butt and gave her such a surprise that she jumped forward, knocking over the IV pole and falling to her knees.

The IV bottle hit the ground and splattered fluid over the floor. The nurse fumbled to quickly recover, cursing as she struggled to regain her composure and get back into a standing position. She didn't know which was worse; the mess that she created, or the embarrassment that she felt.

Once she recovered, she went over to Frida's bedside and checked to see if she was awake. But she wasn't. Frida lay on the bed with all her legs and arms flayed out to both sides of the bed. It was a strange sight. The nurse tried to move her legs and arms back on to the bed and under the covers but it was as if Frida had suddenly frozen into that position permanently. It was impossible to move her limbs.

The nurse placed a call to Dr. Clawson to come check on his patient. Then she went to work cleaning up the mess and reconnecting Frida to a new IV bag. She didn't want anyone to see what had happened. It would be hard to explain why she knocked over the IV pole.

Ten minutes later, just as she had finished cleaning up the mess, the doctor walked into the room, "What happened?" he asked, wondering why his patient was spread eagle.

Gerhard Plenert

"No idea," was the nurse's reply. "She just suddenly flayed herself out like that and hasn't moved since. She's stiff as a board. I can't move her arms or legs back on the bed. I was hoping you had some idea on what I needed to do here. It's the strangest thing I've ever seen."

The doctor didn't answer. He lifted Frida's eyelids to see if there was any recognition or dilation but he saw nothing. He took her wrist and felt her pulse, unnecessarily because he could have looked up at the monitor and seen what her pulse rate was. Then he finally spoke up, "I guess we just keep monitoring her. She seems to be doing fine, but we won't know anything until she comes out of this. That is, if she comes out of this."

The doctor and nurse went to the nursing station. The nurse went behind her desk and sat down while the doctor reviewed Frida's chart and made some notes. Suddenly the nurse jumped up and pointed towards Frida's room. The doctor turned to see what she was pointing at. There, standing at the doorway of her room, was Frida, looking out at the two of them. She started talking, but it made no sense to either of them.

"English?" requested the doctor.

"Of course," replied Frida. "Where am I? What has happened? Why do I feel so strange?"

The nurse had come around, out from behind her desk and took Frida by the arm in order to direct her back to her bed. "You've had extensive surgery and you're not ready to be walking around," said the nurse.

Frida allowed the nurse to lead her back to the bed. The doctor followed close behind.

"Once you get settled into your bed, I'll explain what has happened to you," the doctor told her.

Once she was back where she belonged, the doctor explained how she had had an enormous brain tumor which put her into a coma. She was now in the United States where he had just recently removed the tumor. She was now in recovery from the surgery.

The doctor went on to explain that he was very concerned about the surgery. It had been extensive, and the tumor was very large. He wasn't sure how much brain damage had occurred. He explained that he was thrilled to see her come out of her coma.

"Why do I feel so strange?" asked Frida. "It's as if dozens of things are happening at once. My mind is very jumbled." Then, without realizing it she sent a mental message to the doctor, *"Will I be OK?"*

The message was unexpected and caused the doctor to step backwards. Once he had regained his composure, he realized that this operation was another success. Frida had gained some of these mysterious abilities that his other patients had. He said to her, "You will be more than OK. In fact, I have a couple guys that are going to want to talk to you. They will be able to explain what has happened to you much better than I can since they have also gone through a similar experience."

The doctor took his cell phone and called Stephan. Stephan answered with, "We know. We sensed her abilities. Frida is alive and well and has our powers. We're going to spend the next few days orienting her. We'll be there shortly."

The doctor waited around long enough for Stephan and Cheng to arrive. He introduced them to Frida. He had never been so excited in his life. He realized that he had found a medical procedure that would change the human mind, and through that would be able to change the world. He had planned to leave but couldn't drag himself away. He ended up staying behind to observe the interactions between the three super brains. He watched the interaction, but it was extremely strange. He could see smiles, and even hear laughter, but there was no verbal communication. All communication occurred via mental transfer. He was only an observer. He knew he would have to teach the world about this new capability and maybe someday he would also be able to enjoy these newly discovered capabilities.

Eventually he gave up. He wasn't able to participate in the conservation. All he could do was observe. And that simply wasn't very satisfying. After fifteen minutes of watching, he decided to leave.

Chapter Nine

A New World Order

April, 2020 AD, Davis, California

The doctor decided he needed to get the message out. He wanted to share his discovery with the entire world. Now that he had a critical mass of three successful operations, he felt it was time to get the word out about what he had been doing. He registered himself through the Health Service Network which offered him a chance to broadcast his message over a medical social media site. This was how he would initially be sharing his discovery. He wanted the world to know that a major world-wide transformation was about to take place and that the transformation would be available to everyone. He titled the broadcast, "The XLs: A Medical Breakthrough which will eliminate the need for computers and cell phones." He chose to label his three super brains the XLs because he thought of them as excelling at what they were doing with their new super capabilities. He hoped that the title of his seminar would create some interest. Little did he know how much attention it would generate.

The broadcast was set for one week out and he decided that he was going to use videos of the three

"XLs" as he was calling them. The second day after her recovery he visited Frida's room, where the three were congregated, and asked, "I need you to work together and come up with some kind of demonstration of your capabilities and powers. Ultimately we want to get as many people as possible on the same wavelength as you and so we need to share the knowledge."

"Why don't you have the operation performed on yourself?" asked Frida.

"Because right now I'm the only one that knows how to do it," responded the doctor, "and if something was to go wrong with the operation on me, the knowledge would be lost. I have to get the message out and get this procedure documented before I have someone do it to me. And someone has to successfully perform the operation on other patients before I can allow him to take a risk on my brain. I definitely want to have this operation performed on myself, but we have to make sure the knowledge transfer is solid before we go forward with the procedure on me."

"That's true," agreed Cheng. "Right now you're the only source of the knowledge. Are you going to be operating on anyone else?"

"Not right away," replied the doctor. "I want to document and share the knowledge so that I'm not the only one doing the procedure. That will consume me for some time. After that I, and hopefully several others, will be performing the operation on hundreds of people. For now I need to get the information out there so that I can build up a quorum of individuals that will be involved in this procedure. And that will require some demonstrations. And that's where you come in. I need your help in putting something together."

"Got it," replied Stephan. "Give us some time and we'll come up with something that demonstrates our new capabilities to the world."

"Thanks," responded Dr. Clawson. "I'll come back tomorrow to see how you're doing."

"By tomorrow we'll all be hanging out in our apartment," responded Stephan. "Frida's getting released and we're going to go back to our home."

"Then I'll visit you there," responded the doctor.

Over the next couple of weeks, the doctor and his three patients spent the best part of each day analyzing their new capabilities, documenting numerous examples, and attempting to determine how best to demonstrate them to the world. They planned to demonstrate their telecommunications ability, showing how they could talk to each other no matter how far apart they were. They also planned to demonstrate their multi-processing analytical ability and compare it to a computer, showing how they could out-process even the best computers, and then share the analytical information to their team members without requiring anything to be printed. They tried to make sure the demonstrations were as realistic and verifiable as possible by having neutral individuals watch the demonstrations and certify their authenticity. The biggest challenge was to find someone that the general public would trust. Amazingly, most people, including the ones that were supposed to be their witnesses and who were observing the events, thought the demonstrations were Hollywood stunts.

As they proceeded, they discovered that their talents seemed to be unlimited. They could hold an unlimited number of conversations between themselves simultaneously while they were performing analysis, reading an unlimited number of books, and studying new languages. They attempted to test the limits of their abilities, but the limits were unreachable.

Even Dr. Clawson struggled to understand the full extent of their capabilities. He was especially amazed when he learned about the two specific areas of research that Stephan and Cheng had decided to address. Stephan's search for a hollow earth enticed him. It was always assumed that the earth had a molten core. But Stephan's research suggested that the reason for a belief in a molten core was based on the fact that sound vibrations like an earthquake could not travel through liquid. But similarly, sound vibrations would not travel through empty space. The results would be the same. So which one was it; molten or hollow?

Cheng's research was similarly interesting. Finding a cure for cancer was incredibly complex. If there was only one type of cancer, if all cancers were the same, it could become the focus of attention. But since there were so many different types of cancer, caused in so many different sources, it becomes a series of entirely independent research efforts. The conclusion was that Cheng had to address one type of cancer at a time. He decided on breast cancer as the first surge of his effort. It was the biggest cause of death in women, and he was more interested in helping the ladies than in helping the male population. To him it just seemed logical.

Frida was also interested in jumping into some area of research, but her interests were focused on the world condition. She decided to see if there was anything she could discover in the area of cold energy fusion. She felt that problems like poverty would have a better chance of being solved if there was access to an infinite amount of energy for everyone.

Dr. Clawson was also intrigued by the threesome's attempt to contact other planets and that the XLs even thought it was possible. Frida had also joined in on the idea and had decided to send out a message of her own. She tried a different approach. She sent out the same messages in several additional languages beyond those that Stephan had chosen and sent it to several specific planets. All three of them felt that this search was a long shot, but no one saw any harm in trying.

Over the next week the XLs made their first discoveries. Surprisingly it was the long shot that received the first hit. The three XLs were sitting together in their apartment, going through the information they had scanned in. They were reading every book they could find on each of their target subject areas. They were also researching the internet using the information that was readily available from all sources.

Stephan suddenly and excitedly jumped up and, rather than saying anything verbally, he simultaneously transmitted a message to each of the XLs and to Dr. Clawson. *"I think I've discovered an access point to the center of the earth. I've been observing satellite transmissions and analyzing them for various parts of the earth. My search has focused on finding areas that are rarely visible. I'm assuming that any access point to the center of the earth must be hidden in some way or everybody would know about it. So I decided to try to find places in the earth that lacked visibility."*

Continuing on he said, *"I also used information about lost flights and missing ships, a Bermuda Triangle approach, to see if I could learn anything. The last item that pointed me to this location was mirages. Ships out at sea claimed to see mirages of forests and even buildings in this area. That seemed strange. I have successfully narrowed my search down to one specific location which meets all these requirements."*

Cheng spoke up using nonverbal messaging and said, *"Enough already! Tell us where this location is."*

Stephan continued, *"It's at the northeast corner of Greenland. It's the only place in the world where I can't get a satellite image because it's always overcast. And they have stories of people who claim to have come from the center of the earth."*

"So what do you plan to do?" asked Frida.

"I plan to go there and investigate," answered Stephan. *"I want to see if my analysis is correct."*

Dr. Clawson had been included and was listening in on all the messaging, but he wasn't able to send any of his own messages. He went immediately to visit the XLs and arrived at the apartment. He joined in on the conversation. His communication had to be verbal, even though he was successfully able to receive all the non-verbal transmissions of the XLs. He entered the apartment and said, "I've been listening to everything, and I have a suggestion. I have some funding and I expect to get a lot more once we share our knowledge. I'm willing to use some of that funding so you can go to Greenland and investigate further."

"Will all three of us be able to go?" asked Stephan.

"Do all three of you need to go?" questioned a skeptical doctor.

"It would be fun," responded Cheng.

"We could help each other in the analysis of whatever we find," responded Frida.

"But would it be necessary?" challenged the doctor. "I think it would be a good test to see how well the three of you worked together if you were in separate locations, especially on the other side of the world in a place as remote as Greenland."

"You're right!" agreed Cheng. *"That would be an interesting test. Let's give it a try. Besides it would be easier to maintain our own research here rather than in some remote location in Greenland. Stephan, are you OK traveling to Greenland alone?"*

"Totally," replied Stephan.

"Then it's settled," suggested the doctor. "Stephan is going to Greenland as soon as we have this Webcast completed and the two of you will be supporting him remotely."

"Agreed," answered Stephan.

A couple more weeks had passed, and it was time for the Health Services Network Webcast. Presentations were ready. Video demonstrations of the XLs and their abilities had been made. Dr. Clawson was prepared to make his case for a wide-spread rash of similar operations.

The presentation kicked off with an introduction. The doctor explained the reason for Stephan's surgery, and the complexity of the problem. He discussed the location of the tumor using graphics and charts. Then he explained the extraction process that he went through. He discussed his concerns and any complications.

Next he discussed a similar operation on Cheng and Frida. He explained that the successes with Stephan made it important to see if the process was repeatable. And he tested the repeatability on these two individuals.

Finally, he came to what everyone was waiting for. He explained how this connected with the title of the presentation, "The XLs: A Medical Breakthrough which will eliminate the need for computers and cell phones." He explained the XLs' abilities to photographically record materials, then to read the various sets of material simultaneously, and to run analytical exercises at the same time. Next, he discussed the XLs' abilities to telecommunicate. He presented videos of each of their capabilities.

His final message was that if everyone had this capability there would be no need for computers or cell phones. Everyone could instantaneously communicate with anyone else, and they could do it without interfering or disrupting anything else they were doing. Additionally, he demonstrated how the multiprocessing abilities were stronger and more powerful than any computer anywhere.

After the 45-minute presentation he was barraged with questions. "How is this possible?" "Was the brain damaged?" "What abilities have they lost?" "Can they still function socially?" He was bothered by some of the questions that he considered ridiculous like, "Are they a danger to society?" "Shouldn't we keep them from using these abilities? They may be too powerful for us to control." "Won't this cause them to overexert their brains and cause damage to their brains or other brains?"

Dr. Clawson answered the questions to the best of his ability, and the 45-minute presentation ran into three hours. The consensus from those calling in was that the operations needed to be restricted and that these operations were to be discontinued until the three XLs were thoroughly studied and their abilities investigated. Some individuals even suggested that there needed to be legislation that controlled the activities of the XLs and that restricted any future operations.

The doctor was flabbergasted. Rather than achieving his goal of widespread acceptance and use of the procedure, he was attacked by individuals who were fearful that these XLs may somehow overpower them. Some individuals even suggested that the XLs be confined into a restricted location which limited their movement. They talked about institutions where the XLs should be housed. They would be treated like lab rats in a medical prison.

The doctor ended up regretting that he had shared this information with the general community. These idiots basically wanted him to put his XLs in jail, and that wasn't going to happen. After disconnecting the webcast, the doctor turned to his XLs and said, "We need to get you out of the country immediately. These idiots want to turn you into lab rats. They want to take your life away from you. Rather than sharing this ability with others, they want me to restrict the three of you. So, I think you need to run and hide somewhere where they won't have access to you and won't be able to find you, at least for now until we get consensus that your abilities are an asset and not a threat. The world is just not ready for the dramatic change that the three of you represent."

"This is the stupidest thing I ever heard. They could see in the videos that we aren't a threat. They've watched too many sci-fi movies and they think we are some kind of monsters. I totally agree that we need to get out of here as soon as possible," transmitted Stephan. *"I'm already searching for a new place for us to live. I don't think Greenland is going to be that place even though I want to go there ASAP for my own reasons."*

It wasn't going to be as easy as just packing up and leaving. Each of the XLs were members of a family. And the family relationship couldn't simply be ignored. At this point, their families had all listened to the doctor's transmission about the XLs capabilities. Members of the families were stunned, surprised, and generally in a state of unbelief. Frida's family would be the least affected. They had previously given her up for dead. And although they were ecstatic about her revival, Frida felt the least connected. She decided that it would be best to maintain the distance in the relationship that her tumor and resulting coma had already generated. She knew that future communication would need to be limited while she was in hiding. Maybe, at some future point, when all this attention blew over, she would be able to reconnect with her family. She looked forward to that time, but for now, keeping a distance would be the best strategy.

For Cheng hiding out would be slightly more difficult. He knew that this separation would mean that he would have to temporarily break contact with his children. It would be painful because he still missed his wife, and the children were his way of staying connected with his previous life. But he knew that upcoming break would be critical and unavoidable.

It was hardest for Stephen. He had already sacrificed his job, finding the need to spend as much time as possible clarifying his new powers and syncing up with his XL friends. His family, and especially his parents, were extremely important to him. The thought of being disconnected from them would be extremely hard. Lately they were a little distant and confused about how to communicate with him with his new found capabilities, but that was to be expected considering the strangeness of the XL powers. But he also knew that his family would get past the strangeness of the situation. Family was the most important. Family was everything. How was he going to be able to get along without them? Frida and Cheng had become somewhat of a substitute family and that would help, but it wouldn't be the same. There were cultural gaps. These new friends would never be substitutes for his parents or his siblings. This new superpower was presenting some very painful challenges to him. He wasn't sure he would be able to cope with all the changes, especially as they related to his family.

Chapter Ten

The Escape

April, 2020 AD, Cusco, Peru

Cusco was a beautiful city in the center of Peru sitting at an altitude of about 12,000 feet. It was filled with Inca and pre-Inca artifacts and was a haven for Early South American studies. It was once the center of the Inca civilization. It was civilized enough that few people would ever think of it as a hideout, but it was also isolated. It became the perfect place for the XLs to disappear to.

The three XLs, Frida, Stephan, and Cheng traveled from Denver to Houston using their own passports. Then they used fake US passports for their travel to Lima. The fake passports were necessary for a couple of reasons. They hoped to divert anyone trying to follow them. Additionally, both Frida and Cheng would need special visas to go to Peru on their home passports. The fake US passports simplified the entry process into Peru. They abandoned their cell phones in Houston, thereby eliminating any potential of being tracked that way. They also left their bank accounts and credit cards in limbo, draining as much cash as possible before they departed, and then leaving the accounts unattended.

From Lima they caught a local flight to Cusco. They purchased each of the air tickets separately and used a third name with fake IDs for the final leg of their journey. They hoped this would be enough to confuse anyone trying to follow them.

Once they arrived in Cusco, they picked up new cell phones and made a few calls, finding a hotel for the next few nights. They chose a hotel located in the heart of Cusco, along the Paseo de los Heroes and only 400 meters from the Main Square. The Cusco Kenamari Hotel was close to the Wanchaq Train Station. It featured soundproofed rooms which the threesome considered critical. It had free Wi-Fi, another important feature. The Cathedral of Santo Domingo, which was one of the areas' main attractions, was within the World Heritage historical center situated one block from Cuscos´ central square and three blocks from the Kenamari Hotel. The Velazco Astete International Airport was a seven-minute drive away with free airport shuttles. It was beautifully decorated in the traditional Spanish architecture and well maintained. It became the perfect hideout.

Once they were settled at the hotel, they set up new untraceable e-mail accounts. They had planned these accounts earlier with Dr. Clawson for future communication.

Next, using the hotel as their home base, their new phones allowed them to find a new three-bedroom home that they could rent. Within just a week and they were able to move into this new home as soon as the place was prepared for them. The home was on the outskirts of the city, in one of the more affluent areas. Affluence meant distance. In Peru, as in the United States, people living in affluent residential areas tended to keep to themselves and were more focused on their own lives. That was the type of neighborhood that the three needed.

Now, with everything in place, and with Dr. Clawson using budget money to resolve any of their financial burdens by giving them plenty of cash before they departed, they were free to go back to their research and discovery efforts. They desperately wanted to make a difference in the world using their new found powers.

Fortunately, or unfortunately, they were distracted by the enormous cultural learning opportunities that Cusco offered. Since it was the center of the Inca Empire, it allowed the threesome to visit places like the Sacred Valley, and Macchu Picchu, and Sacsaywaman where one of the great Inca – Spanish battles occurred. The area fascinated each of them and they each became experts on South American archeology.

Much to the surprise of the threesome, one week after they were settled into their new home, they received a message. They knew the message was alien because it was all numeric in a code similar to the one that had been transmitted earlier by Cheng. When they attempted to decipher the code, it come out extremely similar to the message that Cheng had sent. Within the message they found a question specifically asking for their location. But how are they supposed to give their location?

"I have an idea," spoke up Cheng. *"If we send them photographic images of our perspective of the stars, they should be able to triangulate our location using their own star maps."*

"Excellent idea," responded Stephan. *"I'll go out there tonight and map the stars and send them our version of a star chart. Then I'll ask them to similarly send us their star maps. We can see if we're capable of figuring out where they're located."*

"Perfect," Frida said. *"I'm excited to learn more about them. Can you also ask them to send us images of their civilization?"*

"I'll do that by sending them images of us," suggested Stephan. *"Hopefully that will let them know that we would similarly like to see images of them. I need the two of you to pose for me so I can take a pictographic image of what our species looks like."*

"Good enough," responded Cheng. *"Where would you like us to stand?"*

"I think you should get naked so they can see what the human body looks like," suggested Stephan.

"Fat chance of that happening," responded Frida. *"You're not going to get me to pose naked in front of you two perverts, let alone send my naked image across the universe for aliens to see! You're going to have to take the picture fully clothed or not at all."*

"OK! OK!" laughed Stephan. *"I was just joking anyway. I wanted to see your reaction."*

"I was ready to do it," responded Cheng.

"I knew you were a pervert," interjected Frida. *"Next you probably wanted to do some kind of weird sexual pose to show them how we copulate."*

"I'm willing to sacrifice anything for science," replied Cheng.

"OK! OK!" laughed Stephan out loud and in an uproar. He couldn't control himself. *"Let's get this over with. Get posed so I can take a pictograph image picture in my mind."*

Stephan captured the images. Later, in the middle of the night when the stars were at their brightest, he captured images of the stars surrounding the earth at that moment of time. Shortly after using his photographic memory to capture the images, he transmitted the stars and the image of Cheng and Frida to the source of the original message. He had no idea how far he was sending the message, or if he would ever hear from them again.

Two more weeks went by and the threesome had still not heard a response from their new alien contacts. They were now comfortably settled in their new residence. They decided to not worry about receiving a response. Maybe the previous transmission had just been fluke. They returned to their research efforts. Each kept themselves busy solving their versions of the problems of the world.

Their personalities had started to emerge. Up to now they had each been extremely wrapped up in playing with their new toy, a multiprocessing photographic brain. But now they were starting to interact more. Cheng's love of cooking came out and he became the king of the kitchen. He didn't always prepare the food.

When he did it was because he wanted to. With his new capabilities he found that using his physical body to work on preparing food and later sitting down to consume it, didn't stop the rest of his brain from continuing its endeavors. The brain's analysis process seemed to be entirely independent from physical reality.

Stephan loved sports and could often be found sitting in front of the television. He especially enjoyed American football, but that was hard to find on a Peruvian television. So he was slowly becoming enamored with soccer. He watched the matches from all over the world and was starting to identify favorite teams.

Stephan would often frustrate his counterparts because he wasn't the cleanest. He would leave clothes and dishes lying around, much to the irritation of his roommates. He was also engrossed in his grooming. He especially focused on his hair, often spending hours preparing his hair in the mornings.

Frida was more of a mixed bag. She was the pessimist of the group. She would express frustration about things that the other two thought were ridiculous. Things like leaving the light on in a room that was empty or not recycling seemed to be pet peeves. But she also had her quirks. Sometimes it would be afternoon before she climbed out of her pajamas and got ready for the day.

Eventually though, the three compromised on a few routines. For example, they developed the ritual of taking a morning stroll. They even had a route mapped out through their neighborhood and this became their exercise program. This would also be a time for bonding, where they would catch up with each other's efforts.

Every morning at around 09:00 AM they would set out for their walk. It wouldn't always include all three of them. Sometimes only one or two would take the walk. But they did the best they could to keep their bodies as active as possible.

They had also acquired a car. Their fascination with South American culture and history had become somewhat of a combined obsession for the three of them. They enjoyed traveling to the various tourist and archeological sites together to see what they could find. This was happening so often that it had also become part of their routine.

They would go for a ride into the countryside and took turns selecting the destination. All the other days were spent transfixed in their own research.

In the evenings they would have an early dinner, depending on when they returned from their travels. Sometimes they would eat out along the way. Then, the rest of the evening was spent focused on each of their individual research and study efforts. They were starting to become like an old ritualistic married couple. The only problem being that they weren't a couple, they were a threesome.

Romantic attraction hadn't become an issue. Frida thought Stephan was cute, but none of the three seemed interested in romance at the moment. They were just too busy for that nonsense. At one point Cheng had asked the question, *"I wonder if we have babies will they be like us or will they be muggles?"* The reference to muggles was stolen from the Harry Potter books where muggles were the ordinary people of the world. His comment went unnoticed and unanswered.

It had been nearly a months since the threesome came to Cusco. They were settled into their evening routines when suddenly and unexpectedly Stephan spoke up by sending a mental message, *"I think we need to resend our message to the aliens. It doesn't seem right that they haven't responded to our earlier replies."* Interestingly, when someone spoke up, it didn't interrupt anyone's train of thought. All of their trains of thought could continue on. A new train would be initiated for the conversation that Stephan was trying to have.

Cheng was the first to respond, *"I was thinking the same thing earlier. Did we make some incorrect assumptions in the message we sent out? Was there something in the message that may have been offensive? I wasn't coming up with any answers."*

"Or were they just trying to find out our location so they could invade and conquer us?" interjected a pessimistic Frida.

"I don't buy that science fiction doomsday stuff about aliens trying to take us over." inserted Stephan. *"If we went to another planet, it wouldn't be to invade them, it would be to learn from them. I see no reason to assume that aliens wouldn't want the same thing from us. I sure wouldn't want to spend light years of travel time just to find a planet that I could steal from and beat up on. I would want to learn from them."*

"Agreed," responded Cheng. *"Let's try again, each of us sending a message of our own. Maybe these aliens are being selective on who they want to talk to."*

The threesome proceeded to do exactly that. Each sent out a message with a picture hoping that they would be the first that the aliens decided to respond to.

Chapter Eleven

Greenland

April, 2020 AD, Greenland

Another week had gone by and Stephan's traveling urge had returned. He decided he had done all he could here. He needed to leave Cusco and head off to explore Greenland. He was even more convinced that the northeast region of Greenland would contain the access point for the center of the earth. He was going to prove he wasn't crazy, as his family and friends had told him numerous times in the past. He would prove them all wrong.

He checked with Dr. Clawson who readily confirmed that he had the funds to cover the travel costs. Dr. Clawson didn't want to discourage anything his three XLs wanted to do, even if it sounded crazy to the average mind. He was convinced that the superpowers of the XLs would send their minds in directions that the normal mind would never consider venturing in. He didn't want to discourage anything.

With Dr. Clawson's approval, Stephan started researching Greenland. He wanted to learn how to travel around in the country, especially focused on the northeast corner. He was amazed to discover that the total population of Greenland was less than 57,000 people. In the United States that would be considered a very small city. The land mass of Greenland was 2,166,086 sq km, which was significantly larger than Alaska, the largest state in the United States, which was 1,518,800 sq km. In fact, Greenland was approximately the size of the total land mass of the two largest states in the United States, Alaska, and Texas. Yet it has only a fraction (less than 10 percent) of the population of the smallest of the states.

Then Stephan decided to look at the temperature of the country. He was shocked to learn that the daily mean temperature of Nuuk, the capital of the country, was -1.3 F with an average high of 6.7 in Jul and average low of -7.9 in March. Nuuk was the word for "cape" because of its position at the end of a fiord on the eastern shore of the Labrador Sea. Nuuk was the seat of the Greenland government as well as the country's largest cultural and economic center. It had the unique distinction of being one of the smallest capital cities in the world by population. It was also the northernmost national capital in the world.

Stephan was about to leave Peru, which was near the equator, and travel to a country where he would spend his entire time in below freezing temperatures. How was he ever going to be able to buy the type of clothing he needed for this trip in Peru. That would be nearly impossible. He would have to order it on-line. That would cause a couple weeks of delay in his travel, but he didn't have any other option.

The next challenge Stephan encountered was in planning how to travel to Greenland. It wasn't exactly a tourist attraction, so it didn't have a lot of flights in and out of the country. There were only five access points; two. Two from Canada (Iqaluit and Ottawa), two from Denmark (Copenhagen and Aalborg), and one from Iceland (Reykjavik). He would have to travel to one of these locations and from there travel Greenland. After further investigation, the Canada and Iceland options traveled so infrequently (and sometimes not at all) that the only viable option was to travel to Copenhagen and then back to Greenland.

On the Greenland end of the trip, there were only two viable airports with flexible schedules. He would need to travel either to Nuuk, the capital of Greenland, or to the Kangerlussuaq Airport. Timing was critical because both of these locations only had one flight per week to destinations along the central or southeast coast. There were no flights to the northeast, which was the area Stephan was interested in investigating.

After checking all the options, Stephan chose to fly to Copenhagen and then on to Kangerlussuaq. The city was small, with a little over 500 inhabitants, but that was a good-sized town for Greenland where the largest city, its capital Nuuk, had slightly over 16,000 people.

Kangerlussuaq was a settlement in the Qeqqata municipality in central-western Greenland. It was located away from the coast which made it less prone to fog and wind in comparison with other airports in Greenland. Kangerlussuaq Airport was the international hub for Greenland's major airline, Air Greenland.

Stephan managed to arrange for a private plane out of the Kangerlussuaq Airport to take him over the northeast region. He was informed that travel to this area was not always successful. The fog and cloud cover were often very dense and therefore the flights were unpredictable. It was impossible to predict the weather because it would take a couple hours to get there by small plane, and the weather could change dramatically in that amount of time.

The entire northeast Greenland was a National Park which was the world's largest national park. The Park consumed over one quarter of Greenland's total land mass. Daneborg (or Daneborg Station) was a station within the park on the south coast of the Wollaston Foreland peninsula at the mouth of Young Sound emptying into the Greenland Sea. Daneborg served as the headquarters for the SIRIUS Patrol, the dog sled patrollers of the park. The number of persons at the station were few and varied considerably from summer to winter depending on the tourist or expeditionary traffic. Daneborg was the most populated of stations in the park, with an over-winter population of twelve.

Landing anywhere in the northeastern quadrant of Greenland other than at Daneborg was next to impossible. Stephan arranged for his private plane to take him to Daneborg where he would stay for several days. He also booked the same plane to take him for several flights over the northeast quadrant in hopes that he might be able to spot something of interest.

The entire journey from Cusco to Daneborg took a total of four days because of the numerous schedule delays and lay-overs. Getting to Copenhagen took two days and then, since the connections in Greenland were poor, getting to Daneborg took another two days.

Stephan was like a child with a new toy. He was so excited that he could hardly control his emotion. What he wasn't ready for was the negative 11 degree temperature, which was the high for the day. It was the coldest he had ever been in his life. He was already freezing in the plane. He felt like his mouth and nostrils were frozen shut. The plane's heater wasn't strong enough and didn't bring his body to a comfortable temperature. After landing he jumped out of the plane and ran into the terminal, where he hoped he would be able to find some warmth. It was warmer there, but still not warm enough to match what he was hoping for.

Once inside Stephan finally felt as though he could talk. "My gosh it's cold here," he blurted out.

One of the locals sitting by the fire commented, "It's the wind. You just landed on the bay out there, and because it's so flat it gets a little windy. The wind adds a significant chill factor that makes it seem a lot colder."

Stephan, not feeling any comfort from that information, moved closer to the wood burning stove that they used as a heater. "I thought your country was experiencing global warming and melting the country away. I'm not feeling any warming."

The pilot, who had just entered the small station which served double duty as an air terminal, interjected, "I wouldn't mind a little global warming around here. But in reality, all we're seeing is the normal weather cycle. Back in the 50's, 60's and 70's the average low was about -14 and the average high was about – 6 ½ degrees. In the 90's the average high was – 6 ½ and the average low was - 11. Over the last decade the average low has been -11 and the average high has been about -6. So, we haven't seen any significant changes in over 50 years, and yet we constantly hear all this hype about how we're melting away to nothing up here. It's just nuts. If you listen to the news media, you'd think we're getting to be a Caribbean Island up here."

Stephan was settled into a bunk. Private rooms weren't an option. And a sufficient number of blankets to satisfy Stephan had to be begged, borrowed, or stolen. This was a place that required acclimation. It wasn't a place you could just travel to from the equator. In spite of the cold, Stephan wasn't about to give up. He wanted to find access to the center of the earth, and he was convinced it was out here somewhere.

Stephan had trouble sleeping. He couldn't decide if it was the excitement of being this close to finding what he was searching for, or if it was the cold that kept him awake. Maybe it was just the newness of the environment he was in. He didn't know why he felt strange and couldn't sleep, but everything just felt different.

His internal clock was completely messed up. The sun didn't come up in the morning and set at night. It felt like there was no day and night. There was just day. That made it even harder to sleep. He had to constantly check the clock to see what time it really was. Sometimes, when he was looking at a 12-hour clock on the wall, it even became confusing as to which half of the day he was in. A wristwatch with a 24-hour clock was the best solution.

After a good night's rest, Stephan and his pilot were ready to go. For lack of any better options, Stephan requested that they travel north up the coast of Greenland as far as the fuel would allow them to go. They took off, not really knowing what they were looking for. The coastline looked deserted and isolated. It was miles and miles of nothing. It was about 600 miles to the northern tip of Greenland, which was about a 4-hour flight. Along the way Stephan took lots of scenic pictures.

"What exactly are we looking for?" asked the pilot.

Stephan was hesitant to say he was looking for an access point to the center of the earth, concerned that the pilot would think he was an idiot so he said, "I'm not sure but I'll know it when I see it. I'm part of a research team and we're looking for an ideal location for our experiments."

"Maybe if you tell me more about what you're looking for I can help you find it," suggested the pilot.

"For now let's just travel the coastline," responded Stephan.

"Do you want to see the Elephant Foot Glacier?" asked the pilot as they approached 3 ½ hours into their flight.

"Sure," replied Stephan. He had already seen numerous glaciers along the way, but this one was unique and interesting. It had an enormous spillway making the foot of the glacier twice as wide as the main body of the glacier. The glacier formed a perfect crescent around the mouth of the glacier. "Incredible," was all Stephan could think of saying.

They continued their flight, circling over the top of the land mass and started heading west following the coastline. After another 30 minutes the pilot mentioned that they would have to start working their way back to the base in order to refuel. There were no refueling stations at this end of the country. If they went far enough, they would eventually end up at Thule Air Base, a United States Air Base on the northwest corner of Greenland. Private planes would have trouble getting onto the base and getting fuel. This was done only in extreme emergency situations.

Stephan chose to not go to the air base. He thought it would be better to return to Daneborg even though it was further because he wasn't sure what would happen to him on a US Air Base. Being on US soil opened the door for his arrest and the possibility of him getting shipped away to some lab somewhere. Additionally, he was traveling on a fake passport. He just didn't want to take the risk.

The pilot wanted to travel overland for the return to Daneborg but Stephan made the unusual request of asking him to go out to sea about 100 miles from the coastline and travel that same distance all the way back to Daneborg. The pilot thought this was crazy. There's nothing to see out there. Why would anyone want to just see wide open ocean when they could be traveling over the scenic countryside? But Stephan wasn't about to explain his motivation for this strange request. It could only cast doubt on his sanity.

Chapter Twelve

The Greenland Sea

April, 2020 AD, Greenland

The return flight was uneventful. By the time they arrived back at the station they had been in the air about 8 hours and were exhausted, having been seat belted in the same position that entire time. They were both delighted to have their feet firmly planted on the ground once again. Stephan hunkered in front of the fire until he felt warmed, and then went off to the comfort of a bed with eight blankets. His bed wasn't anything special, but it was warm, and that was an important luxury in this part of the country.

The next day the routine repeated itself. After a good night's sleep, they resumed their search. Stephan wanted to go 200 miles off the coastline this time, which seemed strange to the pilot. There wasn't anything out there to see. But Stephan wasn't ready to explain what he was looking for. He wasn't sure how the pilot would interpret his interest in finding a hole to the center of the earth. He didn't need the scoffing and criticizing that he felt would be generated by an announcement of that type. So, he didn't explain his strange request to the pilot.

They traveled four hours north, staying the 200 miles away from the coast. When they approached the half-way point in their fuel, and turned around, Stephan wanted to go out another 100 miles on the return trip. The pilot obliged. For him it was a good paying job and he wasn't about to complain even if it seemed like a stupid request. In his mind he just figured that these stupid Americans must have money to throw away, and he may as well take some of it.

They were about 30 minutes into their return journey when they saw Svalbard Island off in the distance to the east. The pilot started to explain how Svalbard was an unincorporated archipelago of Norway. Administratively it was not considered to be part of Norway and only had about 2,500 people. It was an unincorporated area with a state-appointed governor. Svalbard was the northernmost place in the world with a permanent population. Stephan wondered if these people would know anything about an access point to the center of the earth. That might be something he tried next, if this fly-over didn't yield any results.

After another 30 minutes into the flight suddenly everything changed. In what seemed like the blink of an eye Stephan and his pilot were no longer out in the middle of the Greenland Sea, in the middle of nowhere. Up to now they had traveled in an area where it was rare to find planes or boats. There was nothing here. Even fishermen didn't travel this far out because there were a lot closer places to catch fish, no matter what country you were coming from.

But suddenly everything changed. It didn't feel like the plane had suddenly changed direction, or like the plane had gone down. Their flight seemed to continue on in a straight southerly direction. As far as they knew they were still on course flying straight toward their base. But the cold icebergs and floating ice chunks were gone. The water looked warmer and clearer. The air felt warmer. And off in the distance they could see green. They could see trees, and grassy meadows.

The pilot suddenly became frightened. He was confused and frustrated. It was as if he was seeing a ghost. His face turned pale white. The instrumentation on the plane didn't make sense. The compass and GPS systems went haywire. They kept bouncing between various settings that were inconsistent and meaningless. In his panic the pilot started to turn around, but Stephan stopped him and insisted that he continue forward. He needed to see what was up ahead.

"We have to turn around," insisted the pilot. "We don't know anything about this place. It's not on any map. It doesn't exist. If we get in trouble here, no one will know where to find us. We have to go back." The pilot again started to change the course of the plane.

"I'll pay you double for today if you don't turn around yet," insisted Stephan. "Just continue on a little further and see if you can find a landing spot."

"But we have a limited fuel supply, and who knows what problems we might run into," insisted the pilot.

"If we encounter any problems, we'll turn around immediately," assured Stephan.

The pilot wasn't interested in waiting to see if there were any problems. He wanted to turn around now. But Stephan's offer of a bonus was hard to resist.

They continued flying for another 10 minutes. They saw rivers, lakes, forests, and valleys. But they saw nowhere where they could land a plane. Stephan took pictures as fast as he could. Not much later the pilot again insisted they turn back, or they would be running out of fuel. This time Stephan agreed and the pilot turned the plane around.

It was difficult to explain what happened next, but as they flew back in the direction where they had come from, suddenly, in the blink of an eye, found themselves back in the frozen Greenland Sea. Looking behind them was also the sea. What had happened to the warmth? Where were the green trees and lakes? Suddenly they were back again in the snow, icy waters and cold. The GPS system started working again.

The pilot looked at Stephan and said, "Was I dreaming? Did you see what I just saw? Or did I fall asleep for a while?"

"We both saw it," responded Stephan. "That was what I had come here to find."

The pilot was emphatic, "you tell no one about what just happened. Understood? I have to live in this community, and I don't want to be branded as a crazy man!"

"Agreed," was Stephan's response. He had no interest in putting his pilot friend into an unfriendly environment. Then he requested, "Do you know where that place was? Do your instruments tell you how to get back there again? I want to go back tomorrow and spend more time exploring that location."

"I'm really not sure what happened. We can come back to the exact same location again tomorrow and see if we can repeat the experience," replied the pilot. "Do I get double pay again?" The pilot thought he'd try for a repeat of today's bonus.

"Of course," responded Stephan. He needed this pilot because he was the only one that knew how to get to the access point to the center of the earth. Stephan had memorized the coordinates of the location, but it would take more than just coordinates in order to have a successful return visit. Stephan would need the support and experience the current pilot offered.

Then, looking directly at Stephan, the pilot instructed, "I'll take you back tomorrow. But just remember. IT NEVER HAPPENED!!!"

Stephan was so excited that he could hardly sleep. He had found his access to the center of the world. He had found something that couldn't be explained by natural scientific phenomena. How does the ocean turn inward? It didn't make sense, and yet there it was. An honest-to-goodness access point to the center of the earth. He was excited and anxious to be going to explore it more closely the following day. He had never been so excited in his life.

As on the previous day Stephan and his pilot started out as soon as they were both ready. "I was up a little earlier, so the plane is fueled and ready to go," the pilot informed Stephan.

They flew directly to the location of the "green spot" but the flight still took about 2 ½ hours. Just as on the previous day, as they approached the location of the previous day's encounter, the same thing happened. It was so sudden that it surprised them again. One minute they were in the middle of the sea of ice known as the Greenland Sea, and the next minute they were flying over a wide river in an area that felt warm. Everything around them was green. Where they had just come from was overcast and dreary, but here the sky was cloud free and the sun was up in the sky. The setting was idyllic.

"Let's look for a place to land," requested Stephan. "I'd like to have a look around."

"I have to tell you that I am really freaked out," responded the pilot. "Last night I convinced myself that this was all a big illusion. I was sure that when we returned today, we wouldn't be able to find anything, but here it is again. You may not believe this, but I've never seen anything like this before. I've spent my entire life in Greenland and there's nothing like this anywhere. To see it now out here in the middle of the northern ocean is ridiculous!"

"You need to get around more," was Stephan's response. "There are lots of really pretty places in this world."

"I would love to set the plane down if we can find a place," responded the pilot. "I'd love to walk around a little and see what this place is like. And besides, it would save on fuel and allow us to stay out a little longer." They continued flying on, further and further away from the place where they entered this strange new world. "Where do you think we are anyways? We're obviously not flying over the Greenland Sea anymore."

"I've always heard that there was some type of entrance point to the center of the earth around here and I wanted to check it out and see if I could find it," answered Stephan.

"No way did we fly all the way to the center of the earth in a matter of seconds," challenged the pilot.

"I agree," confirmed Stephan. "This can't be the center of the earth. So, did we do some kind of Sci-Fi thing and enter another dimension? Or were we speed zipped to the middle? Or did we enter into the earth but not go all the way to the center? I really don't know and I'm hoping to find some answers while we're here. The one thing that confuses me is that the sun in here doesn't seem like the sun out there. It's like we're on a different planet with an entirely different sun. How did we get here? I have no idea."

"Well, you're having an interesting conversation with yourself there," came back the pilot. "But you're asking the same questions that I'm asking. What the heck is going on?"

"Hold on!" burst out Stephan. "What's that?" He was pointing out the front and slightly to the right. "It looks like some kind of structure."

"Right you are," responded the pilot as he changed the direction of the airplane.

What they had found looked like a small village. There were several dozen buildings surrounding a central pyramid structure on top of which was a ceremonial building that looked like one of the Inca or Aztec temples of South and Central America. People were running out onto the street pointing up at the airplane as if they had never seen an airplane before. They seemed very excited.

As Stephan and his pilot approached the opposite end of the town the saw a roadway. "I think I can land down there," suggested the pilot. "I'm going to give it a try."

The road was tight, and the pilot had to carefully maneuver the plane between the trees that were on both sides of the road. But he managed to successfully manipulate a safe landing. They had entered an unknown world and they had no idea what they would find once they exited their airplane.

Chapter Thirteen

Sharing the Knowledge
April, 2020 AD, Davis, CA

Dr. Clawson continued his efforts to teach the world about the new found capabilities of the XLs. Sadly, he was labeled a charlatan. Since he wouldn't allow access to the XLs he was also labeled a fraud. He refused to allow access since he knew the scientific community was only trying to turn them into lab rats. He understood that the scientists wanted to study them, but he saw the XLs as people, not something to be prodded and poked. He felt he had already done enough of that himself. And he didn't want them to lose their freedom by being sequestered into some institution for study. He had volunteered to demonstrate his surgery on a new patient, but he was barred from "experimenting" on other humans. He was told he needed to test his process on animals first, like monkeys, before he could experiment with humans. Dr. Clawson felt that this requirement was ridiculous. How do you demonstrate language and memory transfer abilities with monkeys? How would you interview them about their capabilities?

He scheduled another webcast where he tried to "sell" his ideas to the scientific and medical communities. But once again it didn't go well. He had barely finished his introduction of the topic when someone blurted out, "What are you trying to sell here? Science Fiction? Some kind of Superman creation? The brain is a fixed entity. You can't suddenly find a way to stimulate it without drugs of some type."

"That's just not true," responded the doctor. "For example, I'm sure you heard about acquired savant syndrome where some kind of head injury causes the brain to overcompensate in areas where most people aren't able to access. For example, Jason Padgett, a 31-year-old community college dropout was mugged in 2002 and knocked unconscious. At the time he had no interest in academics. Now, he's able to see complex geometric shapes in everyday life. After that Padgett was one of a few people in the world who could draw approximations of fractals, the repeating geometric patterns that are the building blocks of everything in the known universe, by hand. According to an article in the New York Post, in Padgett's eyes even the tree leaves outside his window are evidence of Pythagoras' Theorem. The arc that light makes when it bounces off his car proves the power of Pi.'"

The doctor continued, "Or there is Derek Amato who was able to go straight to the piano after his brain injury and was able to play music without being able to read music. In 2006 he hit his head on the cement when diving into a pool and received a concussion. Days later he was able to play music like a professional. There are only 40 people in the world with acquired savant syndrome. It is possible and brain changes are a reality."

"But you're talking about a complete transformation of the brain," another heckler complained. "You're not talking about some savant capability in art or music or math. You're talking about acquiring all these capabilities using surgery. That's just crazy."

Dr. Clawson explained, "It's happened three times with three entirely different individuals from completely different parts of the world. Two of them were in comas when they came to the operating table. It's not a fluke. The brain can surgically be modified to generate these super intelligent capabilities."

A new caller jumped in, "Can you review what these capabilities are?"

"The big one is a multiprocessing capability," explained the doctor. "These individuals can do multiple functions at the same time. When they're talking with you, they're also processing a multitude of other activities simultaneously. For example, they can be talking to me and talking to each other at the same time, holding entirely separate conversations. Of course, the conversations they have with each other are using mental telepathy and the conversation they are having with me is verbal. Another capability that all three of them acquired is a photographic memory. The way they're using that capability is that they go to the library, scan in the entire contents of several books, each of them scanning different books. Then they pass the books to each other through their telepathy. They use their multiprocessing capabilities to read the books, usually several of them simultaneously, while they're busy doing something else. It's quite incredible. For example, each of them has learned several new languages using this technique."

"If these guys have all this incredible capability, why won't you let us meet with them and talk to them?" asked another heckler.

"They've left the country because they are afraid of becoming lab rats in a cage," explained the doctor. "If it were possible for the scientific community to interview them without locking them up then they would not have run away. But as it is, they're afraid. In our last webcast there were individuals advocating locking them up in some institution so they could be studied. And that scared them, so they took off and disappeared."

"That's crazy," responded the heckler. "You make us sound like science Nazis."

"As I explained," continued the doctor. "These guys read books like crazy. They read hundreds of books a week. And they have read numerous accounts of individuals who were categorized as mentally insane because of some quirk in their mental ability, and they were basically incarcerated in mental institutions as a result. Unfortunately, that's a fact that cannot be denied. These XLs, which is what I'm calling them because of their ability to excel at so many different tasks, know about these stories. And after my first webcast where they saw how aggressive some of you scientists were they became convinced that you would like to do the same to them."

"Well, that's nonsense," replied the heckler. "That's just an excuse. And until we can work with these 'XLs' of yours we won't consider your story credible."

"You know that's exactly what would happen to them," replied another webcast attendee. "It's happened numerous times in the past. I can see why they ran off. To me their running off is a sign that they really do have these capabilities and they're simply afraid to share them with us. If there wasn't anything there, then they wouldn't need to be afraid."

A different person took the conversation in a completely different direction, "In our last conversation you were suggesting that this surgery could completely replace the need for a computer or a phone."

"That's correct," confirmed the doctor.

"What about printouts?" asked the caller.

"Not needed when you can send an image of anything directly to the mind of another," responded the doctor. "Already today we attempt to minimize printouts and look at images electronically. This would be the same kind of thing, except that instead of looking at something electronically, we have a mental image to look at."

The caller continued, "You say this surgery is repeatable and that everyone who has this surgery will attain these capabilities."

"That's correct," responded the doctor. "I only have the three case examples at this point, but it seems to be repeatable."

"Who knows how to do this surgery?" asked the caller. "Only you?"

"Right now, only myself," confirmed the doctor. "I've tried to share the knowledge, but I have been reprimanded and told it would be dangerous to let this information get out because we don't want charlatans cutting into people's brains. So, for now, until it becomes a medically approved practice, I can't share this knowledge. But I am starting to work on documentation that explains the procedure. I'll need to do this in case we have future opportunities to perform the operation."

The same caller continued with his questioning, "You realize that you're saying you can put several entire industries out of business. You're talking about eliminating the computer industry and the cell phone industry. These are enormous factors in the world's economy. You can literally bankrupt some of these economies if you go forward with what you're describing."

"That's like saying don't invent cars because you'll bankrupt the buggy whip manufacturers," explained Dr. Clawson. "You can't hijack progress for the sake of one business sector. That doesn't make sense."

"Why don't you go to another country to perform more of these operations if the scientific community in the United States is blocking you?" asked another caller.

Dr. Clawson explained, "To do that I would need to sacrifice the ability to ever practice medicine again in the United States. It would be considered a breach of my medical oath. I'm not ready to sacrifice that much. Besides, I still have hope that this procedure will be approved in the United States and then I can do more of these surgeries here."

"Well, I think this is just a lot of hocus pocus with no real foundation in science," burst in one of the hecklers. "Without a scientific foundation there's nothing credible here."

The doctor saw that he wasn't even going to get the chance to present his ideas. His presentation was destroyed before it even began. So he asked his audience, "Is there anyone on this webinar that wants me to present the details of the surgeries that I performed?"

No one responded. After a few minutes the doctor relented and said, "I guess everyone just wants to prevent me from doing what I am doing. None of you on this call seem to be interested in making life better. Unless there are any more questions, I'm going to drop off the call." The doctor waited on the call for another five minutes. Then he said goodbye and disconnected the webinar.

The doctor was finished for the day and started packing his materials together in order to depart from his hospital office and head home. He threw a few papers into his bag and headed for the door. Leaving his office, he headed down the hallway to the elevator. On the elevator he traveled to the basement parking garage where he jumped into his car and started driving towards the exit. He weaved around in the hospital parking lot thinking about the things he still needed to accomplish before the day came to an end. As he approached the exit ramp, he noticed two men standing on either side of the ramp. He didn't think twice about the men until it was too late. He assumed they were security guards. As he approached the two men seemed to recognize him. They pulled pistols out of their pocket and started shooting at the doctor. Before he realized what was happening the doctor slumped over onto the steering wheel with his foot pushing down on the gas pedal. The doctor was dead, but the car sprung to life shooting through the parking garage gate and blasting its way towards the street. The car sideswiped a parked vehicle and then shot out into the street where it broadsided a passing truck.

The doctor, and all his knowledge about the surgery, had been eliminated.

The two gunmen raced off into the parking garage to the stairway. They didn't want to be seen coming out of the garage exit in the same direction as the doctor in case someone saw them. They had left their car parked out on the street to the rear of the hospital so they could make a quicker escape. They took the hospital stairs to the main floor. From there they exited out of the back of the hospital and jumped into their vehicle, making a clean escape. They started the 45-minute drive to the Sacramento airport.

En route the passenger gunman made a call. From the other end he heard, "Hello."

"This is your agent in Davis."

On the other end of the line he heard, "Yes?"

In response he said, "The mission is complete. The target has been eliminated."

The other end of the line said, "Good! Our industry has been saved," and then the phone went dead.

Chapter Fourteen

The Knowledge Was Lost
April, 2020 AD, Cusco, Peru

Cheng and Frida continued on their individual research efforts. They would sit in their isolated locations, occasionally going to the internet to download a little more information about a specific topic. To see them at their individual tasks seemed almost mystical. They seemed to be in a trance, almost as if they were comatose, but it was obvious that they were alive and well. Occasionally they would smile, or even laugh, but for the most part they were just quiet. They gave the impression of being organic computers, chugging away and doing their analysis on their specific problems.

"Ready for lunch?" asked Cheng.

"Sure," replied Frida. This had become a daily ritual with them. They started using lunch as their opportunity to escape into the outside world. It was their chance to take a break and get out of the house. They preferred to not spend their lunch time in the kitchen. They were having too much fun. Besides, the food in Cusco was high quality and inexpensive.

The two headed for the front door, which ironically didn't cause any type of disruption to what they were

Gerhard Plenert

working on in other partitions of their mind. The work continued in their minds as if there wasn't any disruption at all. Because of their in-depth knowledge, they had learned a new ability; a new superpower. They were able to run simulations in their brains. For example, they were able to perform chemical experiments and tests based on their enormous database of previous experiments using results that other scientists had performed. They were able to mentally model the results of their own experiments.

As they walked along to their favorite little hole-in-the-wall eatery Cheng asked, *"What do you think of Stephan's efforts?"* They were both still able to communicate with Stephan. Mental communication wasn't restricted by distance. Even with him gone they were still able every evening to get together to share their accomplishments.

"It's incredible," replied Frida. *"I really didn't expect him to be successful. But I'm happy for him and wish him the best. I really never thought he would be able to find an access point. It's all pretty amazing. A world within our world? Who would have expected that? And who is going to believe it?"*

Then Cheng burst out, *"Wait. Are you getting that?"*

"No! Getting what?" asked Frida.

"It was a message from the aliens," responded Cheng. *"They sent a drawing which looks like they are trying to tell us that they are going to come visit us."*

"How do you get that from a drawing?" she asked.

"They show themselves travelling across space in some kind of round ship," he answered.

"*How cool,*" replied Frida. "*I wonder why they only decided to send the message to you. But it doesn't matter. Send them back a message requesting to see some kind of image of what they would like to do when they arrive so we can be ready for them. Ask them for pictures of themselves too.*"

"*Will do,*" was Cheng's reply and he went to work on the transmission.

The two sat down at their favorite table. Cheng, in an attempt to be the perfect gentleman, pulled the chair out for Frida. Cheng ordered his usual fish Ceviche which he loved. Now that he had the opportunity to taste it daily, he wondered how he ever lived without it. Similarly, Frida ordered her favorite Lomo Saltado, a Peruvian steak and potato meal.

Over time Cheng had slowly become enamored with Frida. Similarly, Frida was starting to have feelings for Cheng. Neither could explain their feelings or why they felt so close. Maybe it was because of their common super abilities. It had become hard to relate to anyone else who didn't possess their abilities. Or maybe it was because they spent so much time together.

Frida noticed that Cheng was paying more attention to her and was going out of his way to be nice to her. Pulling out the chair for her was just another example. So she decided to pursue the issue. It seems that even if you have superpowers, sometimes the woman has to make the first move just to get things rolling. "*Do you want to go out together tonight, maybe to a movie or a show?*"

"*You mean like a date?*" asked Cheng, hoping that was what she was asking.

"*Sure,*" she replied. "*Whatever you want to call it is fine with me. It just thought it would be fun if we did something different tonight.*"

"*I'd love to,*" was his reply. "*I'll pick you up at seven.*" He was joking around with her. They lived together so picking her up would mean knocking on her bedroom door.

"*OK,*" she responded. "*But if you're taking me out on a date, then you need to plan everything, like where we're going and what we're doing.*"

"*I can handle it,*" he replied.

Just then the waitress came by. "I have a question for you," she started. "You come here every day for lunch. You sit together. You smile and make eyes at each other. But you never say a word to each other. I don't get it. How can you spend so much time together and never communicate?"

"We communicate," replied Cheng. "We have our own secret language."

"It just seems weird to me that you never talk," replied the waitress as she picked up some of the dishes.

"Don't worry," replied Frida. "We communicate just fine." Neither her nor Cheng wanted to explain any more than that. They didn't want to get branded as freaks. Nor did they want to raise a flag about where they were hiding out.

They finished their meal and headed back to their house. Cheng went to the internet to see if there were any shows that he could take Frida to. He was excited about this being their first date and he wanted to make it special. As he opened the MSN.com website a news bulletin flashed at him, "Doctor to the XLs killed in brutal attack."

"Frida come here," he sent a mental message to Frida. *"Look at this."*

Frida came and looked. *"What was that about?"* she asked. *"Why would anyone want to kill Dr. Clawson? He was a good man trying to do even more good but no one would listen. Now they even went so far as to kill him."*

"Sadly, I'm not surprised," responded Cheng. *"They chased us out of the country too. Clawson kept saying that computers and cell phones would become obsolete. There's an entire industry built around those technologies. Losing them would be extremely damaging to the economies of numerous countries of the world and would destroy companies like Technosoft. Somebody is trying to stop the spread of Dr. Clawson's procedure."*

"That's just horrible," replied Frida. *"I never dreamed it would come to this."*

"How does this affect us?" asked Cheng.

"What do you mean?" asked Frida.

"Are our lives in danger?" explained Cheng.

"Seriously?" asked Frida. *"You seriously think they're coming after us too?"*

"I wouldn't be surprised," he answered.

"What are we going to do?" she asked.

"I think we need to get Stephan updated and have a three-way conversation which includes him," he suggested. *"Whatever we decide will affect him too."*

"You're right," responded Frida, as she sent a message out to Stephan. But there was no response to her message. Instead, she received a flood of images back from him.

Chapter Fifteen

A Brave New World

April, 2020 AD, Greenland Sea

Stephan was excited. He was anxiously trying to share images of the world he was visiting. He sent image after image to both Frida and Cheng showing them the world he had discovered.

When Stephan and the pilot climbed out of the plane they were greeted by several curious individuals who were speaking to them in Hebrew. Luckily Stephan had chosen to study Hebrew earlier because he thought it would be valuable in his study of the Bible. And, to the amazement of the pilot, he started conversing with these inhabitants.

The conversations weren't clean. Stephan's Hebrew was slightly different from the language that the people spoke, but it was close enough for a conversation. The typical questions flowed like, "Where are you from? Who are you? How did you get here?" In the end, Stephan learned that these people considered themselves to be the ten tribes that were expelled during the Jewish Diaspora. When the Assyrians raided Israel and relocated the ten tribes these people didn't stop their migration process northward, and eventually ended up following a mysterious non-existent road that led them to where they now resided.

To Stephan, who loved ancient history, this was an amazing story, and he wanted to spend hours talking with them. He learned that they had administrative centers for each of the tribes. These centers were like state capitals. There wasn't one over-arching government seat. There were ten government seats, one for each tribe. The people that Stephan was talking to were from the tribe of Asher. And they were proud of their heritage.

The locals questioned the flying machine that Stephan had arrived on. They had never seen a machine like that before. They had flying machines of their own, but none like that. Stephan recorded these comments in his mind and planned to pursue more details about these flying machines when he returned.

Stephan asked them how they arrived at the center of the earth, and they responded that they didn't know they were in the center of the earth. Their ancestors followed a road that led them to this Promised Land, and they've lived here ever since. It didn't seem unusual to them.

Stephan was reminded by the pilot that they needed to get going. They had filed a flight plan which would place them significantly overdue, and he didn't want to cause a search and rescue expedition to be sent out to find the two of them. Stephan asked if the airplane's radio could send a message stating that they were safe but delayed, but the radio didn't work. There was no signal. So they came to the conclusion that they would have to depart and return again another day.

The residents of this inner earth world begged them to stay. They wanted to share their world with them, and they wanted to learn more about the outside world. Stephan asked the pilot to leave on his own and come back in two days to retrieve him. The pilot agreed, stressing that he may get a lot of questions about what had happened to Stephan. After discussing options, the two decided that the best course of action would be for Stephan to write a note stressing that he had found something that he wanted to study more closely and that he had requested to stay behind. This seemed to satisfy the pilot.

The plane and pilot departed, and Stephan planned to spend the rest of the day, and all the next day, sharing and orienting himself with the new people he had just met. But then he received the news from Cheng and Frida.

"I can't believe the doctor is dead," communicated Stephan to his two companions. *"Does that mean there will be no more surgeries? Does anyone know how to perform the surgeries besides him?"*

"I think it means no more surgeries," responded Frida in the three-way communications link that they had established.

"I don't think there's anyone else that knows how to do them," interjected Cheng. *"They wouldn't allow him to teach anyone, and I don't think the procedure was ever documented. I think we are the only three there will ever be unless someone else figures out how to do these surgeries."*

"Can we learn how to do it?" asked Stephan.

"Not without some trial and error," replied Cheng.

"*And who is going to let us experiment on them? I keep wondering how this will affect us? Are we in danger too? And I think the answer is 'Yes, we're in trouble.'*"

"*It would probably be smart for us to find somewhere more remote and isolated than Cusco,*" suggested Frida.

"*Well guess what,*" interjected Stephan. "*I'm standing in the perfect place. No one will believe this exists and they'll never come here looking for us.*"

"*But are the natives friendly?*" asked Cheng.

"*I'll be able to tell you more tomorrow after I've spent some time with them,*" Stephan replied, "*but I think they're very friendly and that they're going to be receptive to us temporarily moving in.*"

"*We should be good here in Cusco for another couple days,*" responded Frida. "*Let us know what you learn. Your location may be the best option. No one will ever find us there.*"

"*Will do,*" responded Stephan as he signed off of the conversation and returned to conversing with his new found friends.

At 07:00 PM Cheng went to Frida's bedroom door and knocked.

"*Are you kidding me?*" asked Frida without opening the door. "*You've been sending me messages all day. Since when do you need to knock to talk to me?*"

"*Just trying to do this right,*" was Cheng' answer.

Frida opened the door. She was dressed up in a skirt which Cheng saw as a pleasant surprise from the usual jeans and t-shirt. "*Where are you taking me?*" she asked.

"It's a surprise," answered Cheng. But it really wasn't much of a surprise. There weren't that many options. He was taking her to the local movie theatre to see the latest science fiction movie in Spanish, which luckily, they had both decided to learn now that they were living in Peru.

Cheng had always been impressed by how neat and clean she kept her room in spite of her many mental distractions. He put out his arm for her to take and they left their apartment. Cheng had ordered a taxi and it was waiting for them as they came to the street. Hopping into the cab he instructed the driver to head for the local movie theatre. He was looking forward to a relaxing evening, shoving all of his multi-programmed mental exercises to the back of his mind.

They pulled away from the curb and headed toward the center of town. Cheng and Frida made small talk, acting like they really didn't know much about each other. They were playing the role as if this really was their first date. And they were having fun.

The ride started out uneventful but quickly changed. Suddenly a bullet came crashing through the passenger side of the front windshield and whizzed between Cheng and Frida, crashing out through the back window. Frida screamed and Cheng quickly pushed her down on the seat. He looked around to see if he could identify the shooter as a second shot was fired. This time the shot hit the taxi driver in the head, and the driver slumped down into his seat, his foot still depressing the accelerator.

The car sped up and Cheng tried pulling the driver's body over to the passenger side of the front seat in order to pull his foot off the accelerator, but it was too late. The taxi crashed full speed into the back of a parked vehicle. Cheng was jerked forward, but the front seat held him back. Frida was thrown from lying down on the seat to the floor in front of her. They both received minor bruises, but they had survived.

Unfortunately, the battle wasn't over. Another bullet came crashing through the back window of the vehicle narrowly missing Cheng. *"We have to get out of here quick and run for it,"* was his only thought which he shared with Frida. *"We don't have any weapons to protect ourselves. We need to get away before whoever is shooting at us gets a better shot."*

"Let's go," was Frida's response. They swung the door open, jumped out, and started running away in the opposite direction from where the shots were fired. They heard several more shots ring out but were too focused on getting away to look back and see who was shooting.

Cheng felt a pain in his left thigh but assumed it was because of the shock of the taxi crashing into the car. They ran to the end of the block and rounded the corner to the right, hoping this would put them out of the shooter's line of sight. It seemed to work. There were no more shots fired, but they didn't stop running. They kept rounding corners for several more blocks, zigzagging their way through the town.

As they ran they talked. *"Who is shooting at us and why?"* asked Frida.

"I wonder if it's connected with Dr. Clawson's death?" asked Cheng. *"If it is, then they're trying to get rid of us too."*

"It sure didn't take them long to find us," complained Frida.

"They must have found something in Dr. Clawson's home or office that led them to us," responded Cheng. *"That's the only thing that makes sense."*

"I wondered if the money that the doctor sent to Stephen for his travels was going to give us away. They may have followed that lead. Well, we can't go back to our apartment," suggested Frida. *"You know they'll be watching for us there, whoever they are."*

"Unfortunately, you're right," agreed Cheng. *"Whatever we have there is now lost forever. So what do we do?"*

"Head for the airport," recommended Frida. *"We need to distance ourselves from here. Let's get on a flight to the international airport in Lima. Then, while we're on our way there we'll have to think about what to do next."* Then she noticed a red stain on Cheng's hip. Pointing to it she said, *"What's that?"*

Cheng took a closer look and explained, *"I guess I must have gotten shot after all. It looks like it just scraped me and gave me a minor cut."*

"That's not a minor cut," stressed Frida who was concerned for the welfare of her close friend. Across the street was a pharmacy and Frida insisted, *"We're going over there to get some bandages and antibiotic ointment. Then we can fix you up when we get to the airport."*

"Good enough," replied Cheng, who was also concerned about being shot even though he didn't want to show weakness to Frida.

After getting the bandages Frida said, *"Now we can go to the airport. I don't suppose this was all part of the date you had planned. Or was this your way of getting out of taking me to a movie?"*

"I just wanted to make our first date special. But this is not the kind of special first date I had in mind," agreed Cheng as he waved down a cab. He instructed the cab to take them to the airport. He knew they would have no problem getting a flight to Lima since there were several every day. But the big question that needed to be answered was, *"Where do we go once we get to Lima?"*

"I really don't care except it needs to be a place where we don't get shot at," demanded Frida.

"Then middle earth it is," responded Cheng.

Chapter Sixteen

Escape

April, 2020 AD, Cusco, Peru

Cheng and Frida arrived at the airport and were able to book a flight that departed 70 minutes later for Lima. Fortunately, they always carried their various multiple passports with them when they left their apartment. Keeping their passports on them was a recommendation by the Foreign Service office as a good practice in case someone was injured. Money was also available to them through a variety of foreign bank accounts that the doctor had set up.

Next they decided to communicate the news to Stephan. He needed to know that he was probably also in danger. They started their three-way communication with Frida saying, "Stephan. *We have some bad news. Not only is Dr. Clawson murdered, but we are also under attack and had to leave Cusco quickly. We were getting shot at and the only thing that makes any sense is that they found out about our location from something in the doctor's home or through his help to us. Now they're after us as well. We wanted to let you know so that you were aware of the danger.*"

"*Where are you going?*" asked Stephan.

"*We have no idea,*" replied Cheng. "*For now we're just trying to get to the international airport in Lima and then we'll have to see where we go from there.*"

"*Come to me,*" suggested Stephan. "*The place I have found here in the center of the earth is extremely friendly. I'm sure we can hold out here. And no one would ever think of looking for us in the center of the earth. The bad part is that we lose all communication with the outside world. No news. No internet. Nothing from the outside world. We'll be totally isolated.*"

"*We were hoping you would say that. Right now, breaking all contact sounds pretty good,*" explained Frida. "*How do you suggest we get there?*"

Stephan explained the travel routing. He told them to travel to Copenhagen and then from there on to Kangerlussuaq, Greenland. He suggested that they get one-way tickets for each leg of the journey separately and use different IDs. That way it will be more challenging for anyone trying to follow them. He explained that from Kangerlussuaq they would have to take a private plane to Daneborg in the northeast part of Greenland. Stephan told them that he had a pilot that knew the way to Daneborg and could bring them all the way to the center of the earth. He explained that the pilot didn't want anyone to know anything about this entrance to center earth because it would ruin his reputation. But that he knew how to get there, and he would be an excellent guide. Stephan indicated that he would not move from his current location because of the potential threat. He would stay where he was and just wait for them there. He would send his pilot back to Kangerlussuaq to wait for them.

"Then it's settled," explained Cheng. *"We're off to the center of the earth to join Stephan."*

"I agree," confirmed Frida. *"It definitely seems like the safest place to go."*

Stephan mentally sent Cheng and Frida the books with the lessons for Hebrew that he still retained in his photographic memory. They committed to learning the lessons before their arrival to the center of the earth. They threw the lessons into one of their mind's partitions and let it go to work teaching them the language as they engaged in other activities.

Travel wasn't too challenging. About the only requirement was that they didn't want to have any layovers in the United States. They found a KLM flight that was routed through Amsterdam. It required a four hour wait in the Lima airport and then about twenty hours of travel time to get to Copenhagen, but they didn't mind. As long as it kept them from being attacked and shot at, they were OK with the waiting.

Frida and Cheng were constantly nervous as they waited in the airport before boarding the plane. They were always looking around to see if anyone was paying them notice. They didn't feel completely safe until the plane lifted off the ground and they were in the air. Then they felt reassured that whoever was after them had failed. They could finally relax a little. But they wouldn't feel completely safe until they arrived in Center Earth with Stephan.

They watched as many movies as possible during the 12 ½ hour flight to Amsterdam, realizing that this was probably the last chance they would have to see any movies in a long time. After that the planes from

Amsterdam to Copenhagen and on to Greenland wouldn't offer movies and the center of the earth would leave them completely isolated.

Cheng and Frida successfully made it through their two transition points in Amsterdam and Copenhagen without incident. They were on their way to Greenland.

Stephan spent the evening with his new friends. They were extremely accommodating and helpful. He worked his way through learning the cultural nuances and became comfortable with their way of doing things. He became relaxed around them and before long it started to feel more and more like home.

He found the food a little strange. They seemed to have the same types of meats and vegetables that he was used to, but the way the food was prepared and the spices they used generated a strange taste. The foods were spicier than he was used to. But he knew he could get used to anything, even their strange meals.

Meals were open and shared in a common area. Everyone in the community contributed to the meal. And if there was anyone who couldn't contribute, like visitors or disabled, they simply joined in with everyone else. No one was going to be denied a meal.

For food preparation, there seemed to be roles. Some individuals were the bakers, others had the vegetables, and still others were responsible for preparing the meats, etc. He learned that no one was assigned to a particular role. They just picked a role and worked in it as long as they wanted. And if they wanted to try something else, they were free to do so.

He also found it quite unusual how they engaged in regular prayers. Not just around meals but as a forerunner to any activity that they had planned. It was just the way they conducted themselves. Their lives were religiously focused. All things came from God and all things belonged to God. Ultimately, they considered themselves as borrowers of God's gifts to them.

The houses were normally just two rooms. One room was the living room area where everyone lounged and talked. Sleeping was in a second large separate room using a shared floor that was cushioned with mats. The entire family slept together including any guests. There weren't designated sleeping places. Everyone just laid down and went to sleep wherever they wanted.

The following day Stephan went with various individuals to see where they worked and how they worked. There were all the traditional resource functions like mining for metal ores, farming, milling, and food preparation. There was also a more hi-tech role where individuals had sophisticated mechanical devices which were used for recording and tracking information. He learned that they had a sophisticated method for genealogy. They tracked the heritage of every member of the community. He also learned that they kept detailed data about the weather, harvests, mining, etc. They could tell you information about the cyclic weather cycles going back over a thousand years, much more detailed than anything the outer world had to offer. And they could access all of this in seconds. They also had books, but not in the form that Stephan was familiar with. These books were in rolls rather than single pages. The entire book would be in one roll with index tabs which made searching the book easy.

Stephan was amazed at how efficient their world was. In some respects, they were behind the outside world, but in other aspects they were ahead. For example, their medicines seemed extremely advanced. They had found cures for diabetes, colds, and cancer and had completely eliminated these and many other diseases from their society. In fact, the idea of prolonged sicknesses seemed somewhat foreign to them. They would ask questions like, "Why would anyone stay sick for a long time? Do they believe in self-degradation?" These questions led Stephan to wonder if there was anything that couldn't be cured by these people.

Leadership of the group was by senior religious authority. Religion was also their government, their judicial system, and the way punishment was carried out. When Stephan asked if they had crime they answered, "We still have teenagers, and they like to misbehave."

Stephan discovered that they used a type of stone that they referred to as a seer stone, which was their method of communication between the various groups in center earth. It worked a little like a phone but had broader capabilities. For example, if someone wanted to view a different part of their world, he could use the seer stone to do so. It didn't require cameras and monitors. You simply instructed the seer stone in what you wanted to see, and it showed it to you. Or if you wanted to talk with someone you just told the stone, and the other person became visible. Then a conversation could be held. The other individual didn't need to have a seer stone as well. All that was needed was for one person to have this stone and then they could communicate. They could see each other, talk to each other, and even smell or feel each other. Stephan was baffled by how this technology worked. It immediately became his goal to learn about how something that appeared to be a rock could have these sophisticated capabilities.

The days were clearly defined. There was 8 hours of nighttime every night, every day of the year. There were no clearly defined seasons. They would have rainy days and hot days, but they weren't on an annual cycle. There was no end of the many surprises that Stephan encountered. This was a strange new world, and Stephan was going to love learning about it.

The following day, around mid-day, Stephan's pilot returned. Stephan explained that he would not be leaving. He would be staying there permanently. He instructed his pilot to pick up his friends in Kangerlussuaq, bringing them to Daneborg, and then on to center earth. The pilot was delighted to have the assignment because Stephan paid well. And then he departed.

Chapter Seventeen

Reunited

April, 2020 AD, Center Earth

During the four days that Stephan was waiting for his companions he had made arrangements for housing. Preparing a house turned out to be an interesting endeavor as well. Stephan wanted a place with a living room, bathroom, and three bedrooms. But the citizens of center earth insisted that he shouldn't have three bedrooms. That he should have just one combined bedroom. They couldn't understand why anyone would want to hide out in their own private bedroom, they felt it was unsanitary and unsocial. Eventually, since they were building the place for him, he had to give in and let them build his home in the way they desired. The house would be constructed typical to all the other homes, which had one large living area, a large sleeping area, and bathroom.

Next came the selection of a building site, which again Stephan deferred to his new friends' best judgment. Designing and selecting the building site took about two hours. Then it came time to build the place. Stephan assumed that the construction of their new home would take a couple weeks, but he was surprised when the basic structure was in place in about two hours. It became a community project, and everyone was involved. The whole town seemed to have specific roles in building a house and they all jumped in performing their specific duties.

Stephan was amazed at how quickly the structure went up. He noticed that they were using a rock to hold up the structure. But it wasn't a large rock. In fact it was quite small, about the size of a man's fist. This rock had strange antigravity properties. It rose like a balloon. But when Stephan held it in his hands he could tell it was definitely a rock. The builders used this antigravity rock to help lift up the roof, allowing the workers to connect it to the walls. He found this incredible and fascinating and noted that he was definitely going to research how it worked.

Next came the inner walls and ceiling. This was all put on in about one day, again with the benefit of the antigravity rock which was used to lift and hold things up.

With the structure in place, people started showing up with mats and pillows which amounted to the furniture. Tables and chairs were reserved for the common eating area outside the living quarters. They weren't used in the homes.

The timing was perfect. As the community was wrapping up the mats and the furniture, a plane could be heard overhead. It was heading for a landing on the same road where it had landed previously. Stephan ran to the site eager to see if his companions had arrived safely. They were just getting out of the plane as he approached. He waived to them in the distance. When

126 | P a g e

he was within earshot he asked, "How was your trip here?"

"That was the strangest thing I've ever lived through." It was Frida's comment as she and Cheng exited the plane in center earth. "One minute you're freezing in a world of icy cold seas. And the next minute you're in some kind of garden paradise. It's incredible."

"It's definitely strange," replied Stephan as he gave Frida a hug and shook Cheng's hand. "I'm delighted you made it. This is the strangest place on earth; or should I say in earth. You haven't even seen strange yet. Things are really different here."

"What do you mean?" asked Cheng.

"You'll see," replied Stephan. "I don't want to spoil any of the surprises that are ahead of you. And believe me, there are a lot of them."

There would be plenty of surprises. These people had lived isolated from the outer world for about 2,500 years, since the first Jewish dispersion. During that time they utilized the resources of the world they lived in to develop an entirely different way of life with an entirely different set of tools. It was as if they didn't live on the same world. They had a world all their own. In many ways their life seemed better than the life of those living on the outside. But the threesome would also identify shortcomings of this new way of life. Only time would determine if their life here would be considered better than on the outside. At least for now they felt confident that no one would be hunting them here.

Stephan made arrangements with the pilot to return in exactly one year. He made the false assumption that he wouldn't be needing contact with the outside world anytime in the near future. He invited the pilot to join them for lunch, warning him that the food was unusual but extremely healthy. The pilot joined them, had lunch, and then bid his farewells, promising to return in one year.

Now the threesome were on their own. Their scary experiences on the outside had initially forced them into hiding and had now caused them to flee for their lives. They were convinced that it would be dangerous to share their capabilities with anyone here in this new world. They would try to fit in and adapt as best they could. They vowed to each other that they would do nothing that would cause them to stand out. They were now citizens of center earth.

May, 2020 AD, One Week Later, Center Earth

Stephan, Cheng, and Frida quickly became comfortable with their new environment. They had learned the basic Hebrew language prior to their arrival at Center Earth and they were picking up the nuances and changes that had occurred to the language in the last 2,500 years. There were many new terms and a large amount of slang that had crept in.

They were also fascinated by the focus and the standard of life. For example, if you managed a work crew, the manager had to be multi-talented. If the crew was working out in the field, the manager had to play music or sing for the workers. This was considered critical to giving the workers focus and enthusiasm. The manager had to be an entertainer. Not in a way that would distract the workers. Rather, in a way that would invigorate them.

Gleaning was also the norm. Workers would put in their normal workday, which could be any number of hours, not a strict eight-hour day. They worked by the job rather than by time. And after they had completed their task, they were allowed to glean. So, if they worked in the fields, they were allowed to go through the field and pick a few things for themselves after they were finished their workday. However, since meals were communal, there wasn't the need for a lot of gleaning.

Each of the three companions took on different tasks. They wanted to learn as much as possible about this new world. And they decided that they could share their experiences. Cheng worked at mining. Frida worked in the fields. And Stephan worked at what the outside world would consider to be technology. He wanted to learn about anti-gravity stones and seer stones which had the ability to project images and messages so they could see in any other part of Center Earth at any time, without cameras or recording equipment. He was interested in learning about any other type of technological tool that he hadn't yet encountered, and he was sure there were a lot of them.

It was on their fifth day in Center World when one of the local residents came to Stephan and requested, "You have to make a trip. Our tribe leader wants to meet with you in the main city of our tribe. He wants to learn what the outer world is like. He wants you to come tomorrow."

Stephan wasn't sure how to carry out the request so he asked, "How far away is he? How do we travel to his location? How long will the journey take? Will we be coming back here?"

"You will fly about ten minutes to get to his location because he is a long ways away," responded the local. "Our leader is sending a travel ship to our location in the morning to collect the three of you. Coming back will be your decision."

"What is a travel ship?" asked Stephan.

"It is very different from what you came here on," responded the resident. "It is hard to explain. You will see it tomorrow."

May, 2020 AD, Center Earth

The next day a circular shaped flying vehicle suddenly appeared overhead. There were no engine sounds indicating its arrival. It was just there. Then it slowly descended into the middle of the community. A ramp opened out of the side of the vehicle and two individuals disembarked.

The town's people treated the visitors with a great deal of respect. Stephan and his companions were gathering together to observe the spectacle. He commented to his two companions, "They must be from some central government post. Everyone treats them as if they have some powerful position."

Just then, as if they had heard his comment, one of the locals explained, "They are representatives of our

High Priest class. They are here on behalf of the prophet and head of our tribe who has asked that you be brought to him."

"So they are religious leaders, not political leaders?" asked Stephan.

"Actually, they are both," replied the local. "Our political system and religious systems are one. The Assyrians, Egyptians, and Babylonians, all considered their political leaders, whether they were king or Pharaoh, to also be their religious leaders, and sometimes even their god."

Then he continued to explain, "You will be going to visit our Senior High Priest and Prophet at the temple in the center of our Tribe's territory."

"When do we go?" asked Cheng.

"Immediately," was the response.

"How long will we be gone?" asked Frida, wondering if she needed to take anything with.

"You can come back today, if you want to, or you can stay longer if you like," replied the resident. "It is up to you how long you want to stay. Come with me and I will introduce you and then you can get going. You don't want to keep the Senior High Priest waiting. That would be discourteous."

The threesome were escorted to the two visitors and were quickly introduced to Abbott and Barak. Abbott spoke first, "We are here to escort you to our High Priest Chaviva at the temple. Are you ready to go with us?"

"Of course," replied Cheng.

"Then let's step aboard our air transport. The trip from your current small town of Jericho to the capital city of Samaria will take about ten minutes," commented Abbott. That was the first time the three XLs had heard the name of their town. They had been staying in Jericho, but there were no walls surrounding the city as described in the Jericho of the Old Testament. There were no signs with the name of the town. There was no indication that the town even had a name.

All five entered the flying saucer looking vessel. Inside it looked like a circular living room, with cushions and pillows around the outside of the circle. There wasn't anything like seatbelts. It was just open seating. There were some windows around the outside which immediately caught the attention of Frida, Stephan, and Cheng. They watched the scenery as the vehicle quietly and slowly rose into the air and then suddenly took off at an extremely high speed. What was unusual was that there was no jerky feeling. They didn't sense the acceleration. It was more like watching a movie, even though they understood that it was them that was moving at this extremely high speed.

Stephan noticed something that he hadn't observed in the past. He noticed Frida and Cheng standing tightly next to each other. But it was more than just standing, they were physically in contact with each other. Their shoulders were touching. At one point Cheng put his arm around Frida's shoulder and gave her a hug. At another point, when they thought he wasn't looking, Frida gave Cheng a small kiss on the cheek.

Stephan felt like he was out in the ozone. How could he have missed what was obviously going on here? How could he have missed that Frida and Cheng were developing a relationship? Stephan had been so wrapped up in his world of learning that he had blocked himself from the social side of life. But obviously these other two XLs hadn't missed that opportunity. They were getting along just fine. They were working on their intellectual lives while at the same time not ignoring their social lives.

It was a wakeup call for Stephan. He realized that he shouldn't ignore the social side of life in his pursuit of the intellectual. Then another thought hit him. How was he ever going to find a mate if there were no other girl XLs? Frida, the only female super, had been taken by Cheng. So there was no one for Stephan. Suddenly the idea of being alone in his work scared him. He didn't want to be alone forever.

Stephan returned the focus of his thoughts to the flight he was on. He was fascinated by the technology of Center Earth and asked Barak, "What propels your vehicle? What makes it raise up in the air, and what moves it along so fast?"

Barak responded, "We use our antigravity tool to lift the ship and that helps if we want to float in the air. Then we use a tool that we call the shifter. We just tell it where we want to go and it shifts us there. Maybe someday, when you have more time, I will let you talk with the people who build and maintain our traveling vehicles and you can learn more about how they work. They're extremely efficient and use only the fuel from the sun."

"I would be delighted to learn more about how this flying ship operates," commented Stephan. "I am extremely interested in its technology. It is unlike anything the surface world has ever experienced."

"We would be delighted to teach you," replied Barak, "but I am not the one to do the teaching since I am not a technologist. I will find you someone more suited. Maybe, if you decided to stay over until tomorrow, I can have someone meet with you then."

"That would be wonderful," exclaimed an excited Stephan. "I would be extremely grateful for the chance to meet with your technologist."

"Then I'll arrange it," explained Barak, and Stephan went back to looking at the scenery out the window.

True to their word, ten minutes later the flying saucer came to a sudden halt and slowly started its vertical descent, landing right in the middle of what appeared to be a large game field. It reminded them of the playing fields that the Aztecs and Mayans were known to have in South and Central America, which seemed a little strange since these peoples had never been to South America.

The ship's stop was so sudden that watching the abrupt halt through the windows caused the threesome to have queasy stomachs even though they didn't feel any type of surge from the stop. Off in the distance they could see a temple raised up on a pyramid perch, which looked like the large rectangular box extremely similar to the temple that Solomon would have built over 2,700 years earlier in Jerusalem.

As they exited the vehicle, they were greeted by a couple more individuals who proceeded to lead them toward the temple. They explained, "You will be meeting with High Priest Chaviva. He is interested in your story of how you arrived here and why you're here."

Chapter Eighteen

The High Priest
May, 2020 AD, Center Earth

The walk from the flying saucer towards the temple was fascinating to the three XLs. Up to now Jericho had been their only experience in Center Earth and they assumed that all the cities would be similar. They were not ready for the surprise that awaited them. Compared to Samaria, Jericho was just a small farming and mining town. Whereas Samaria covered at least 100 times the land space of Jericho, and possibly even more. The number of people in Jericho was about 1,000, but the number of residents in Samaria was about 200,000. And this was just one of the 10 capitals for the lost tribes that now lived in Center Earth. Their guides told them that their tribe of Asher was one of the smallest of the tribes. Some of the other tribes were hundreds of times larger.

As they worked their way toward the temple they passed by a commercial center, which included a multitude of shops. The shops included craftsmen, clothing, food, and all the elements that you would expect to find in a vibrant community. In Jericho there were a few small vendors who traveled door to door and used small handcarts to transport their goods. But here in Samaria the citizens utilized vehicles that were powered by silent engines similar to what the XLs experienced in the flying saucer.

"Why don't they use these vehicles in Jericho?" questioned Cheng.

"Jericho is more conservative than most of the rest of the communities," explained the guide. "They believe in staying closer to nature and avoiding unnecessary technologies. For example, the vehicles that we use for air and ground transport, you won't find in Jericho unless they were being used by a visitor like you. They believe that a closer adherence to the scriptures will bring them closer to God. And in reality, they do seem to be more spiritual than many of the other communities which tend to get distracted by the newer technologies."

"That's interesting," responded Frida. "It reminds me of the Mennonites or the Amish that we have on the surface. They also don't believe in the use of modern technology."

"That's the same kind of idea," explained the guide.

"That's why the people in Jericho kept saying 'if we come back' like if they weren't expecting us to come back again," explained Stephan.

"They're testing you to see if you're going to get enamored by the technology," explained the guide. "They want to see if you want their conservative lifestyle or the more modern life style. Honestly, there are a lot of days when I wished I'd chosen their simpler way of life."

"As advanced as you are, there still seems to be a lot of open and untouched land," commented Cheng.

"We engage in land rotation here," explained the guide. "We believe that no place should be inhabited more than 20 years. The only exception to that is the temple itself. Other than that, once a piece of land was inhabited for 20 years, the people must move out and move to a new location, and the place where their previous structure stood is then plowed under and used for farming or growing trees, or some other different activity than what it was used for in the past. Then, after 20 years of farming it can again be used for homesteads or businesses. This helps us keep strength in the land. And that's why you see so much green when you're up in the sky. We don't allow any more than 25 percent of our land mass to be used for housing at any one time. Right now, we are ahead of the game. We only have about 18 percent used for housing."

"Wow," exclaimed Stephan. "That's an incredible concept. On the outer surface it seems like we have cities spring up in the best agricultural areas, and then the cities expand and take over the agricultural land, and before you know it the good land is all covered by cement. The land that's left is the land where nobody wants to live, like Nevada."

"That would never happen here," replied the guide. "We do just the opposite. If there is land that cannot be rotated into farming land or tree farms, for example because it is solid rock, that type of land is exempt from the rotation requirement, and a lot of people who want a homestead that can be passed from generation to generation will build on this rotation exempt land. These structures also tend to be built more solidly. But they are often more remote."

"How ingenious," expressed an excited Frida. "I wish we had that type of environmentally conscientious approach on the surface. We have numerous cities that are built right up against the mountains, and the land in the foothills and mountains isn't good for farming, but do you think they build their houses in that land. No! They build the area out in the flats which is good agricultural farmland and end up destroying the farmland because it is cheaper to build there. I've heard about cities in the more liberal parts of the United States, like Sacramento, California. Their city grows out into the farmland rather than into the rocky foothills. But I'm sure there are dozens of examples all over that have that same problem. We could learn a lot from you!"

The guide continued, "If you look around, this entire city is built on a small rocky mountain. Not even trees were growing here. That's why we built this city here. Look at the construction of the buildings. They're rock and cement. They're intended to be permanent. But if you remember the houses in Jericho, they were built with wood."

"That's right," exclaimed Stephan. "They put a house up for us in just one day."

"That's right," the guide continued in his explanation. "They are temporary and will need to be rotated."

The pace of the travelers had slowed considerably. The questions had caused the guide to stop and explain Central Earth's environment and culture, which he was delighted to do.

"Tell us about your government," requested Cheng. "How does the political system work?"

"We're broken up into ten tribes which are named after ten of the twelve sons of Jacob who was renamed Israel, who was the son of Isaac, who was the son of Abraham. Each of the ten tribes has their own central city which has a temple and ruling High Priesthood. That priesthood makes the decisions for the tribe. The leaders of each of the tribes gets together once a year to discuss inter-tribal concerns. But usually there aren't many concerns, and this is just a big reunion. Then, within each tribe you have a collection of independent cities and townships, each with their own governing religious leader who also acts as the mayor. That's what you encountered in Jericho. It's one of these small townships under the tribe of Asher."

"And Samaria is the capital?" asked Cheng.

"Correct," replied the guide.

Samaria was geographically slightly higher than the surrounding area allowing for a scenic overlook of the entire region. It was beautiful and green. Seeing something out in the distance which looked like it might be another city, Cheng asked, "Is that another city in a different tribe?"

"Still our tribe," explained the guide. "It's the city of Bethsaida. Slightly smaller but very similar to Samaria. Everything you see, as far out as you can see, is Asher. We would have to travel on the sky mobile if we were going to visit one of the other tribes."

"Do you visit the other tribes very often?" questioned Frida.

"Of course," was the guide's reply. "We trade with them regularly. Especially when it comes to meat products and fish products which we're not that good at. The Asher tribe is best at manufactured goods and mining. And that's what we use for barter."

They finally arrived at the foot of the temple complex and started to climb the 120 steps that led up to the temple's entrance. They passed several guards who formally watched over the temple grounds. From this raised view they could see far out into the distance.

Entering the temple, they found it to be an enormous stone structure with stone cuts that were one foot thick and more than twenty feet by ten feet rectangles each weighed over 20 tons. They were used for the walls and the roof of the structure. It was quite impressive and beautifully made of the finest materials in all of Center Earth.

They passed through several chambers until they finally arrived at a closed door. The door was granite, about ten feet high and five feet wide. It was mounted on a single pivot, both on the top and the bottom of the door. The pivot was so accurately balanced that they were able to move the door open by pushing against it with just one hand. It easily rotated and opened, and they entered the temple.

The guide introduced the High Priest Chaviva who was standing inside the temple conversing with some of the other High Priests. The guide and the additional High Priests exited the room and left the threesome alone with High Priest Chaviva.

"How are you doing?" asked the High Priest. "Do you like our world? I understand that you're from the Old

World. I've never been there, and I am curious about what it's like."

Cheng started the conversation, "We love it here. It's beautiful and people are extremely friendly."

"Glad you like it," exclaimed the High Priest. "I'd like is to ask you a few questions about the Old World. What is it like? What is the political and religious structure? How many people are there? Please just give me a description and then I'll ask more questions when I'd like a deeper understanding."

"Gladly," replied Cheng as he started to describe the outside world's mixture of cultures. He described the different countries and nationalities. He gave estimates of the population as he remembered them. He described the wars and the conflicts between the countries."

"My gosh," exclaimed High Priest Chaviva. "That sounds like a terrible place to live. No wonder God has tried to keep us isolated from the Old World. I'm somewhat nervous about your arrival here because I don't want a flood of people eager to take what we have away from us. It happens to us time and time again. People come in and see the opportunity and try to steal from us. Sadly, we find it necessary to get rid of them before they do too much harm and I don't want that to happen again. So, my question to you is, 'What is your purpose for coming here?'"

"We came here because someone in the outer world was trying to kill us," explained Cheng.

"Are you criminals?" asked Chaviva. "Why would anyone be trying to kill you?"

The threesome saw that they were trapped into a tricky situation. Stephan sent out a message to his friends because he wasn't sure what to do. *"Do we tell him our entire story? Or do we make up some kind of short-cut lie?"*

"Let's leave out the XLs business," suggested Cheng. *"I'll start it out and you flow with me."* Then Cheng addressed High Priest Chaviva, "We are not criminals at all. We are being chased by criminals. We were part of a research program that developed a new way to record and transmit information. Unfortunately, the existing high-tech infrastructure would be destroyed if this new idea was implemented and that would mean an enormous economic loss. So, the individuals behind this structure tried to stop further development. They established laws and went after the leader of our research team and executed him. Then they went after the three of us because we are the only other three who know how this technology works. Fortunately, we were warned off by the execution of our leader and we escaped. But not until we were also shot at several times." Cheng pulled up his shirt and showed Chaviva the wound he had received in Cusco.

Stephan jumped in, "Simultaneous to all that occurring, I was on a hunt for the Lost Ten Tribes, and I thought they may be here somewhere. I had just found you when all of this was occurring, and I invited my colleagues to join me. That is why we are here now."

Chaviva looked skeptical. He had no reason to doubt their word, but he thought it was worth a challenge. "Is this new technology something we can use here?" he asked.

Stephan explained, "The problem is that we don't have the complete understanding of the process. We were the experimentation tools that were used by Dr. Clawson, the founder of this process. So we have no way to repeat it. But the people that are after us don't know that we don't know. They think we know how to do this, when in reality, the only one that could have repeated the process has already been killed by them."

Chaviva sat quietly for a moment, reflecting on what he had been told, and then he spoke up, "I have received spiritual confirmation that you are telling me the truth even though on the surface your story is full of holes. But I have no reason not to believe you. You are welcome here and I would like to have more conversations with you about what the outside world is like. Maybe we can spend some time today and then you can return again in the future so we can talk even more."

"That would be wonderful," exclaimed Stephan. "I would love to spend more time with you. I want to learn about your world every bit as much as you want to learn about mine. I have already scheduled a meeting tomorrow with someone to discuss how your anti-gravity processes work."

"Maybe all three of you can come back tomorrow and while you are meeting about the anti-gravity tools, I can meet with the other two of you to discuss life on the surface," requested the High Priest.

"That would be perfect," commented Frida.

They spent a couple more hours together and then the three returned home to Jericho using the flying saucer that had brought them. It was decided that since the flight was so short it would be easier to return to Jericho for the night and then return to Samaria the following day than it would be to set up a place to stay for just one night in Samaria.

Chapter Nineteen

Samaria

May, 2020 AD, Center Earth

The following day the threesome once again returned to Samaria. En route Stephan raised the question, *"What do you two think about where we're living? I get the impression we could stay in Samaria if we like that better. But whatever we do I think we should do it together. We should stay a unified threesome."*

"*I rather like life in Jericho,*" commented Frida. "*I like the relaxed, yet productive environment. I feel right at home there.*"

"*I agree,*" responded Cheng. "*And since coming to Samaria is so easy, we can come here any time that we want to experience the big city.*"

"*Then it's settled,*" responded Stephan. "*We stay in Jericho for now.*"

The day after arriving in Samaria, Frida and Cheng were escorted off to spend the day with Chaviva. This time the meeting also included several of the High Priest's associates who had begged him to be included in the conversations. They wanted to hear more about the outside world as well.

The group spent the day sharing stories about each other's history. Then they went into a detailed discussion about current events. Life in Center Earth was mild in comparison to life on the surface. In Center Earth they had the occasional skirmishes, and sometimes even wars between the tribes. But there was never the threat of mass extinction, as existed with the thermo nuclear bombs during the Cold War. Center Earth had their tyrants and crazy rulers, but not to the extreme of Hitler, Stalin, Idi Amin, or Pol Pot.

They also discovered numerous cultural differences. Center Earth was strongly religious based, retaining its roots to the twelve tribes. Some of the tribes were more economically successful than others. Unfortunately, these tended to be the ones that moved away from their religious roots the quickest and moved toward sectarianism. But not surprisingly, whenever tragedy struck, religion once again became important, no matter how economically successful the tribe may have been.

Another major difference was that Center Earth was not focused on a central power or authority. They functioned as an organization of ten individual city-states, much the way the old Greek Polis' functioned in the heyday of Greek civilization. Some of the tribes were even broken down further so that there was a collection of independent Polis communities within the tribe, similar to the way Jericho functioned.

The day passed by quickly and Frida and Cheng were disappointed when it came time to leave. They had found a level of friendship and had built a relationship with the Center Earth people that felt like they had been friends their entire life.

During this same time Stephan had been taken by a different guide to visit with Abigail, a senior scientist working on the anti-gravity project. Introductions were cordial. It was obvious that both were nervous.

"I am Stephen, from the outer world town known as Vacaville, California, in the United States of America," suggested Stephan.

"I have no idea what any of that means," responded Abigail.

Stephan continued, "The outer world is composed mostly of salt water, and the land masses are blocked into continents. I am from the continent called North America, which is composed of three countries. I am from the middle country. In technology, we are considered the world's superpower, however economically we are ranked second."

"What do you mean by economically?" questioned Abigail.

"In the outer world, money rules, and most success is measured in terms of money," responded Stephan.

"Not here," replied Abigail. "Here we define success by family status and church status."

"But I've noticed that some people are dressed more elaborately than others," challenged Stephan. "Doesn't that mean that they are richer?"

"In your terms yes, but to us we look up to the overall status of the person's family, and the clothes they wear is often a facade which we are not influenced by," insisted Abigail.

"That makes sense," responded a doubtful Stephan. But he didn't want to alienate this lady. He wanted to learn from her. Add to that, Abigail was hot and being a typical male, he treated a hot lady with more gentleness than he would have treated a male.

Gerhard Plenert

Abigail was average height, about five foot four, with dark eyes. She had long dark brown hair which was clean and perfectly combed. She was 25 years old and had a great smile. It didn't hurt that she had a pretty face and a cute figure. She wasn't anything like the scattered geeky looking female scientists that Stephan had been familiar with and had gone to school with.

Abigail returned the conversation to the reason for their meeting, "I understand that you're interested in our technologies. I was told that you're especially interested in our gravi-push-pull mechanisms."

As she went on with her explanations Stephan had no idea what Abigail was talking about. He knew she was trying to explain Middle Earth avionics. She started spewing out words that meant nothing to him. For the most part these were words that had been invented by the Center Earth scientific community to help them understand and explain what they were working on. After Stephan was successful in getting Abigail to "dumb down" her explanations, the discussion started making more sense. She started defining and explaining the terms she was using. Stephan was soon able to jump in on the conversation and ask intelligent questions.

The anti-gravity technology turned out to be much more complex than initially imagined. It wasn't just one simple tool that was used by Center Earth. It was actually a collection of several discoveries which were all linked together to create a tool they now referred to as anti-gravity.

The foundational discoveries involved an understanding of how energy was transmitted. Correct understanding and use of energy facilitated the ability to leverage large objects and move them in ways that were unknown to the surface world.

These foundational scientific discoveries also involved a redefinition of gravity. Gravity was not caused by mass. Rather, it was caused by friction. The Center Earth scientists understood that it was the movement of the earth through space which caused gravity, and not its weight. This explained why the earth could be hollow, and still have the gravity levels that seemed to be measured by mass. It also explained why the pull of gravity at different locations on the earth was different.

There were also several more foundational discoveries and as Abigail went through them, Stephan was completely amazed. Several of the principles that the surface scientific community considered to be basic truths, were contradicted by the Center Earth scientific community. Stephan felt like he had entered an entirely different dimension. He felt like he was no longer on the same earth. Each new explanation, and each new discovery, excited him more. There was so much that he could learn from these people.

At one point Stephan was standing next to Abigail and he accidently bumped into her. At first he was apologetic. He wasn't sure what Center Earth protocol was when it came to touching someone from the opposite sex.

"I'm sorry," he started to say.

"Don't worry about it," smiled Abigail. "It's no problem." After noticing that she laughed rather than feeling offended he decided to repeat the accidental bumping.

As Stephan and Abigail spent the day together, they both started to feel a strong attraction. It was a magnetism that grew slowly over time and became increasingly stronger. Soon the bumping became a game. He would bump into her, and she would in turn bump into him. After a while they developed a comfort level that encouraged closeness. It became so strong that Stephan started to become infatuated with Abigail, not just because of her scientific expertise, but because he thought she was hot.

Stephan would become more engrossed in the way she spoke to the point where he almost wasn't hearing what she was saying. He had never felt this way before. This had become a strange feeling which he liked but at the same time it made him feel uncomfortable.

The day started with the two of them just smiling a lot and acting courteously. Then, after a couple hours, when they had become more comfortable with each other began joking with each other. Soon joking turned to flirtatious bumping and teasing. A couple more hours and then there was increased occasional physical contact, like a hand on the shoulder or a slight hug. As much as he enjoyed the science that Abigail was explaining, Stephan was even more overwhelmed with the attraction he was feeling. He didn't know what was appropriate for Abigail's culture and he didn't want to offend her and ruin everything. This fear caused him to be reserved in his actions. He moved slowly, but he was excited and wanted desperately to develop a relationship with her.

Abigail also felt the same resistance to push the relationship too quickly. She didn't want to push and ruin a good thing. But as Stephan explained some of the looseness and openness of the surface world societies, she wondered why he was so slow at taking her hand or even giving her a serious hug. As the day started to come to a close, she started to become concerned that she might never see Stephan again and she decided to push the issue. At one point, when they were standing close together watching an experiment, and as Abigail explained what was happening, she decided it was time. She leaned over and kissed Stephan on the cheek.

Stephan looked surprised! The suddenness of the kiss made him take a step backwards and he stumbled slightly. Abigail became concerned that she had somehow overstepped her bounds and started to pull back. But Stephan quickly regained his composure and refusing to miss out on this opportunity put one hand on each side of her face, pulled her face toward his, and slowly kissed her on the mouth.

After the kiss he said, "Thanks for opening that door. I was afraid to break a cultural barrier. But I wanted so much to kiss your pretty face. It was driving me nuts."

This time it was Abigail who was slightly stunned. She realized that Stephan's feelings for her were mutual. She had hoped it was mutual, but she was never-the-less stunned by the suddenness of his response. She decided to let him know that she approved. She came back at him and kissed him in return, but this time it wasn't a quick peck, this time it was a long, drawn-out kiss. Both of them felt like they had just achieved nirvana.

"You're welcome," responded Abigail. "I thought I'd better make the first move since you seemed hesitant. But now I hope you know that my feelings are mutual. I want to spend more time with you. I want you to move here to Samaria so we can work together more often."

"I would love that too," replied Stephan. "Will you help me make the move and find a place to stay?"

"Of course," responded Abigail.

It was amazing how quickly life had changed. Suddenly for Stephan, being with his friends was no longer important. Being with Abigail was what he wanted more than anything else in the world. He couldn't wait to let the world know. He immediately sent out a message to his two friends, *"I changed my mind. I want to stay in Samaria. You guys stay in Jericho. I want to move and live here. Sorry."*

Within seconds he received the message back from Frida, *"Don't worry. We'll stay in touch and work together just as much when you're living here as with you living with us. Apparently, you found something here making the move worthwhile."* Secretly Frida and Cheng were glad to have Stephan move away so they could spend more time together and alone. Stephan was a bit of a third wheel in their relationship. Now they would be able to spend more time together.

"Her name is Abigail," was all Stephan needed to say, and Frida and Cheng understood completely.

Chapter Twenty

Visitors

May, 2020 AD, Center Earth

Life started to become routine as the days and weeks passed by. Stephen had found himself a new role working in the technology labs of Samaria. Cheng and Frida continued their agriculture and mining roles in Jericho. They missed their old homes, but they were now extremely comfortable were starting to feel at home in this new world.

After having lived in their new environment for about one month, Cheng suddenly and unexpectedly received a message from the aliens, the same one that had contacted him previously. He had completely forgotten about their previous efforts to try to communicate, having been distracted by the new world that they now lived in. The alien message was coded, similar to the coding used for the SETI Arecibo message that he had sent out to them. But the message came with numerous unexpected surprises. The DNA code that he had described in his message for the people on earth came back from the aliens with three rather than two strands. The alien DNA was a triple helix rather than the double helix. There was a triangular bond rather than the double bond that influenced and affected them in every aspect of their life, unlike the dual male-female bond that existed in life here on earth. The aliens DNA strands were shorter, and they were linked differently than anything on earth.

Another major alien difference was that rather than a pair of sexual opposites, these aliens came as a triad. It wasn't just a man and a woman who came together to create a child, it was a threesome that was needed. Creation for these aliens required three sexually different individuals, it was a man, a woman, and a non-man, a term Cheng invented because he didn't know what else to call this third partner. Cheng wasn't sure how this worked. The message he received wasn't specific enough to explain everything. But he could see that there were some dramatic differences.

The triad relationship raised all sorts of questions in his mind. What did the family look like? How did the social relationship work and what were the roles of each of the individuals in the triad? The entire social structure of these aliens must be dramatically different than what he was familiar with on earth.

The bodies of these aliens had a lot of similarities with the bodies of humans. They had a head, a body, which had two arms, one on either side, and two legs. But the sexual organs were significantly different. And the coded message that he received wasn't enough to explain how all of this worked.

Cheng forwarded the message to Frida and Stephan who immediately responded with comments about how strange and unexpected these aliens were. Because of their super abilities the threesome were able to converse without interrupting their other work They were able to talk about the aliens with no one noticing. *"I don't get how all this works,"* responded Frida. *"This just doesn't seem right somehow."*

Stephan chimed in, *"In their message I see what I think is a comment suggesting that they are sending a group of envoys to come and visit us."*

"Where do you see that?" questioned Cheng.

Stephan explained why he interpreted the message to suggest that the aliens were coming. Frida and Cheng looked at what Stephen was focusing on and readily agreed that Stephan's interpretation seemed reasonable. *"Meeting them is going to be even stranger than coming here to Center Earth,"* commented Cheng. *"These aliens seem extremely advanced. How are we going to deal with them? They're going to see us as completely backwards. Maybe contacting them wasn't such a good idea. This is going to shake out like one of those Sci-Fi movies where the aliens come and find us backwards so they use us for slave labor or food or something like that."*

"Quit talking like that," complained Frida. *"You're freaking me out."*

"We have to be optimistic and assume the best," suggested Stephan. *"We need to assume that they are friendly and that there is a lot we can learn from them."*

"I sure hope you're right," explained Frida. *"Regardless, it's too late for us to do anything about it now. Is there anything we should do to prepare for their visit? Should we warn someone?"*

"Not sure how we can do that," explained Stephan. *"Our pilot won't be back again for a year, so we can't*

talk to anyone. And even if we were able to talk to someone, what would we say? Do you think they'll believe that we can talk to aliens and that we invited them to come to earth? We need to get ready? But if we involve anyone else they're going to think we're completely crazy."

"We're not as isolated as you think," explained Cheng. "We can send a message to the pilot and tell him we need him to come to Center Earth. I think we'll surprise him, but I think we can figure out how to get out of here anytime we like. I think you're right in that even if we get out of here and spread the message, no one will believe us anyway. Who speaks to aliens and invites them over for dinner? That's science fiction craziness."

"Should we at least communicate with them and ask them a few questions?" asked Stephan. "It would be useful to know when they are coming and what they plan to do while they're here. It would be helpful if they were able to transmit some of their language by sending symbols or pictures and sounds across to us. It would also be helpful to see some images of their world. Cheng, would you be willing to do that since it seems like you've become the point of contact for us?"

"And don't say anything like 'Dinner is waiting'," requested Frida. "I'm not sure I like that idea."

"Don't worry," replied Cheng. "You'd be desert anyway!" Then, addressing Stephan's request Cheng said, "I'll try to get some answers to your questions. They're reasonable questions and the answers would be helpful."

"This is all very exciting!" explained Stephan and the discussion of the aliens ceased. The three were left with their thoughts. They reflected how dramatically their lives had changed within the last few months, and it all started with the risky removal of a tumor.

October, 2020 AD, Five Months Later near the Moon

It had been months since Cheng requested more information from the potential alien visitors. He had repeated the message several times using various symbols and images, but never received a response. The threesome had convinced themselves that there must be some social protocol that made his request unreasonable or possibly even insulting. These were completely different creatures from those that existed on the earth, and so nothing should come as a surprise. Or maybe they simply had no clue what he was talking about. After all, a common language had not yet been established.

It had been about five months when Cheng finally received another unexpected message. It came in the form of an image. It was a picture of the moon, with the earth off in the distance. The message was clear. The visitors were here.

Cheng responded to the message with a repeat of his earlier request. But again, there was no response. A couple hours later he received another image. This time it was of Bangalore, India from a distance of about 50,000 feet. Cheng wasn't sure how to interpret the image. Was it an invitation to meet? Or was it a warning or threat? He quickly realized that this process was going to be more complicated than working with the Center Earth people.

Cheng shared his information with the remainder of his XL team and asked, "What do you think they're trying to say?"

Frida and Stephan tried to interpret the images. "I'm not making any sense of it," commented Frida.

"I agree," supported Stephan. "There just isn't enough here to come to any conclusions. I don't have any answers, just more questions."

"Should we try to meet with them," asked Frida.

"I think we should just wait and see," suggested Cheng. "Like Stephan said, we just don't have enough information to decide what to do next. Hopefully we'll get more information so we can make a reasonable decision."

"Let just stay hidden here in Center Earth and watch to see what happens," commented Frida, somewhat tongue-in-cheek sarcastic. "Let's wait to see if these aliens are aggressive or friendly. Then, if they're nice, we can still go out to visit them. But if they're not so nice, maybe we'll just want to stay away."

They unanimously decided that they would wait to see if the visitors were here to suck away earth's resources, or if they were just curious about the earth and its inhabitants.

Chapter Twenty-One

Another Visit

October, 2020 AD, Bangalore, India

Rajesh was riding his motor scooter to visit his cousins which was just a short fifty-minute ride through the traffic to the other end of town. His wife was sharing the seat, sitting behind him with one arm around his waist and the other arm holding on to his ten-year-old daughter who was sitting on her lap. The daughter held on to his two-year-old brother. Sitting in front of him with his feet propped up against the handlebars was another five-year-old son. This seemed risky, but Rajesh was careful not to go more than about 20 miles per hour. He wasn't rich and barely survived on his income working at the clothing factory. He couldn't afford a second scooter, let alone a car. So this was the way they had to travel.

His cousin was celebrating a birthday and the entire family was expected to be there. He wasn't about to be left out of fulfilling this family obligation. The road was extremely dusty. But even worse was the thick blanket of smog that covered the entire city. Bangalore was classified as the most polluted city in the world. Rajesh knew that this wasn't healthy for his family, but he felt trapped. He would never be able to find work outside of the city. He considered himself lucky to have the job he had since his skills were limited. Additionally, being classified an untouchable made it impossible to move up any social ladder. So, he maintained as best he could.

The traffic was really bad that day. He found himself weaving between a multitude of cars and buses, and a barrage of other motor scooters. He had made this trip so often that he was numb to all the risks. He had become used to this environment and couldn't see any changes in his future.

He heard a sound. He wasn't sure what it was, but it was loud enough to be heard above all the traffic noise. It seemed to be coming from everywhere at once and from all directions. He noticed some people looking up in the sky causing him to look up as well. He didn't notice that the car in front of him had slammed on his brakes. Luckily, he was only traveling about 5 MPH at the time. He bumped into the back end of the car causing his entire family to come crashing forward and falling to the street. Luckily no one was seriously injured, but there were plenty of cuts, scrapes, and curse words.

After making sure his family was safe, Rajesh looked up again and found the source of the attention. It was a ball. It looked like a perfect round ball with the diameter of a five-story building. As best as Rajesh could tell through the distortion of the thick smog it was about 300 feet off the ground. There were no windows or identifying marks. It was a big floating ball which glowed. The ball seemed to emanate light, but Rajesh couldn't tell if the light was being emitted by the ball or if it was a reflection from the sun.

The floating ball rotated and spun in an erratic motion. It didn't move away from the spot where it was positioned. It just rotated. Rajesh didn't know what to make of it. He had never seen anything like this before, not even in the movies. Movies were the authority on all things alien. Was there something alive in this ball? Was it a ship of some kind? He couldn't tell.

Rajesh was so fascinated with the ball that he didn't notice his wife beating on his shoulder screaming that she was scared and wanted to get away. She was begging him to get going so they could move away from this place. Slowly Rajesh's wife's shaking brought him back around to reality. But, as he started to look away from the ball, it suddenly disappeared. He didn't even notice it move if it moved at all. It was just gone. Did it become invisible, or did it move really fast? He just wasn't sure.

He reassembled his family on his motor scooter. Luckily there wasn't any damage to the bike because of the accident. He was ready to go and once again headed off to the birthday party of his cousin.

October, 2020 AD, near Perth, Australia

Kiffin loved sheep and his 2,000-acre sheep station south of Perth was his pride and joy. He raised sheep for wool and meat, and he was good at it. He was respected by his neighbors as a good friend and confidant. He was tall, nearly seven feet with a sun beaten and weathered rugged look. He was the complete cowboy image sitting upright on his horse, his hat on his head, looking out in the distance as he surveyed his station.

It was a bright, sunny, beautiful spring West Australia kind of day. The weather was perfect; not too hot, in the mid 80's. The sky didn't have a cloud anywhere. As he spied his sheep off in the distance, he could see that all was well. Then suddenly, and unexpectedly, he was covered by a shadow. It was so sudden that it scared him. His reaction was to sit back in the saddle and slouch down slightly, as if something was about to hit him in the head. After a couple seconds, when he had recovered from the initial surprise, he looked skyward to see what was causing the shadow. There, above him in the sky, was an enormous ball. It looked like the kind of ball his kids might have been playing with, but it was enormous. It hung there, floating in the sky. It seemed so close that he wondered if he could reach up and touch it. After a few more seconds, when he saw that nothing was happening, he felt a little braver. He reached up to touch the big ball but found that it was too high, just out of his reach.

He started to feel uncomfortable sitting under this big object, so he decided to ride away from it. He thought he would ride out and look back at it from a comfortable distance. But he was too slow and too late. The ball bounced on the ground right where Kiffin's horse was standing.

It would be several days before anyone was successful in finding Kiffin's body. And then all they could find was a smashed and flattened Kiffin, pancaked on top of his horse, and pressed into the ground. The bodies of the man and his horse were so flattened at ground level that they didn't even make a bump.

October, 2020 AD, Planet Earth

News of the bouncing ball traveled quickly. The ball had visited most of the continents, including Antarctica. At first the news media demonized it as some type of military experiment gone badly. No one wanted to suggest that it could possibly be aliens from another planet. That was too science fiction for anyone to accept. Everyone hoped for some kind of earth-bound explanation. If anyone were to dare suggest that it might be alien, they would be scorned and ostracized. Only the crazy wacko extreme nut cases would come up with an off-the-wall explanation like that.

There was no end to all the news commentaries with their guest expert scientists, and all the crazy theories they proposed about terrorist attacks, or a new kind of spy probe, or science experiments gone bad. Unfortunately, none of the conspiracy theories held any water. They didn't seem to fit. It was all just beyond explanation. This ball seemed to randomly bounce around the world, including bouncing on the water as if it was as hard as the ground.

Several attempts had been made to engage the ball. Jet fighters had charged it and attempted to communicate with it using every form of signal imaginable, including sound, light, and every wavelength known to man. But there was no response.

There was no indication whether the ball had occupants or if it was controlled remotely. There was no power source like engines which would explain the balls' ability to float in the sky. The experts were baffled and didn't know what to do next.

After a couple weeks of the ball bouncing around the world, fear started to set in. The bounce of the ball had caused the occasional death and had destroyed a few buildings, and had even sunk a ship, but it had not made any threatening motions which would imply evil intentions. It just bounced. But the unknown has always been the greatest cause of fear.

The United Nations held a special session to discuss the "Ball Problem" as it had become known. Just weeks earlier the term "ball" had implied a game. But now the same term brought fear into people's mind. The UN was tasked with identifying a solution. The world wanted to know what the ball was.

Following a general session which was open for discussion to all nations, the UN held a special session of the Security Council to discuss the "Ball Problem." Of the 15 members in the Security Council, 10 of the members voted for an attack on the ball claiming that it was dangerous and had killed several people in various countries around the globe. They voted to wait until the ball was somewhere safe, like over the ocean, and then it should be sprayed with weapons fire including missiles with ever increasing force until it was destroyed.

The dissenting votes on the Security Council stressed that there might actually be people in the ball and that destroying it might kill an unknown number of individuals. They stressed that the ball hadn't actually demonstrated any intent to do harm. The harm it had inflicted seemed accidental. They were concerned that fear was ruling the decision, and not logic.

Never-the-less the vote stood and the decision of the council to move forward with lethal force was implemented. The next step would be to identify the best timing for the attack. United States troops were assigned to carry out the assault. They would wait until the ball was over an ocean. Then the attack would come in waves. The first wave would be missiles shot from a team of three fighters. Then the fighters would disperse and watch what happens. Next another wave of fighters would move in with a heavier payload and repeat the exercise. This would continue, with an ever-increasing payload with the hope that eventually they would see a reaction of some type. In spite of all their preparations, no one was ready for the unexpected. The "ball" disappeared.

October, 2020 AD, Arecibo Observatory

The Arecibo Observatory was a radio telescope in the municipality of Arecibo, Puerto Rico. It was established by the National Science Foundation. The observatory's 1,000 ft aperture is the world's largest single-aperture telescope. It is used for several areas of research including radio astronomy, aeronomy, and radar astronomy.

Butch was busily monitoring the screens. The telescope was focused on a specific galaxy, and the readings were coming in as anticipated. He leaned back in his chair, letting the data recording continue freely, not anticipating any surprises. The hum of the recording became rhythmic and hypnotic. He became a little too comfortable with the boredom and started to doze off. Suddenly, and unexpectedly there was a loud screech over the speakers causing Butch to jump up out of the chair. He quickly turned down the volume on the speakers and went over to the monitors to see if he could identify the cause of the problem.

Reviewing the display on the monitors Butch saw that they had been recording a steady osculation, nothing special, everything seemed normal, and then there was a sudden, unexplainable series of enormous spikes. It was completely strange. In the past there would have been the occasional bird or plane that interfered with the signal, but nothing quite as dramatic as what he was now seeing. It appeared as if the entire telescope had somehow been blocked. No signal was getting through at all; not even a distorted one.

The entire event was so strange that it made Butch get up from his chair and walk outside to see what was going on. Had the telescope collapsed? He wasn't sure what he would find, but he couldn't resist looking.

Looking out over the telescope Butch saw nothing. Then he looked skyward and was in total disbelief. The entire area was covered by a giant floating ball. It was sitting so close to the ground that he felt like he could almost reach up and touch it. He even reached up and tried, but he knew it was futile.

The ball rested quietly over the top of the telescope. It completely covered the telescope and the surrounding area. And it just floated there, doing nothing, completely obstructing the ability of the telescope to pick up any recordings.

October, 2020 AD, White House Situation Room

The United States military surrounded the conference table. It was the Secretary of Defense who spoke up first, "We have a United Nations Security Council directive in hand which instructs us to go and blow this big bouncy ball out of the sky, and you're telling me that there's nothing we can do?"

"Unfortunately, there isn't," responded the Secretary of the Air Force. "The darn thing just disappeared. We have no idea where it went. We haven't come up with a way to track it other than visually observing. It's not metal and isn't emitting any signals that we can recognize. It has no definable engine noise or anything else we can track. It just has its size. And visual tracking is challenging because it moves so fast that it's easy to lose."

"So I guess we're saying the attack is off for now," responded the Secretary of Defense.

"I don't see where we have any other choice," replied the Air Force. "We'll stay on alert just in case it resurfaces, but for now we'll just have to stay on hold."

Chapter Twenty-Two

Silence

November, 2020 AD, Center Earth

Normally when there was no news it was considered to be good news. But the three visitors to the center of the earth found the silence disturbing. It had been nearly three weeks since the last communication from the aliens. They knew that the aliens had made it past the moon and were probably somewhere on the earth. They saw the images of Bangalore. But where are they? Have they made contact? What were they doing?

Cheng sent out numerous requests but there was never a response. He was convinced that either the aliens were hiding out, or else they weren't friendly. Stephan, on the other hand, insisted that the three must have violated some cultural barrier or taboo. He was convinced that something had angered them, and they were now refusing to respond to any communication. He wasn't sure what it was. Maybe it was the repeated persistent messages that Cheng was sending out. Maybe the simple act of requesting information was intrusive. He wasn't sure what it was, but he was convinced that these aliens were friendly and that the threesome had somehow alienated the aliens.

Having lost Dr. Clawson, who was their primary contact with the world outside, the threesome had no idea how to communicate with the outside world. If they sent a message to someone, then they would probably scare them. Whoever they contacted would be resistive to telling anyone about being contacted because they might get labelled schizophrenic. There was no one out there that they could trust.

They wondered if the aliens even tried to contact the people of earth. Maybe they just looked at earth and decided it was too backwards to work with. Maybe they already left. It was frustrating not knowing.

"Maybe we can work with the pilot? asked Stephan. *"He's already familiar with our strange adventures. He may not be surprised by our ability to communicate."*

"That's exactly what I was thinking," responded Cheng. *"Why don't you give it a try?"*

"I'll let you know what I learn," replied Stephan.

November, 2020 AD, Seattle, Washington

A senior security official was reporting into the CEO of Technosoft, "The hit on the three XLs, as we're calling them, was a failure. The asset that was sent to do the mission arrived too late. They simply vanished from Cusco. We're not sure what happened to them. They're obviously getting help from somewhere."

"Are you kidding me?" the CEO was in a tirade. "I have the top security team of any company in the world. You guys are highly valued military assets. And you allowed three inexperienced geeks to escape your grasp? What's going on here? This is crazy." After fuming for a few minutes, the CEO settled down a little and asked, "What are your next steps?"

The security officer continued, "We learned that there are some individuals who are trying to replicate Dr. Clawson's surgeries in the attempt to learn how he did them, but we have managed to invoke legislation that doesn't allow human experimentation. Without that they'll never know if the experiment was a success."

"That's not what I'm interested in. I want to know about the threesome," challenged the CEO.

"They simply vanished," replied the officer. "We have individuals working their trail. We followed them going to Lima and getting on a plane to Copenhagen. And that's where my team is working on trying to figure out the next leg of their journey. We'll find them. My team has always been successful. But the trail has been a hard one to follow. One thing that confuses us is that only two of them seem to be following this route. We're assuming they're following the third super, but we're not sure. The only thing we know for sure is that the third one is not in Peru."

"I need them eliminated and discredited," replied the CEO. "We can't have people thinking that there is something better than computers or cell phones. That would be devastating to the entire electronics industry. We have to put a stop to this for the sake of the world's economy. Millions of people will be put out of a job."

"And you'll lose your status as one of the richest men in the world," thought the officer to himself.

The CEO continued," I don't care what it takes; we have to find these three and put a stop to this fantasy. And we need to stop the experimentation on the process. We need to have it discredited as a foolish fantasy that had no basis in reality. It's ridiculous to think we're going to charge around the world and do surgery on everyone's brain. That's just not practical. And the only way to put a stop to this nonsense is to show it for what it is; utter nonsense."

November, 2020 AD, Davis, California

The University of California, Davis medical center was frantically attempting to recover Dr. Clawson's knowledge. They searched through his handwritten and computer notes and his video recordings in an attempt to learn how he had performed the surgeries. They experimented with monkeys that had brain tumors, in some cases these tumors were medically induced, in an attempt to replicate the surgery. But all attempts were failures. Either the monkey died or, if it recovered, they couldn't come up with a way to test it for multiprogramming capabilities. It was impossible to get a good test without a human subject, and the use of human subjects for this specific experiment, even if they were willing to sign releases, had been outlawed.

"I can't believe that the power brokers would destroy something that has the potential to do so much good in the world," grunted Dr. Wagton. "Money definitely has more influence in Washington DC than common sense."

"Perhaps if we talked with the three XLs that Dr. Clawson created we can learn more about the procedure," suggested one of his aides.

"No one has any idea where they're at," replied the doctor. "The government scientists wanted to turn them into lab rats and Dr. Clawson helped hide them so that wouldn't happen. But no one has any idea what happened to them after that. And now that he's gone, I'm sure they're more scared and therefore more cautious about their safety than ever."

"Can you blame them?" responded the aide.

"Here is what I want to do," Dr. Wagton started to explain without answering the question. "I want our little team to travel to another country and attempt these surgeries on patients in these foreign locations. I think the monkey trials will continue to be failures because their brains, as similar as they may seem to be to the human brain, they are still different. So I need to perform these surgeries on humans. And I'm looking to see who is willing to travel with me."

"You know what that means?" a second aide spoke up. "It means we can't return to the United States or else we can be arrested. The way the law is written it doesn't allow an American citizen to do this surgery. It's specific to the U.S.A. citizen, not to the operation being physically located in the United States."

"Yes," replied the doctor. "After doing the surgery we would be stuck with staying overseas for seven years until the statute of limitations runs out, or until the law gets changed. We have the medical community already trying to change the law. But that's unpredictable and unlikely since the money power brokers were the ones that caused the law to be enacted in the first place. And no congressman is going to go against the guys with the money, especially if they fund their campaign. I'm not counting on any change to any of the laws. I'm going to go do this, but I don't expect anyone else to join me on this little adventure, especially if you have families that would be placed at risk."

The first aide chimed in, "You may be able to get around the law by going overseas, but you won't be able to get away from the hit squad. They'll be out there after you if you do this."

"That's the bigger concern," agreed the doctor. "But I don't know what else to do. The only other option is to give up. And I don't like that option."

"Another option is to have the lawyers keep pushing and wait until the law gets changed," replied the second aide. "And not do anything till then."

"But that's the point," responded the doctor. "If I'm overseas doing this, then I'll be that much ahead when the law does indeed finally get changed. Showing success will help to put pressure on Congress to make a change."

"I guess you're set on doing this regardless of the danger you're putting yourself and your family into," replied the second aide.

"I guess I am," confirmed Dr. Wagton, but in his mind he was rethinking the risk that he was putting his family into. Up to now he was just focused on his own personal risk. But there would also be a risk on his family. Was this worth it? He wasn't sure.

November, 2020 AD, Center Earth

Stephan had taken a chance and had transmitted a message to the pilot. He asked him if there was any way that he could return to Center Earth earlier and bring an update of what was happening in the outside world.

The response from the pilot was nonexistent. The threesome had forgotten an important principal. The pilot didn't have the ability to send a message. It was a ridiculous and foolish attempt to try to communicate with him.

"*You know,*" commented Stephan, "*unless that pilot had our powers, he wouldn't be able to send us a message. I sent a message to the pilot, but there's no way for him to answer us.*"

"*Probably the only thing we accomplished was to freak him out,*" suggested Frida.

"*I wish I could have seen his face when you sent out the message,*" commented Cheng. "*I'll bet he was a bit surprised by it all.*"

"*After bringing him to the center of the earth I'm not sure if anything we do would surprise him anymore,*" suggested Stephan.

The threesome gave up the attempt to communicate and considered it a waste of time. However, two days later, much to their surprise, the plane that had brought all of them to Center Earth was suddenly flying over Jericho.

The pilot landed in his usual spot on the street outside of Jericho. Cheng and Frida ran to his location in order to talk to him. Cheng sent a message to Stephan letting him know that the pilot had returned. Stephan immediately arranged for one of the Center Earth air transport vehicles to bring him from Samaria to Jericho. He informed Cheng and Frida that he would be arriving shortly.

"What's up," asked the pilot as he stepped out of the plane.

"We are thrilled that you received our message," replied Cheng. "We weren't sure how you'd react to it."

"Actually, I was quite shocked at first," replied the pilot. "I didn't like the idea that you could poke into my mind. But then, after I thought about it I came to the conclusion that nothing you guys do surprises me anymore."

"For your information, we can't peek into your mind anymore than when we're talking to you verbally," explained Cheng. "We can send you messages, just like we can talk to you now. But that's it."

Cheng invited the pilot to join in the mid-day meal and they headed off to eat. This allowed a sufficient amount of time for Stephan to get to Jericho so that he could join in the conversations.

After arriving, Stephan joined the group. He went straight to the pilot and apologized, "Sorry about freaking you out. We're desperate to learn about what's going on in the outside world. As you can guess, the news down here is limited. We received a message from some aliens many weeks ago, but we haven't heard anything since and we're dying of curiosity."

The pilot explained how a ball had been bouncing all over the earth and he wondered if these were the aliens that Stephan was talking about.

"I really don't know," explained Stephan. "We communicated with these aliens in the past, but we really have no clue about what's going on now. We haven't heard from them since they first passed by the moon. They're not responding to our messages."

Cheng suggested, "One of us should probably go out to the surface and see if that would improve communications. Maybe there is a problem with us being inside the earth."

"I was thinking that too," replied Stephan. "I'm not convinced it will work, but we should try everything we can. I'll go to the surface with the pilot and see if I can open up a channel of communication. It's worth a try."

"But the next question is, 'What do we do if they respond?'" questioned Frida.

"That's the million-dollar question," replied Cheng. "The problem is that the answer to that question depends on their response. At least if Stephan is on the surface, we can communicate with him and work out a plan."

"Let's do it," responded Stephan. "Can we go right now?" he questioned the pilot.

"Of course," answered the pilot. Stephan and the pilot climbed on board the plane and headed for Greenland. He wrote a quick note to Abigail and had the pilot of the Center Earth air transport vehicle deliver it back to her when he returned to Samaria. Stephan had not yet braved the need to share his super XL abilities with Abigail, and so he hesitated to send her a mental message. He didn't want to scare her off. Maybe, if their relationship continued to develop, the time would eventually come when he would need to share his abilities with her. He hoped she would react positively and not freak out.

Chapter Twenty-Three

Aliens

November, 2020 AD, Greenland

Stephan and his pilot arrived safely in the North-East Greenland National Park Daneborg Station without incident. Stephan decided to spend one day there before moving on. He wanted to see if their previous attempts at communicating with the aliens from Center Earth was the problem. He hoped that there was just a blockage and that the blockage was now eliminated with his arrival on the surface. He hoped they weren't just ignoring him.

He sent out a message. He did not receive an immediate response. Surprisingly, about three hours later the big ball that had been traveling the earth was suddenly overhead. Everyone at the station stepped outside to look at the ball as it slowly moved down to the earth as if it was landing. The place it stopped was over the bay, landing on the frozen icepack.

Stephan continued to send messages, hoping that one of his messages might finally get through and get a response. But still there was nothing. Stephan sent images to Frida and Cheng letting them know what was happening. They were amazed and stunned.

The ball just sat there. It had been stationed on the ice for about one hour when suddenly it started to rotate in place. It appeared to be spinning faster and faster. Then, unexpectedly, a door opened near the ground side of the ship. The spinning continued, but it didn't seem to have an effect on the open door. The door stayed in one place, but the rest of the ball continued to look like it was spinning. A platform quickly moved out of the opened door and stretched out to the surface of the ice.

No one appeared. The spinning ball with the open door just sat there for over ten minutes. Then Stephan heard a voice in his mind which said, *"Enter!"* He looked around to see if anyone was moving towards the ball, but no one reacted to the voice. Then he realized that he was the only one who had heard the voice. Not knowing what else to do, Stephan walked toward the ramp and then walked up the ramp, slowly heading toward the door of the alien ship.

When he arrived at the top of the ramp, just before he entered the ship, he was stunned. There was nothing there. It was a big empty ball, just like the inside of any ball would look. He was confused. He didn't want to take another step because he would just fall into the ball and slide down the side to the bottom.

Again, he heard the alien voice in his head, *"Enter!"*

Stephan stepped forward. To his amazement he didn't fall. His foot touched a surface, but he couldn't see it. He moved forward taking another step. Again, it held up. The floor that wasn't there fascinated him so much that he had to reach down and touch it. As he tried to touch the floor, his hand went right through it, as if there was no floor there. But his feet held strong. His feet didn't sink even though his hands couldn't find a floor. It looked like he was floating in midair in the center of an enormous ball.

He stood there floating in the middle of the ball for about five minutes with nothing happening and hearing nothing. Then, in what seemed from nowhere, a door opened. But it was more like a hole in the wall opening up except there wasn't a wall there. It was just a door in the middle of the open air. Stephan could see through the door and next to the door, all the way to the other side of the ball. However, a door did indeed open and out stepped an alien.

The alien was about five feet tall. It had the general body structure of a human, having a head, a body, two arms, and two legs. The head didn't look like a normal human head. It was a perfect circle. It was a ball with some minor identifiable features like eyes and ears. The eyes were vertical slits rather than the normal horizontal human slits. And the eyes had the ability to move around the head. They weren't attached in a fixed position at the front of the head as with humans. These eyes could rotate to the side of the head, or to the back, and even to the top of the head.

The ears were holes. They didn't have the outside structure that human ears have. And they also moved around the ball head freely, just like the eyes. What Stephan assumed was the mouth was just a circular hole. There was no noticeable nose. Stephan assumed the mouth hole must serve as both the mouth and the nose. Maybe the mouth was just for breathing or eating. It didn't seem to be used for speaking.

There was no hair or chin or any other features that distinguished the front of the head from the back. The alien could have turned completely around, and Stephan wouldn't have noticed any difference.

The alien wore clothing, which seemed strange as well. His arms and legs were covered with sleeves, and the main part of his body was covered with something that looked like a girl's one-piece bathing suit. Stephan could see skin between each of the sleeves and the body suit. The legs were also partially covered, just like the sleeves. There was a gap between the leggings and the body suit. Each of the five pieces of clothing was a different color. It looked quite strange.

Stephan had no idea if this was a male, a female, or a non-man. He had no idea how to tell the difference. But for now, it really didn't matter.

The alien's hands and feet were also covered with something that looked like gloves. They were made from leather or some type of plastic.

The alien didn't speak verbally. He just transmitted a message to Stephan's mind. "*Welcome,*" he said, which seemed a little strange to Stephan since the alien was visiting his world and Stephan should be the one welcoming him. Stephan received the message in sixteen different languages including English, Russian, Spanish, Chinese, and several more that he couldn't identify.

Stephan returned the message in English, "*I am happy to finally meet you. English is the most universal language on this planet and that's the language I speak. Can you tell me more about why you're here and how I can help you?*"

"We wanted to learn about your world," explained the alien. *"We have found that there are very few of you who can communicate with us. It took a long time to find you so we could communicate with you. We kept getting messages from one of your kind, but we couldn't locate the source of the message. We are not able to communicate verbally, and it seems that most of the population of this planet can only communicate verbally. What makes you different than the rest? What makes it so you can communicate when no one else can?"*

"My friends and I are different," responded Stephan. *"We can communicate in ways others cannot. The other people on this planet are intelligent except that they can only communicate verbally."* Stephan was concerned that the aliens may be thinking that the other inhabitants of the earth were inferior. He didn't want the aliens to be left with that impression even though he knew that the rest of the citizens of earth didn't have the XLs capabilities.

"There was a time when we could communicate verbally," explained the alien, *"but my people rarely used this form of communication and over time we have lost the ability. We can make some meaningless sounds with our mouths, but they are not intelligible worlds. We are very interested in your capabilities. We have come here to understand your species and your culture. You have made it easy because you have many recordings and transmissions to learn from. We came here to learn from you."*

He continued, *"We find your culture extremely interesting. You are a very simplistic culture. Your DNA has only two strands whereas our DNA has three. You only require sexual interaction between two individuals, which seems so incomplete and unsatisfying to us. We require three. You have two sexes, men and women, and we have three, a-men, b-men, and c-men. You believe in the dichotomy of good and evil or truth and falsehood. We understand life as a trichotomy of ultimate truth, intended falsehood, and reality. We find your people a simplistic disappointment. Life is not just black and white, as you say. Life is much more complex. Maybe your black and white approach to life is the reason you have so many brutal wars. We tend to be able to find a middle compromising ground and as a result many of our disputes are solved quickly."*

"I am sorry that you see us as a disappointment," explained a defensive Stephan. *"But at this point I see your race as a disappointment as well. You are judgmental and have diminished us as inferior without ever having had meaningful communication with any of us. Anyone that can pass judgment having only heard one side of the story is intellectually inferior."*

"You explained that you look for truth, evil, and reality," continued Stephan. *"You stressed your superior belief in a triad. Why have you only looked at one perspective rather than all three before passing judgment?"*

Stephan wasn't about to let this alien discredit the entire human race. But apparently Stephan's bluntness and defensiveness were offensive to the alien and the visitor walked back through the door where he had entered. It was strange because he just started to walk backwards. His eyes flipped around to the other side of his head and suddenly what had previously been the back side of the alien was now the front side. He just flipped directions.

After passing through the door the alien closed the door and the alien along with the door simply disappeared.

Stephan was disappointed at his own boldness. He didn't expect the alien to become offended so easily. After all, the alien had been blunt and offensive to him. Still, he didn't expect the alien to just walk out. Stephan felt stupid, as if he had just ruined the earth's one and only attempt to communicate with an alien species. How could he have been so dumb? He turned around and started to walk towards the ramp of the ship where he had entered assuming that the conversation with the alien was finished. He was halfway to the exit when he received the message, *"Wait."*

Stephan turned around to see the mysterious inner door open again, but this time from a different location than previously. Or was it the same location? It was difficult to tell because the ball was spinning and everything on the inside looked the same. Stephan still hadn't figured out how there could be a door in the middle of the air, and a floor that didn't exist. All of this was an incredible mystery.

Stephan walked back to approximately the same location where he had previously stood. This time two aliens came through the door. Neither was the same as the one that was there previously. Or at least Stephan didn't think either of them was the same because the clothing color was different. He wasn't sure. He couldn't tell by the face because the facial features were constantly changing. So he wondered if the clothing colors also changed.

The aliens continued, *"Why are you leaving in the middle of our conversation?"*

"I thought you left," responded Stephan. *"I thought we were finished."*

"How could we be finished? We don't even know your name or what to call you," replied one of the aliens, but Stephan couldn't figure out which one was communicating with him. There was nothing in their expressions that would indicate that either one was sending him messages. The messages could have even been coming from someone who wasn't there with him. He just didn't know.

Stephan explained, *"Our planet is called earth and we are a combination of numerous races, but we all have the same basic genetics. We all have a common root, even though science hasn't been able to exactly figure out what those roots are. We have lots of theories, but no answers. My name is Stephan."*

"Explain what you mean by Stephan?" asked the aliens. *"Is that the name of your race?"*

"No," he explained. *"That's the name that belongs to me individually."*

"I still don't understand," questioned the alien. *"Let me explain my world and then you can help me understand what Stephan is. We have lines of individuals. Each individual is labelled by the three partners who conceived it. For example, in my case my a-men parent is called Gartig, my b-men parent is called 847, and my c-men parent is called X2R, which means that I am part of the group called Gartig-847-X2R-b. The*

last b is because I was born a b-men and that is my sex type as you would call it. There are approximately 900,000 Gartig-847-X2R-b's." Pointing to his companion he said, *"He is also a Gartig-847-X2R-b. We are all identical and interchangeable. We all communicate with each other constantly and each of us knows what the other is doing. In that way we share each other's experiences and learn from each other."*

"Help me understand," requested Stephan. *"You have three names, but your parents only have one each. So if you have children, what part of your name contributes to the child's name?"*

"Your race is indeed intellectually inferior if you ask a question like that," replied the alien in an offensive tone of voice. *"Obviously since we are b's our child's second name would be our b name which is 847. That seems like a ridiculously basic question."*

At this point Stephan was becoming extremely irritated. These aliens were arrogant and rude. They didn't seem to recognize how foreign their culture was from human culture. The alien spoke up again, *"Any one of us Gartig-847-X2R-b's can do the functions of the other. We are completely interchangeable and so we all carry the same label. So how does Stephan work?"*

Stephan was tempted to say that these aliens were stupid for not understanding how Stephan worked, but he was more interested in learning than in fighting back so he resisted expressing his sarcasm. He explained, *"We don't use the same type of designations. For us each individual is unique. Generally, we have three names where our last name comes from our father, similar to you, but our mother and father pick our first* two names. *We do not have an automatic designation for the first two names the way you do. We also have a nationality which is defined by our citizenship, but this does not become part of our name. For example, I'm an American. The other two individuals you have been communicating with are from Malaysia and Hungary."*

"*Do they have a food shortage?"* questioned the Alien.

"*No. Why would you ask if there is a food shortage?"* asked a confused Stephan.

"*You said that one of you was hungry,"* responded the alien.

Stephan went on to explain that hungry was both the name of a country and a need for food. But he kept going in circles trying to explain the concept, so he gave up and changed the subject by asking, "*How many people are on your planet?"*

"*Most of my people live on one of three planets, two in one solar system and one in another solar system close by. We also have colonies on several other planets and moons. Our total population is around 60 billion, about ten times the number on your earth,"* explained Gartig-847-X2R-b.

"*You came here very quickly.*" Stephan was digging for information. "*What were you hoping to gain by coming here?"*

"*I don't understand gain,"* responded the alien. "*We came here to learn. Maybe there is something you know that will be useful to our civilization."*

"*Are you also going to help us learn?"* questioned Stephan. "*Like how you are able to travel so quickly?"*

"*No,*" replied the alien very matter-of-factly as if it should have been obvious. "*We don't do that. We learn from you but we do not share our knowledge with you.*"

"*Why not?*" asked Stephan, once again frustrated by the alien's arrogance.

"*It's just not what we do,*" explained the alien, sounding as if he was surprised that Stephan didn't understand. "*But from what we've seen so far, there's nothing that you have to offer. Your people cannot even communicate with us. We are dealing with dumb animals here. Your planet's resources are worth more to us than your knowledge. It has resources that we could use, so we're going to come and do some mining.*"

"*What do you mean by saying you're going to do some mining?*" asked Stephan. "*Should I make arrangements for you to talk to someone? Where are you going to do the mining?*"

"*We don't need to talk to anyone,*" responded the alien, obviously not understanding why he needed to talk to anyone. "*You're not using the materials so we're just taking what we need and that you are not using anyway.*"

"*What are you taking and where are you taking it from?*" asked Stephan.

Gartig-847-X2R-b replied by showing Stephan an image of a spot in Nevada, about the size of New Jersey. "*We will take what we need from here.*" Then he explained, "*We already have a mining ship on its way and it will take the resources that we need.*"

"*But what are you taking?*" asked Stephan, but he was sorry he asked because the answer was undecipherable. They didn't use our chemical designations and the name wasn't translatable. So he asked a different question, "*What do you use it for?*"

"*We use it as a coating on our bodies,*" replied the Alien. "*It is a shield which protects us from some of the radiation problems we have on one of our planets. It's a rare resource and hard to find. It's impossible to create. Only nature has the forces necessary to create this substance. On your planet it was created when the continental plates collided in that part of your continent.*"

Stephan was a little surprised by this answer. He expected them to say they were taking an energy resource or a food resource. But finding out they were here to steal materials that are used to manufacture a body lotion sounded strange. But the larger problem was that they planned to mine a portion of the United States and that would be considered an invasion by the United States government. It would be considered as aggressive behavior. The reaction of the US government would probably be to attack. Stephan knew he would have to warn someone in the government.

Stephan continued to probe, "*There will be people living in that area. Will they be hurt?*"

"*Everything will be destroyed,*" responded the alien. "*We will be removing the earth for a depth of about one of your miles. There won't be time to move inhabitants around. We will extract the materials we need and we will redeposit the waste that we don't want. Then the area will be yours again. All animal, plant, or human life in the area will most likely be destroyed.*"

Chapter Twenty-Four

Invasion

November, 2020 AD, Greenland

Stephan continued mentally conversing with the aliens. In the meantime, using one of his parallel programs, he was sharing his conversation with his companions in Center Earth. Using another parallel program, he attempted to contact leaders of the United States and Nevada to inform them of the pending mining operation. He sent messages to the minds of the President, the Nevada governor, and numerous other leaders in the hope that there would be a response. But he wasn't sure if they received the message. The non-XLs could only receive messages, not send them. They might react negatively to having a message dumped into their minds just like the pilot's initial reaction was a negative one and one of disbelief. The politicians would most likely ignore it. When protecting image was critical, letting others know that they were receiving mental messages might cause them to be thought of as crazy!

Feeling he had done all he could to inform the leaders of the alien's intentions, Stephan continued his conversation to learn more. He asked, *"When will your mining ship arrive?"*

Gartig-847-X2R-b's responded by explaining, "*The mining ship should be here in one more day your time. It will take them about 20 days to complete their operation. Then we will leave this planet because we have found only three people that we consider worthy of our communications. The remainder of these people are too primitive. We may come back again sometime if we need more resources.*"

Stephan was disappointed that the relationship with the aliens couldn't be stronger. He asked, "*Is there anything you can teach us that would help us to advance and grow?*"

"*Nothing that we think you are ready to receive,*" responded the alien. "*From what we see, anything we share with you will just be used as a tool for aggression between the various earthly indigenous species. We didn't come here to create more trouble on this primitive planet. From what we see, you already have too many ways to kill each other off.*"

"*Will I still be able to communicate with you in the future?*" asked Stephan. He decided that learning about their technology was off limits for now, so he decided to learn more about their strange way of life. He desperately wanted to establish some form of on-going relationship. "*We want to learn as much as possible about your culture.*"

"*What do you want to know?*" asked the alien.

"*For example, do you have marriage?*" asked Stephan, trying to keep the conversation going.

"*Yes, but again not the way you do,*" explained the alien. "*Our marriages require a trichotomy relationship. There has to be an a-man, a b-man, and a c-man. Once married any a-man of that type can come together and* be united with any corresponding b-man and c-man of the correct type. This means that most marriages were created millennium ago and we are free to have sexual relationships with married partners of the correct types and which have been previously consummated. There is rarely a need to create new marriage relationships. We do require strict adherence to only having relationships that have been cemented in a marriage. My Gartig-847-X2R-b type has marriage relationships established for 54 different types of unions. In that collection of 54 marriages, we rarely find it difficult to make a sexual connection. We can easily find an appropriate a-man and c-man as needed. And as I explained before, I am Gartig-847-X2R-b and I can get married to any a-man and any c-man but once married I can only have relationships with similar a-men and c-men. In my case, my offspring would carry my b-man label forward which is 847.

"Creating a marriage is quite complicated because it happens so rarely. Our community votes on the marriage and must approve it before it happens. And we need the majority of the a-man, b-man, and c-man types to agree that they want to engage in this marriage before it can be organized. It becomes quite an elaborate process. And afterwards, the marriage celebration is also quite elaborate. With our system all men types will have a fair opportunity for reproduction. It keeps social order by keeping our population mix in balance."

"*What a mess,*" thought Stephan to himself. "*I like it better our way.*" Then he asked, "*Do you have love?*"

"*We heard that concept mentioned numerous times on your plant, but we aren't able to grasp its meaning. Can you explain it to me?*"

This question left Stephan stumped. How do you explain love? He wasn't sure so he started with, "*When one person has a strong attraction to another person, and that attraction grows to become more than just friendship, we call it love.*"

"*What causes this attraction?*" questioned the alien.

"*Sometimes it's good looks. Sometimes it's personality. Different things can cause the initial attraction. But when it becomes stronger than just attraction, that's when love comes in,*" stumbled Stephan in his explanation.

The alien didn't respond for a few minutes. He seemed to be processing what he had just learned. Then he explained, "*We have love in our triad, but the community tells us who to love. Not some arbitrary meaningless attraction. We have attraction to a man-type, not to an individual the way you do. If we like a man-type, then we can propose a triad marriage with them, but the community still has to approve. But once we are married to that man-type we can have relationships with any man of that type.*"

Stephan was offended. What did this alien mean by meaningless attraction? Then he threw back, "*We used to have planned marriages here on earth, but we've advanced beyond that. We now allow individuals to determine their own matches. We found planned marriages to be archaic.*"

The alien didn't seem to get the stab that Stephan had thrown his way. He continued on with his same train of thought, *"Our relationships are primarily for reproduction. Our marriages are planned in order to keep a social balance. Our relationships are with our same type. So, using your logic, my best friends are all the other Gartig-847-X2R-b's. I don't have friend relationships with any other man-type, only for sexual reproduction purposes. I interact and work with other individuals, but my best relationships are always with Gartig-847-X2R-b's."*

"I understand," commented Stephan, even though it really didn't make sense to him. He just wanted to move on with the conversation. *"So let me make sure I understand. If a Gartig-847-X2R-b was married into one of these triad relationships sometime in the past, before you, then you're stuck with also maintaining that same triad relationship?"*

The alien was silent for a few moments as if confused by the question. *"I think I understand your confusion. Yes, if a Gartig-847-X2R-b was already married into a triad then I have the option of maintaining that triad. But you must remember that I have 54 of these triad relationships, and I don't necessarily have sexual relations with all of them. So there are plenty to choose from. So you are correct in saying that I am committed to one of these 54 relationships for reproduction. But we don't worry about sexual preference or attractions the way it is with you. So maintaining that previously established triad makes the most sense. But it's not a requirement or a restriction. If I want to set up another triad, another marriage, I can do that as long as I first go through the approval process."*

Stephan still wasn't comfortable with what he was hearing so he asked, *"Are you saying that it's possible that you are already married into a triad the day you are born, and that you can have sex within that triad anytime without personally getting married?*

"Of course," responded the alien as if Stephan was dumb for even asking the question. *"We don't spend half our lives trying to decide how we're going to reproduce. We have a structure in place. It's not so rigid that we can't change it or add to it. But if we're happy with the existing structure, and for the most part we are, then it's already there for us. It's so much easier than the way you do it. Nearly every one of your visual displays discusses some aspect of what you call love or sex. We don't have that problem. We already know where our relationships are going."*

By visual displays Stephan realized that the alien must be talking about television or movies. Stephan decided that he had had enough of this conversation, and he was glad to be human. These aliens were way too mechanical. He couldn't imagine being assigned to someone for love and sex. He liked Abigail and he liked how that relationship was going. The mechanics of the alien lifestyle was something he really felt uncomfortable with.

Stephan decided to pursue a different topic. *"How do you decide what your career is going to be? How do you decide what work you are going to do?"*

"That is also largely determined by our class," explained the alien. *"For example, Gartig-847-X2R-b's*

are considered good leaders and spokespersons and so we have several options within the leadership group that we can pursue. I chose to be a leader on this mission. I wasn't the only one who made that choice so within the Gartig-847-X2R-b's a random selection was made and seven of us were chosen. But it really doesn't matter because as I experience this journey, all the other Gartig-847-X2R-b's are also able to experience it with me."

Stephan was at a loss. These aliens were so foreign to him that with every explanation they raised more questions than answers.

Stephan had spent about four hours with these visitors, and he was growing extremely tired. He wondered if being on board this alien ship was somehow draining energy out of him. He started to feel as if he was going to collapse. He explained, *"There is something wrong. I am feeling sick and need to get off of this ship."*

"Understandable," was the alien's response. *"Our mix of oxygen is different than on earth and if we were to get off of this ship, we would also feel weak."*

"Will we be able to talk again in person?" asked Stephan.

"Probably not," explained the alien. *"As soon as the mining ship arrives, we will be returning back to our planet. There will be no more reason for us to stay around. But we can continue to communicate even though it will not be in person."*

Then Stephan made a request which he knew would be a stretch, but he thought he'd try anyway. *"Would it be possible for me to come with you and visit your planet?"*

The alien explained, *"That would require us to develop an environment for you that you could live in. We don't have the air you breathe, the food you eat, the means of comfort that your people seem to require like chairs and beds, and so on. You would need to create your own ship and then come and visit us. We can't accommodate you within our ship. You would die within a day."*

With that comment a fear of dying suddenly surged through Stephan and he decided he better exit the ship. He headed for the door through which he had entered. Once through the door, he was immediately blasted by the cold, but he began to feel better right away. He was thrilled by the experience with the aliens, but he now had a bigger mission; trying to find a way to keep the aliens from destroying Nevada.

Chapter Twenty-Five

Nevada

November, 2020 AD, Winnemucca, Nevada

Blake was out in the backyard petting Baby, the new pony that had just been born two days earlier. The horse cuddled up to him, showing no fear or hesitation. It made Blake feel good that this little pony trusted him and felt a closeness to him.

It was strange weather for November. There had been some light snow flurries over the last week, but none of it stuck. There wasn't any snow on the ground. The temperature was in the 50's which for this time of year felt like spring weather.

Blake was in his early twenties and was home on break from college. He had been attending the University of Nevada, Reno, studying fire science. He was 5 foot 11, dark hair, dark eyes, with a perfect tan.

His home was just north of Winnemucca, Nevada, off of Highway 95 where his parents had a small 30-acre ranch. Their house was a double-wide mobile home, which seemed to be the standard home for most people who lived in the area. Blake's father worked in one of the local mines, and his mother was a waitress at one of the truck stop restaurants downtown. There wasn't much out where he lived except scrub brush, but it was home, and Blake loved it there. It was a place where he could relax and get some head space.

Off to the west Blake could see an enormous dust cloud building up. At first, he didn't think much of it but then he realized that there wasn't any wind blowing. He wasn't sure what would cause such a large amount of dust. As he watched, the cloud kept getting larger and larger. He guessed that it was still a good twenty miles away. The size of the cloud looked as though it must be at least four or five miles wide.

It didn't make sense that such a large dust cloud could be caused by some farming or mining equipment, especially when there wasn't any wind to stir it up. Blake was fascinated by the billowing and growing cloud. He struggled to find an explanation for what he was seeing, but there was none.

He noticed that the cloud was slowly coming straight towards him. He decided to bring Baby to the small barn which would serve as a shelter. He walked the horse into the structure and securely locked him into his stall. Then he tied a damp towel over the horse's nose and mouth, hoping that would help shield the horse from the dust.

He secured the barn by closing and locking the windows and doors. He was confident that the horse would be safe until after the dust storm blew by. Then he left the barn and headed over to the house. He was surprised to see that the dust cloud had covered nearly half the distance towards him from where it had been when he had brought Baby into the shed. He entered his parent's home and locked down all the windows and doors. He didn't want the house to be filled with dust.

Feeling confident that he had done all he could to protect himself from the oncoming dust storm he slouched down on the couch and flipped on the television. He thought he'd see what Dr. Phil had to say. He was mentally keeping score on how often the doctor used some of the same phrases. He even had a tally sheet on the wall where he marked off some of these catch-phrase statements like, "The best predictor of future behavior is past behavior."

As the television came on, programming was overridden by a news flash. A report was saying, "We don't know how much damage is being done, but it seems like everything in the way of this dust storm is being completely destroyed. There is something happening which is causing the dust storm and it is plowing up the ground to the depth of several hundred feet. Entire mountains have been erased." They flashed pictures of the before and after of one of the nearby mountains, Blue Mountain. The mountain had completely disappeared.

Blake looked out of the window to see if the dust cloud had moved any closer and was shocked to see that it was traveling over Winnemucca Mountain, which was just a short distance of less than two miles west of his home. He was in a panic. What should he do? Obviously, this mobile home wasn't going to withstand the force of a dust storm that had the strength to completely eliminate an entire mountain. He decided to run for it.

Blake ran out of the house and jumped into his car. He started heading south towards Winnemucca. It seemed to be the best option. Traveling east or west was suicide. And traveling north was nothing. So, heading to town seemed the most logical. And maybe he could meet up with his parents.

He started driving like a maniac. Speeding wasn't a concern. Staying alive was more important. He jumped from Old Highway 95 where his parents lived, and then on to the main Highway 95. His speed was approaching 120 MPH.

As he looked off to the right towards the approaching cloud, he saw that the cloud was moving faster than he anticipated. He tried to push the car to go faster, but it had topped out. There was no more speed in that old clunker. The race was tight. The cloud was closing in as he raced on. And then the cloud was on top of him. Dust started pelting the car. First the side window was getting sprayed. Then the front windshield. It quickly became impossible to see anything. And then, with a crushing and grinding force, Blake and the car disappeared.

November, 2020 AD, Carson City, Nevada

"What a nightmare!" belched the governor at his advisors as they sat around the conference table. "What's going on up there in Winnemucca? Can anyone tell me anything?" He didn't confess to the message he had received a few hours earlier warning him of a pending attack by aliens on Nevada soil. It all just seemed too preposterous. But now that it had become a reality, he didn't dare admit to having ignored the warning.

The commander of the Nevada National Guard had traveled from Reno to share his insights, "We tried to fly over the area but all we could see was dust. It's just one thick dust bowl moving along at about 20 MPH. Flying into it would be suicide because the engines would stall out. And from the sides or from above all we see is dust. There has to be something in the dust, but we can't make it out. And radar images are garbled and distorted because of the metals that are being pulled up from the ground and mixed into the dust. We can't see inside that cloud."

"We need to stop it," commanded the governor. "It's already killed several people and it may just as easily roll over one of our towns or cities which would kill thousands. Do we know anything about what's causing this thing? What can we do to stop this thing? It has to be stopped."

The general from the Guard continued, "The first thing I would recommend is the evacuation of Winnemucca. If that thing turns south, it would wipe out the entire city in a matter of minutes. The second thing I would recommend is that we fire a couple missiles into the middle of the dust bowl and see what it hits. Obviously, we're not going to do any more damage than is already being caused and we may just get lucky and stop it."

The governor looked around the room to see if there was any dissention to this plan from any of his aides. He only saw heads nodding in agreement. No one disagreed. No one had any better ideas. The governor looked back at the general and said, "Do it."

The general responded, "Then I have your approval to activate the National Guard reserves?"

"Absolutely," responded the governor. "Do whatever you have to do to protect the citizens of this state."

The general immediately stood up from his chair and left the conference room. He proceeded to call his headquarters and gave the command to activate the reserves and mobilize the guard to Winnemucca so that the city could be evacuated. He also ordered the Air Guard to get a couple fighters ready complete with missiles. He ordered them to contact him when the planes were ready to go and then he would give the command to attack the dust storm. On the surface, the idea of attacking a dust storm with missiles sounded a little ridiculous, but that's what he was doing. He had no better options.

November, 2020 AD, Winnemucca, Nevada

The Nevada National Guard Commander received the call, "We're ready. Weapons are loaded."

"Proceed with the attack," responded the general. "Connect me into the command central so I can listen to the attack as it takes place."

"Yes sir," was the response from the other end of the line.

It was about twenty minutes later when the general received the call he had been waiting for, "The two fighters are in position and ready to engage the target. One is going to shoot at the target from the front, aiming about thirty feet above ground level. The second is shooting from the top down into the center of the dust cloud."

"Proceed," commanded the general. Then he listened in on the attack.

"Team A dropping two missiles into the center of the dust bowl."

This was followed by the second plane broadcasting, "Team B is sending two missiles into the center of the dust bowl parallel to the ground."

It was a matter of seconds before the missiles arrived at their target. The whirling of the dust was so great and so broad that the explosion of the missiles, if there was indeed an explosion, wasn't noticeable.

The fighters stayed in the area to report on any changes. They reported, "It looks like we had an affect. The movement of the dust cloud seems to have slowed down."

"Excellent work," responded the governor.

Then a frantic broadcast occurred from Team B, "Team A was just destroyed. A beam of light was shot out of the center of the dust cloud, and it struck Team A. We're leaving the area in order to get away from this here as quickly as possible in case they . . ." The message was cut short.

Chapter Twenty-Six

Planning A Bigger Attack

November, 2020 AD, Carson City, Nevada

"What do we try next?" asked the governor.

The National Guard general responded, "We are in the process of evacuating Winnemucca toward the south-west in order to get some distance away from the dust cloud. Beyond that we're not sure where this cloud is going because right now it isn't moving close to any other major population centers. It just wiped out a small mining town before we could warn them, but we are warning other farmers and miners that are in the path of the cloud. We have helicopters searching the area because some of these guys don't have cell phones. That's all we can do for right now to protect citizens. We'll keep monitoring it closely. We have also sent an urgent report and status update to President Rogan."

The general continued, "The hit did temporarily slow down whatever it is that is doing all this damage. It didn't slow down for long. Now it's back to full speed. But we've learned that we can slow it down. What we need is more fire power. I recommend that you contact the President and get a Presidential order commanding the Air Force to hit this thing with everything they have short of nuclear weapons. We don't want to contaminate the area unnecessarily. I think we can stop this thing with conventional weaponry."

"I had similar thoughts," confirmed the governor. Turning to his secretary he commanded, "Get the President on the line here in the conference room so we can all talk to him."

President Rogan was sitting in the situation room of the White House, and he immediately connected with the governor. "The President here. I am in the situation room with my cabinet and the military commanders. I understand I have the governor of Nevada on the line along with his advisors and the Nevada National Guard Commander. Is that correct?"

"Correct," confirmed the governor. "I appreciate you taking the time to talk to us."

"We were just talking about you," responded the President. "We have received an update from the guard unit out there. The situation looks bleak. What is your evaluation?"

The governor explained that the current level of fire power had slowed down the invader, but that his team was of the opinion that more fire power would be needed in order to put a stop to it. Then he warned, "They shot back and took out our attack team."

"Have you tried any form of communication?" questioned the President.

The governor explained, "We believe it's the same aliens that had the bouncing ball and that had been traveling all over the world. Communication with this group would be just as futile. We believe that the ball was stripping us for resources, and that they have found what they were looking for here in Nevada and now mining it. We also believe that if we don't put an end to this, there will be more attacks, and next time it could be in major population centers such as New York or Los Angeles. We need the full force of the US Air Force to put an end to this immediately."

"Apparently you've had a mind melt with the people around my table here because they're all saying the same thing," responded the President. "Talking about mind melt, Governor did you get any premonition that this might happen?"

"I did Mr. President, but it seemed preposterous at the time," replied the governor.

"Same here," replied the President. "My team thinks it may have come from those XLs that have disappeared."

"You could be right," replied the governor.

"I recommend that in the future we take these premonitions seriously," instructed the President. "But I'm not sure what we could have done to prevent this disaster even if we did take it seriously. I wish I knew how to communicate with the XLs. They may have additional useful information that could help us. Unfortunately, they went into hiding after the attacks on their doctor and even my CIA has no idea where they're at."

"You're correct about the XLs Mr. President," answered the governor. "So what can we do about this situation now that we're in it? Can we get a full force attack?"

The President looked around the situation room table and asked, "Any dissention to an attack?"

The Secretary of State spoke up and said, "It may cause them to strike back harder. But we really don't have a choice. We can't just allow them to continue tearing up our country and killing our people. We need to at least try to stop them."

"I agree," responded the President. Then looking at the Secretary of the Defense he commanded. "Hit them and hit them hard. But no nukes yet."

"Understood," replied the Sec Def, which is the Washingtonian short speech for Secretary of Defense, as he stood up and left the room followed by the secretaries of each of the branches of the military.

Then the President returned to addressing the conference phone call and said to the governor, "They're on their way."

"Thanks," replied the governor.

"By the way, I want to talk to you on our secure line," requested the President. "Can you go to your office so we can have a short private conversation?"

"Right away," replied the governor as they disconnected the conference call.

Shortly after the governor arrived in his office and closed his door his private line started ringing. It was the anticipated call from President Rogan. "Hello," answered the governor.

"The President here," was the reply. "Are you alone?"

"Yes," answered the governor.

"Apparently we both received that message into our minds about the attack by the aliens," suggested the President. "Tell me what you were told."

The governor explained the message that he had received, and it was identical to what the President had received.

"I'm convinced that it was the XLs," explained the President. "Apparently, they can communicate with these aliens. We need to get in touch with them somehow and see if they can help us."

"But how are you going to do that?" asked the governor. "Getting in touch with them may be as hard as getting in touch with the aliens. They're on the run for their lives, especially after their mentor Dr. Clawson was executed. They know they are in danger."

"I would like to offer them protection, but I have a feeling that they are better at protecting themselves than we would be," explained the President. "Even my CIA and Security Forces have no idea what happened to them. We've tracked them to Cusco, Peru, but apparently, they were attacked there. Luckily, from reports that I've heard they successfully escaped and now they've completely disappeared from the face of the earth."

"How about broadcasting a message around the world's media that we need to communicate with them?" suggested the governor.

"I suppose that would work, but it seems a little desperate. It also assumes that they are monitoring the communications systems of the world. But we really don't have any other option," explained the President.

"I'll try and see what I can come up with. Let me know if you hear anything."

"I'll get in touch with you immediately if I hear anything more," responded the governor. "We should connect a couple times a day as we go through this crisis so that we're in sync with each-other's activities."

They disconnected the call, and the President called his press secretary into his office. "We need to send a message out on the world's news media which says something like, 'XLs we need your help. Please contact me. We will give you protection. The President of the United States.' Then give them one of our phone numbers that exclusively ties to our call center and let the call center screen any crazies. Hopefully we'll hear from them."

Chapter Twenty-Seven

A Bigger Attack

November, 2020 AD, Washington, DC

"Are you serious?" exclaimed the President. "All this destruction is just to make hand lotion?"

The President had sent out a world-wide message to the XLs requesting their help. Stephan, who luckily was still in Greenland and hadn't returned to Center Earth, saw the message, and relayed it to his two cohorts. In turn, the XLs sent the president a message directly saying they would not consider leaving their hiding place but that they would be willing and eager to help in any way that seemed reasonable, without them endangering themselves. They thanked him for his offer to help protect them but the XLs suggested that the fewer people knew about their location the better.

In a message to the president, they explained what they knew about the aliens and that one of the XLs had met with some of them. The aliens only communicated telepathically. The aliens felt that humans were inferior and therefore not worth their time. But they found some rare resources on earth that they wanted. They explained that this mining project was focused on a mineral that the aliens needed for a lotion that would protect against a special form of radiation.

The XLs instructed the President to post a message on U-Tube and that he should always use a special code so they would always be able to find his messages. Stephan gave the code to the President. Then, when they spotted a message, the XLs would listen to the message, and they would respond telepathically. That would have to be the procedure used to communicate.

Stephan mentioned that he had tried to discourage the aliens from doing their mining project but that they cared very little about what he had to say. They were going to do what they wanted to do regardless. He also mentioned that he had tried to communicate with them since the start of this mining operation and that they had been nonresponsive.

Stephan attempted to explain that the aliens did not see this mining activity as an aggressive act. They seemed to think that since we weren't' using these resources here on earth, that they were available to the aliens for the taking.

Shortly after communicating this message to the President the XLs received a shocking scream into their minds. It was a scream of fear and pain. It was so loud and strong that it took them completely by surprise and left them momentarily stunned.

"*What was that?*" communicated Stephan with Frida and Cheng.

"*I have no idea,*" replied Cheng. "*It was obviously a cry for help. It seemed almost like a death cry. But it was in an unrecognizable language.*"

Frida suggested, "*Do you think it was the aliens? Do you think they were hurt in an attack by the Air Force?*"

"*That's probably right,*" responded Stephan. "*When the alien screamed, he opened his mind to see more about him. Did you see that too?*"

"*Yes,*" replied Frida. "*It was a little scary. They have an extremely strange planet and strange lifestyle. They live entirely underground. Everything above ground is contaminated in some way. They even travel underground.*"

"*The thing that struck me was that this alien that we have been meeting with wasn't a good guy,*" responded Cheng. "*He is some kind of rebel or possibly even a criminal.*"

"*I was working on that vein of thought myself,*" responded Stephan. "*These guys are the bad guys of their culture. We're not dealing with honest and trustworthy people here. We're dealing with criminals. This is extremely bad news. We have been sharing our secrets and information with the wrong guys.*"

"*We better let the President know,*" suggested Frida.

"*We can do that, but what's he going to do?*" asked Cheng. "*He's already treating them as the bad guys. What more can he do?*"

"*Let's let him know anyway,*" suggested Frida. "*But we need help if we're going to conquer them. We need to send a message to their home planet and see if there is anyone that can help us. They may know how to shut these guys down.*"

"*Or maybe they're all bad and all we're doing is opening the door for a larger group of people,*" replied Stephan.

"*Stephan, you communicate with the alien's planet and see if you can get help,*" instructed Cheng. "*Frida and I will update the President.*"

Stephan did exactly as instructed. He sent a message to the leadership of the clans of the alien home planet. He mentioned that people from their world were here on the earth and that they were destroying major sections of the planet. He asked them to help end the destruction. He pleaded with them to come and help control the behavior of these destructive individuals.

He hoped that this wasn't a mistake. Maybe everyone on that planet was the same. Maybe they were all willing to sacrifice a lesser species like the people on earth. Maybe the access to this mineral was more important than the survival of another species. Maybe we were all expendable. Stephan didn't know what to do, but he knew he had to try something.

November, 2020 AD, Nevada

Ironically the United States Air Force's drones were located at Creech Air Force Base in the same state as the alien attack. The drones were chosen for the attack on the aliens in case the aliens decided once again to shoot back. The base was in southern Nevada near Las Vegas. Creech was the USAF command and control facility used for Overseas Contingency Operations of remotely piloted aircraft systems. It was the base for the Unmanned Aerial Vehicles (UAVs) that are used in Afghanistan and Iraq.

At the orders of the Secretary of Defense a dozen of these vehicles were quickly armed with four each of their most powerful missiles and deployed. They were all in the air within one hour of receiving the command to get armed and ready. They were instructed to find and simultaneously attack the dust cloud that was working its way across the northern part of Nevada. They were informed to proceed without waiting for further commands assuming that any hesitancy in firing at the dust cloud may give the aliens an advantage.

At first the idea of attacking a dust cloud seemed ridiculous to the Air Force pilots. But when they learned that two of the Nevada Air Guard's fighters had been shot down earlier in the day, the deployment took on a more serious tone.

The first of the drones arrived on the scene and was positioning itself for an attack when suddenly there was a shot fired from the middle of the dust. All they could see was a bright streak of light and the UAV was blown completely out of the air.

The pilot of the destroyed UAV broadcast the report, "Apparently these guys were waiting for us. They just attacked and destroyed my aircraft. They didn't even give me a chance to get into position."

The Sec Def, who was listening in on the activity, immediately commanded, "Send in the second drone but keep a distance and send the missiles in rapid fire succession. Don't get too close and don't go slow. Directly and quickly attack the target."

The instructions were followed, and the second UAV fired its missiles when it was still several miles away from the target. The four-missile payload streaked towards the target when once again the flash of light appeared from out of the dust. At first it struck one of the missiles, and then it struck a second. But the other two missiles were too fast for the light to destroy all four.

There was no apparent impact from the two missiles. The dust cloud continued moving forward at the same speed as before.

"Now we know how to attack them," explained the Sec Def. "Apparently they only have one gun to shoot with and if we send in the entire payload of all the UAVs at the same time, most of them will get through to the target."

"Understood," was the response from the commander on the ground at Creech. He gave instructions to the remaining ten pilots to execute a simultaneous attack.

The payload of the remaining ten UAVs was released. Three of them were immediately blown out of the air. The remaining 37 missiles all entered the dust cloud at the same time. This time there was a noticeable disruption. The dust cloud was splattered in various directions and for a brief moment a ship of some kind was partially visible. The cloud was significantly reduced and seemed to hover immediately around the ship. Most importantly, the dust cloud stopped moving forward.

The structure of the ship within the cloud looked like an enormous rolling pin, but it was too covered with dust and dirt to distinguish any features. But it had indeed stopped rolling forward.

"We stopped them!" exclaimed the commander on the ground at Creech AFB.

"Excellent," agreed the Sec Def who was on the open call with the attack team.

There were high-fives all around the control center. The pilots had to bring their eleven aircraft home. Ten of them were brought back directly and one was left to do high altitude surveillance of the area. They were watching to see if there would be any changes. They wondered if the cloud would completely settle to the ground and disappear. They wondered if there would be any aliens who survived and would leave the ship. They used the last drone to watch for movement or action of any type.

The alien ship, still surrounded by a small dust cloud, sat in a stalled position for over fifteen minutes. Then the unexpected occurred. The dust cloud slowly reformed and the entire operation started once again to move forward at full speed. It was as if nothing had happened. The bad news message was quickly transmitted to the governor and the Sec Def who in turn relayed the message to the President.

Chapter Twenty-Eight

Plea for Help

November, 2020 AD, Nevada

The governor contacted the President on their secure line, "What do we do now President Rogan?"

"I have a million people running around trying to figure out what to do," replied the President. "They even raised the question of nukes, but I nixed that. We don't want the entire state of Nevada as a nuclear waste zone. So, they're trying to come up with other alternatives. Unfortunately, we have already hit them with some of our best firepower, and the effort seemed futile. Did you hear from the XLs?"

"Haven't heard anything. We have nothing we can do out here but get everyone out of their way," responded the governor. "Right now, the mining machine is not headed for any major population centers, but that may happen and then the problem escalates."

The President explained, "I received a message from the XLs, and they explained that you are being mined for a mineral that they use for some kind of radiation resistant lotion. Apparently the XLs had actually met some of these aliens. That's why they were able to warn us about the attack. But it sounds like it was a very one-sided conversation where the aliens told them what they were going to do and all the XLs could do was nod their heads and listen."

The president continued, "I sent back a message using U-Tube asking them how they were able to contact and communicate with the aliens. Apparently, the XL's thought they would send a telepathic message out to some of the planets that are believed to be habitable, and these guys are the ones that showed up. But apparently these aliens can't communicate verbally, only telepathically, and so they can't communicate with anyone on earth except the XLs. Apparently, these aliens consider us an inferior species because of our lack of ability to communicate telepathically. That puts is in a very unfortunate situation. We can't directly communicate with the aliens, and the XLs are afraid to come out into the open to communicate."

The president continued to share, "I just learned that apparently our last hit did have some effect. According to the XLs one or more of the aliens was badly hurt or even killed. They screamed out in pain and the XLs were able to receive that message and learn a little more about them. It looks like the aliens are outcasts or criminals of some type. So the XLs are going to try to communicate with the home planet and let them know what kind of destruction is occurring. The XLs are hoping that someone from that home planet will come to earth and help us. It's a long shot, but what else can we do? We're at the point where we're willing to try anything."

"I understand," replied the governor. "I wish I had more to offer. It seems like we're at the mercy of the aliens. Hopefully they'll get what they want soon enough and then be off."

"That would leave us with the risk of them coming back again at some point when they run out of suntan lotion," responded the President. "I don't like that option. Hopefully we can find a way to get rid of them permanently and keep them from wanting to come back."

November, 2020 AD, Greenland

Stephan had decided to stay in Greenland since he had now become the primary contact with the aliens. No one else on the surface of the earth could communicate with them. Additionally, he felt guilty because he had invited them to come to earth and had even shown them the way. Now he had unleashed a band of alien criminals on the earth. Logically, he shouldn't really blame himself for that because he couldn't have known the destruction the aliens would inflict. Nevertheless, he felt a need to stay within communication range of the aliens so he could relay any messages to the President. He needed to stay close to the internet so he could receive any of the president's U-tube messages. He couldn't do that in Center Earth.

Stephan was calling it a day. He was about to crawl into the only place he really liked in the entire part of northern Greenland, his bed. As he was starting to tuck himself in he received a message from the alien home world. It had come relatively soon after his request and the suddenness of it surprised him. It wasn't good. The message said, *"Leave us alone. Stay away. Don't communicate with us again."*

Stephan was stunned. These aliens had seemed so friendly before when he had met them. Now they were being rude. He decided not to respond. He didn't forward the message to his friends because they would probably already be asleep. He decided he would let the President and everyone else know in the morning that there would be no help coming from the alien home planet.

Around the middle of the night Stephan was awaken out of a sound sleep. Once again, he was slightly shocked at the abruptness of the message he had just received. It was another message from the aliens. But the tone of the message was completely different from the one he had received earlier in the evening. This time the message was positive. The message was, *"We are sorry to hear that one of our renegade groups has attacked your planet. We will send someone out immediately to rectify the situation."*

Stephan was so surprised he didn't know what to think. Additionally, he was sleepy, and the sudden awakening disrupted his thought process. Finally, he decided to send a response directly to the sender of the message which said, *"Thank you for your help. We have been unsuccessful in getting them to stop destroying our land and killing our people."*

A few minutes later he received a response. *"We understand your urgency,"* explained the responding voice. *"We will arrive shortly."*

Stephan was confused by the conflicting messages. He decided that the first message must have come from the aliens who were responsible for the mining operation. They didn't want to stop what they were doing, and they didn't want Stephan to interfere. They hoped to squash his attempts to get help.

The second message must have indeed come from a concerned leader who was trying to keep his citizens under control. The news couldn't be any better.

"Excellent," thought Stephan. *"We're going to get help."*

The morning didn't come soon enough for Stephan. He was anxious to share the good news. First he contacted Frida and Cheng. They were ecstatic about the news. Next, he sent a message to the President, who he knew was probably still asleep, but who would welcome the news. Stephan was thrilled but also knew that he needed to be reserved and cautious. Everything to do with these aliens had been a surprise up to now. He had no reason to believe that this would be the end to the alien invasion. He just didn't know what to expect next.

November, 2020 AD, Seattle, WA & Greenland

The CEO of Technosoft was livid. "Can't you guys do anything right? You're telling me you can't find three derelicts? How hard can it be? You had them in the palm of your hand in Cusco and you let them outsmart you. Are you kidding me? They're playing you all for fools. I need them eliminated. I need to stop this fantasy of everyone having some kind of superpower. The idea that they can eliminate the need for computers and cell phones is ludicrous and needs to be put to an end. It's unrealistic to think that everyone in the world is going to have brain surgery."

The Technosoft task force commanding security agent, hired out of the CIA to lead their Special Operations division, explained. "We are following up on the best lead yet. Someone has placed pictures on U-Tube showing that the alien ball opened up with some kind of ramp, and one of the XLs went into the ball. We're not one hundred percent sure it was one of the XLs, but it sure looked like Stephan. Anyway, we're tracking the source of that U-Tube video and it originates from northeastern Greenland at a national park out there. We're guessing that the XLs are hiding out somewhere there. We have a group of agents heading out there right now. They've landed in Greenland at the only viable airport and they're catching a light plane out to the location where the alien ship landed. They should be there in about four hours."

"Excellent," commented the CEO. "I needed a little bit of good news. Keep me updated on the progress of this team. Also, I keep hearing about this doctor who is trying to replicate the surgeries. I understand he is going somewhere outside of the United States to perform some experiments. I could use some good news that his experiments have failed."

"We'll take a look at that as well," commented the Special Operations agent. Just then the satellite phone that he was carrying started ringing. He put the phone on speaker so the CEO could listen in. He answered with,

"What's going on? Please be informed that our CEO is on the line."

"Hello sir," came the response across the line. "We have good news for you. We found the pilot of the XLs. He knows where they're hanging out and he told us he would bring us to their location. We gave him some sob story about trying to find them to tell them about a relative that recently died and he bought the whole thing. He says that the place where they're holding out is incredible, but we don't know what he means by that. Anyway, we'll keep you updated on the progress."

"Wow," exclaimed the CEO. "That's really good news. Keep up the good work."

Thirty minutes later the Technosoft Special Operations team of three was sitting on the plane heading to North-East Greenland National Park and Daneborg Station. They were proud that they had made their connection with the pilot who was intimately familiar with the XLs and their hideout. But then they became worried. The pilot started telling them about this place where it was warm and green and it was out in the middle of the ocean. They started to think that this pilot was crazy. Maybe he had made the whole story up about being the guide for the XLs. Maybe this entire trip was a waste of time. But they had seen the U-Tube video of Stephan and several people had told them that the location was in Daneborg. At least that part was true, even if this patch of green out in the middle of the ocean turned out to be a fantasy. Anyway, now they were committed to making the journey. They had to follow this through and see if Stephan was really there. They had to find out the truth.

They were about two hours into their four-hour journey when everything changed. Suddenly the pilot screamed, "Missile coming straight at us from 10 O'clock. We're done for. I have no idea where it's coming from, but it doesn't matter. We're history." Then he crossed himself and started praying, "Our Father who art in heaven, hallowed be thy name, thy kingdom come, . . ." The agents started praying too, but they never finished.

As they prayed the agents leaned forward to look out of the front windshield, but by the time they were able to take a good look it was too late. The entire plane erupted into a ball of fire which could be seen for a hundred miles in the winter darkness out in the middle of nowhere in Greenland.

Chapter Twenty-Nine

Life Goes on in Center Earth

November, 2020 AD, Center Earth

Abigail was distressed. She was sure Stephan had feelings for her and that they were going to spend some time together, but now he disappeared, and she hadn't heard from him for over a week. She had received his note which the pilot of the air transport vehicle delivered, but it was short and didn't offer much of an explanation. She was scared that somehow something had happened to Stephan or, worse yet, that he had changed his mind about joining her.

Abigail decided to travel from her home in Samaria to Jericho and visit Stephan. Even if it was bad news, she was certain that not knowing was worse. The trip was short. Upon arriving in Jericho, she found Cheng at work and asked about Stephan. Cheng took her aside and explained, "This has to be kept in strictest confidence." Then he looked at Abigail for agreement. After she nodded her head in agreement he continued, "The world on the surface is being invaded by aliens. Unfortunately, these aliens can only communicate telepathically, and Stephan was needed to do the communication. He ended up being the chief negotiator between the aliens and the surface people who apparently aren't able to communicate with them."

This was complex for Abigail to grasp. She was still uncertain about the idea that there were people living on the surface. This had always been a rumored part of Center Earth's history, but a large part of the population was convinced that it was just a fairy tale which was shared with children to scare them into obedience. Now she was also being told about aliens from another planet. And she was being asked to believe that Stephan could communicate telepathically. She started wondering if this was just a way to get her to dismiss Stephan and to get her to leave him alone.

Cheng continued, "Stephan is also concerned that you would probably be wondering what happened to him. Unfortunately, he has no way to communicate with you. Communication between the surface and here in Center Earth is only possible through messages transferred mentally. Stephan could send you a message to your mind, but you wouldn't be able to respond."

At this point Abigail was convinced that Cheng was feeding her a lot of manure. First the surface world nonsense, then the aliens, and now mind transfer of information. All of this sounded like a great science fiction novel. But it didn't make sense to her.

Again, Cheng explained, "Stephan wanted to send you mental messages, but he was convinced that you wouldn't understand how it worked, and since it was only one directional, he was afraid that the whole process would scare you."

Abigail decided to call Cheng's bluff, "Have Stephan send me a message. I want to hear that he is okay."

"Okay," Cheng agreed. He was thinking the same thing and had already sent a message to Stephan telling him that Abigail had come looking for him. He asked Stephan to send a message to Abigail.

Suddenly Abigail's expression changed. She had the look of mystery and shock on her face. She had just received a message from Stephan, *"Hi Abigail. I am sorry that this is the only way I can communicate with you. I miss you a lot and look forward to returning to Center Earth so I can be with you. Please ask Cheng to send me your response."*

It took a couple minutes for Abigail to compose herself. Suddenly she realized the possibility everything Cheng had been telling her was true after all. After she had had a chance to process what had just happened, she asked Cheng to send Stephan a message. "Please tell Stephan that I received his message and that I want him to communicate with me regularly, even if I can't respond. I just need to know that he is okay and that he is planning to be with me."

Cheng relayed the message to Stephan after which Abigail received the message, *"Thanks. I will stay in touch. I will send you images of what is going on here on the surface, but you must not share this information with anyone."*

Abigail was thrilled. Stephan still had feelings for her. Their separation was just temporary, and they would be together soon. A big smile crossed her face. She thanked Cheng for the help and headed back to the air transport vehicle which would take her back to her home in Samaria.

None of the XLs realized that Stephan was now stranded on the surface. His pilot, the only person that knew how to travel between Greenland and Center Earth, was gone.

November, 2020 AD, Center Earth

Later that evening, at the evening meal, Cheng told Frida about Abigail's visit. *"Why did you wait till now to tell me?"* questioned Frida. *"You could have told me when she was still here, but now she's gone."*

"What difference would it have made?" asked a confused Cheng.

"I just want to know what's going on," complained Frida. *"I don't like being kept in the dark."*

"Nobody's keeping you in the dark," protested Cheng.

"Next time tell me right away," protested Frida.

Cheng, knowing that he had to keep harmony with Frida if he was later going to be able to cuddle up to her and seduce her, agreed. *"Okay, I'll keep you better informed."*

"Thanks," said Frida in a calmer voice. Then Frida went on to explain, *"I've been wondering if we should take a trip around Center Earth and learn more about its culture and geography. We've spent our entire time here in Jericho, except for a couple visits to Samaria, all of which has been really nice, but I know there is a lot more out there and I think we should learn as much as we can. What do you think?"*

Cheng was completely in agreement. He had been thinking the same thing. The visit to Samaria had aroused his curiosity. He had originally assumed that everything was like Jericho, but after Samaria he realized that Jericho was an exception. He wondered if Samaria was more typical, or if the rest of Center Earth was also unique. *"I definitely agree,"* he responded. *"I was wondering what else was out there. They don't have a television with a travel channel here so it's hard to know what other surprises Center Earth holds."*

"Good," exclaimed Frida. *"You go out there and figure out how we get around to these places and let me know when we're ready to go. I'm ready anytime."*

Cheng felt manipulated. But he wasn't surprised. Frida had dumped him with the busywork tasks of arranging for travel before when they came to Center Earth. But he wasn't sure how it would be handled this time without the internet. He decided that he was going to have to ask a lot of questions.

It would take several days before Cheng had the logistics figured out. He learned that he needed to communicate with one of the air transporters, which served as a type of taxicab, and use them to figure out how the arrangements would be made. He managed to catch one during the next day and he learned that the process for getting to other tribes in other locations involved a form of air hitchhiking. You had to find out who was going where and then get them to include you on their ride. Most travel was for commercial purposes for the delivery of goods between locations. It would be on one of these goods transport missions that Cheng and Frida would travel

.

After getting a few more details about where to find these transport vehicles, Cheng explained the process to Frida. They made the decision to leave for their tour in two days.

November, 2020 AD, Center Earth

For Frida and Cheng's travels around Center Earth, their first jump was to Samaria which was the transport hub for the tribe. That turned out to be the standard for all tribes; the tribe's capital also served as the transport hub. They had already visited there in the past, but this time they decided to walk around the city a little on their own in order to get a feel for its pulse. They no longer looked like strangers. They had lived in Center Earth long enough that they were now categorized as residents of Jericho based on their clothing.

They held conversations with many of the local citizens asking them what sights they should see. They had a relaxing and enjoyable day. Eventually it came time to look for food and a place to spend the night. They asked people if they could direct them to a place to stay and were surprised by the response. There wasn't anything like a hotel. Rather, they were invited to spend the night in people's homes and to share a meal with them and their family. They readily accepted the invitation, not just because they needed a place to stay, but primarily because this would allow them to get involved in the culture and to learn more about the people. Spending an evening meal and conversation with locals would be a great way to learn more about the culture.

The meal wasn't communal the way it had been in Jericho. In Samaria the meals were within each household, but it had the same sense of informality that they experienced in Jericho. The meals were shared by the extended family, not just the immediate family, and as mealtime arrived, people started showing up from all directions. It was more like a daily reunion than just a meal.

The meal was mostly composed of raw vegetables and fruits. That had also been the case in Jericho. The only meat that would ever be included was fish or foul. But they never ate mammals. There was a lot of seasoning with a large variety of herbs making the meals a culinary feast.

After the meal, the conversation centered on Cheng and Frida. The Samarians were as much interested in them as they were in the Samarians. Initially it felt like they were being interrogated to see if their story about an outer earth was real. The Samaritans seemed hesitant to believe in an outer world which many in their scientific and sectarian community had declared as false traditions. They asked challenging questions about how Frida and Cheng arrived in Center Earth and why didn't they leave and go home. Frida and Cheng gave them lots of stories and explained life on the earth's surface. It took time and lots of explanations, but eventually Frida and Cheng won them over and their new friends became believers. Then the questions from the Samarians became more constructive. They started asking questions about what the people were like, what the government was like, what technologies existed, etc.

Frida and Cheng had their own questions as well. They were curious about the legal system. They were trying to match the Center Earth structure to what they were familiar with on the outside. They were looking for governments and laws and borders. None of these seemed to exist. There were ten tribes, each living on a foundation of the Mosaic law. They each used the Torah as their basis for government. Each tribe was administered over by a group of religious leaders referred to as high priests. These priests were selected annually out of the entire tribe's collection of high priests using a lottery system. They were placed in office and ruled as a tribal council for one year, as well as administering over any religious ceremonies. Since each of the tribes had the same legal basis, using the Law of Moses, they managed their affairs in a way that had a level of harmony. There were disputes, but they were mostly about trade pricing and timelines. But these were considered normal and were negotiated between the various councils of each tribe. If the dispute could not be solved easily a neutral tribe was selected as the arbitrator and its council would be brought in as the mediator.

The Samaritans, along with all the other Center Earth cultures, were based on the Law of Moses. This provided a foundation of morality standards which were exceptionally high compared to the earth surface. When it came time for going to bed, everyone migrated to the sleeping room together. The mats were strewn across the floor, as they were in the homes in Jericho, and there were no distinct designated sleeping areas for anyone. However, there was an understood separation of the unmarried males and females. The sexes each had separate sides of the room. Married couples slept together wherever they wanted.

Frida and Cheng ended up spending four days in Samaria. Each evening was shared with a different family. From there they went on to visit the capital cities of each of the other tribes, starting with Dan, then on to Issachar and the remaining tribes. Each tribe seemed to have their own cultural flavor in how they decorated their buildings and how they arranged their food, but the foundational structure of their belief systems and their legal systems aligned fairly closely to each other. In the end, Cheng and Frida made lots of new friends. They were invited to speak with the High Priest leaders in each of the communities. Some seemed more accepting than others of their earth surface stories and about coming to Center Earth from the outside. But in the end, they were all friendly and welcoming, even if they thought Frida and Cheng were crazy.

During this time Frida and Cheng had developed a level of closeness between each other that went beyond just being friends. At one point, while they were on a private walk through one of the towns, Cheng became brave and took her hand, watching to see how she would react. Seeing that she didn't resist he became a little braver and asked, "*I like the time we're spending together. I think we belong together. What do you think?*" Then he held his breath.

Frida's first thought was, "*It's about time.*" Then she answered Cheng by not saying a word. Instead, she stopped, turned towards him, put her hands on each side of his face, and kissed him on the mouth.

Cheng's face became beet red. He was thrilled and embarrassed all at the same time. In spite of his multi-processing brain, he suddenly went brain dead. He didn't have enough processors to be able to react. It was just too much.

From across the street a man yelled, "Stop that. It's not allowed," and he wagged his finger at the two of them.

Both Frida and Cheng were embarrassed, and Cheng also turned red. Apparently they had crossed a taboo barrier. They continued their walk just holding hands. But both of their minds were reeling, attempting to figure out what this meant and what would be the next step in their relationship. They both felt like they were floating.

While visiting the tribe of Reuben they were invited to meet with a group of scientists who grilled them with a barrage of never-ending questions. It felt like an interrogation. In the end they were sure that they didn't convince anyone. The scientists were convinced of their own theories and weren't very open minded, much the same as scientists in the outside world. What Frida and Cheng were saying was outside of the acceptable scientific parameters and therefore had to be rejected.

Eventually Frida and Cheng returned to Jericho, which had come to feel like home to them. They were glad to be back even though they had enjoyed their travel experiences touring the various tribal capitals. To their surprise, the citizens of Jericho hadn't traveled to the other capitals and they were interested in hearing stories about Frida and Cheng's travels.

When they were once again alone, Cheng asked Frida the question that he had been dying to ask since the kiss that she gave him. It came out in a burst, which wasn't how he had planned it, but in his panic he just blurted out, *"Would you marry me?"*

Frida, with a smirk on her face replied, *"Not if you don't get down on your knee first and ask me formally."*

Cheng was glad to do that and repeated the question.

This time Frida answered with, *"Of course. I never thought you'd get around to asking. I was starting to think I was going to have to ask you just to get the whole thing moving."*

Then came the time for planning. Cheng asked a couple of the community members what the marriage process was like, and they were surprised to find out that their wedding announcement had suddenly become a community event. The entire community became involved in the planning, right down to deciding what the best date would be for the marriage. It seemed like all the marriage planning escaped the hands of Cheng and Frida. They had lost control. But they didn't mind. They were in love and that's all that mattered. They were too starry eyed to care about the details.

Chapter Thirty

Stephan

November, 2020 AD, South Africa, Seattle,
Greenland

Dr. Wagton had migrated his attempt to replicate the XL's surgery to South Africa after learning that their medical facilities were comparable to the United States, but their restrictions on experimental surgery were not as stringent. South Africa was the location where a large number of leading-edge surgeries had been attempted in the past, such as heart transplants.

He identified several candidates that should imitate Clawson's brain surgery, attempting to find individuals who had similar brain tumors as Stephan, Cheng, or Frida. He made arrangements for four experimental candidates to travel to South Africa. He wanted them to arrive around the same time that he arrived.

The doctor also studied numerous videos and notes from the past surgeries, hoping to replicate the process. Most of the surgical information had disappeared around the time that Dr. Clawson was killed. But Dr. Wagton documented what he was sure was the exact process that Dr. Clawson performed in the past which eventually resulted in the initial three XLs.

Dr. Wagton had developed a relationship with doctors from Pretoria during some recent medical conferences that he attended. He took advantage of these relationships when he was arranging for the surgeries in South Africa.

After arriving he planned to perform a number of tests to assure himself that the four patients that he had selected were viable candidates. Using this data he planned to prioritize the patients for their surgeries.

The doctor traveled from Sacramento, through Denver and on to Pretoria with his team of three assistants. He had chosen individuals who had worked with Dr. Clawson in the past. He hoped their experience might help him successfully replicate the process.

They arrived at the OR Tambo International airport in Johannesburg where they were met by a driver. Their route took them on the R21 freeway north toward the capital of Pretoria. This was going to be a 40-minute drive. Initially they drove through an industrial area but soon they were out into farm country. It was a pretty countryside and, in many ways, reminded them of Colorado. Soon they passed through a mining area where they could see the mines off on both sides of the freeway.

About two thirds of the way along their route they passed Doornkloof East and the M31 interchange. This was the point where they entered the suburbs of Pretoria. As they crossed the interchange, they didn't notice the two pickups that were joining them on the freeway and following close behind. The taxi driver thought it was strange that they were following him as he traveled at the speed limit. They could easily have passed him.

As the vehicles came to the N1 overpass one of the pickups started to pass the doctor's taxi. The other continued to stay behind. The one passing drove towards the front of the doctor's vehicle. He was a half a car length ahead in the fast lane. As he reached the top of the overpass the pickup quickly veered hard left toward the front of the doctor's vehicle, ramming it hard and driving the doctor's car into the small railing. The railing buckled badly but held. Then, the second pickup coming from behind slammed into the back of the car pushing it through the railing. The car was pushed forward another five feet, but still held. The pickup in the back pulled back about 20 feet, and then charged forward again hitting the back of the car. This time the car flew off the top of the overpass and over the side. The car fell down towards the busy N1 toll road below. The car had turned on its side so that the passenger side of the car was on the bottom and would be hitting the pavement first. The roof of the car was facing the on-coming traffic. The car hit the ground just in time for a cement truck to slam into the roof of the car crushing everyone inside.

The crash eliminated the last of anyone who had any knowledge of Dr. Clawson's super operation. As if that wasn't bad enough, the car burst into flames burning the laptop and all the notes that Dr. Wagton had in the trunk. At this point anyone who had ever had any interest in the super XL medical procedures was now fearful for their lives. Both Dr. Clawson and Dr. Wagton had been brutally executed. And the knowledge of how to do an XL operation had been permanently lost.

November, 2020 AD, Seattle, WA

"What do you mean we lost the flight in Greenland?" questioned the Technosoft CEO. "What happened?"

"We're not sure," replied his special operations chief. "Our team was on board with the pilot that helped sequester the XLs, but the plane never arrived at its destination. And it didn't appear to have landed at any of the other airports in Greenland. And there aren't that many to choose from. They may still be out there somewhere. Maybe they had a forced landing for some emergency. But we haven't been able to find them. They're just gone.

"But I do have some good news," he continued.

"What's that," asked the CEO.

"We've successfully eliminated Dr. Wagton and his team in South Africa," responded the security agent. "Apparently they had an accident on their way from the airport to the hotel. Everyone in the car was killed."

"Good," replied the CEO. "That should discourage anyone else from experimenting with this XL nonsense."

The CEO continued, "Let's get back to the problem with the XLs themselves. If we lost the pilot who was the only one who knows where the XLs are, then what do we do next?"

The security agent responded, "Apparently Stephan, the super that was seen going onto the alien ship, is still in Greenland. If we can capture him, we can use him to lead us to the other XLs. I have dispatched another group of agents to see if they can find him. We know where he was when he met with the aliens. I'm hoping they can catch up with him before he leaves and rejoins his friends."

"Good," replied the CEO. "I'm glad we're not just sitting around waiting for someone to find the other team that's lost out there somewhere in Greenland."

"I'll keep you posted on any progress," replied the agent.

November, 2020 AD, Greenland

"I can't come home until we have a solution to the aliens tearing up Nevada," replied Stephan mentally to Frida and Cheng. *"A second troop of aliens is on the way and they're supposedly going to stop these guys. But we'll have to wait and see what happens. You're just going to have to wait on your wedding until I get there. You can't cheat me out of a good party just because I'm working and you're traveling around and vacationing."*

"We'll wait," responded Frida. *"But hurry it up."*

"Also, my pilot had to leave because he was offered double his normal pay to bring some people here to this remote spot of land in Greenland," responded Stephan. *"Hopefully he'll be here soon so I can return."*

"*I know Abigail is hot to have you back,*" snickered Cheng.

"*I'm hot to be back,*" replied Stephan. "*It just doesn't feel safe out here. Not only is it freezing cold, but there's nothing to do out here. And I constantly feel like someone is looking over my shoulder.*"

"*I'm a little concerned about these people that are paying so much to come out there where you are,*" challenged Frida. "*Doesn't that sound a little suspicious? Maybe I'm just being paranoid, but it wouldn't hurt for you to be extra careful Stephan. You never know what their intentions might be. Hopefully they're not after you.*"

"*I thought of that too,*" replied Stephan. "*I'll definitely be careful and watch for them.*"

Stephan was at a loss on how to keep himself occupied. He was becoming more and more antsy by the minute. The other residents had resigned themselves to their fate. They were comfortable sitting and watching television, even though there wasn't much to see. They spent more time flipping through the channels of their satellite connection than actually watching anything.

At one point they dialed into the news. The big news of the day was about his pilot. Apparently, he had disappeared along with his passengers. As Stephan looked at the image of the passengers, he suddenly became convinced that these guys were assassins that were obviously in search of the XLs. This put Stephan into a bit of a panic. Somehow these assassins had been able to track him down. Had the President betrayed him? Or possibly one of his aides? Then Stephan realized that it was probably the image of him visiting the alien ship that had given him away. That image had been broadcast around the world. With the image out there it was simply a matter of identifying the location where the picture was taken.

Next his mind shifted to wondering what had happened to the pilot and his passengers. The pilot was extremely experienced and had amazed the XLs several times. It was surprising to think that he disappeared without a trace. At the very least he should have broadcast a distress signal. But the search crews haven't been able to find anything.

Suddenly Stephan realized that he had an even bigger problem. How was he going to get back to Center Earth? That pilot was the only person that knew how to get there. Was Stephan going to be stranded in the outer world forever? Stephan had to sit down to think about his dilemma.

Stephan sent a message to Cheng and Frida, *"I'm stranded here for sure. It looks like our pilot went down and they can't find him anywhere. And when I look at the pictures of the crew that was with him, they sure look like a bunch of thugs. They don't look like they're coming out here for a vacation. I think they were probably sent after us."*

"That makes me wonder if the President had anything to do with their disappearance?" questioned Cheng. *"He did tell you he was going to help protect us. Maybe he found out about the attempted hit and put a stop to it."*

"I hope so," replied Stephan. *"Actually, that's probably the best explanation of what may have happened. I was thinking that the President may have*

sent these guys after me. But I'll bet you're right. He was probably the cause of their demise. That still leaves us with my problem. How am I going to get back to Center Earth?"

Frida jumped in, "I wonder if one of these flying saucers that they have down here can come out and pick you up."

"That's not a bad idea," responded Cheng. "I'm not sure if they'll get lost once they get to the surface, but it's probably our best shot. That's probably more likely than Stephan trying to find another pilot who is willing to take him to Center Earth. Let's go to work on trying to see what we can come up with."

"I would sure appreciate your help," replied Stephan. "At some point I want to go home. And Samaria and Jericho are now my home."

"Baloney," replied Frida. "What you really want is to get back to Abigail."

"Sounds like a good idea to me," responded Stephan and that was the last of the messages.

Chapter Thirty-One

Assassins

November, 2020 AD, Seattle, WA &

Kangerlussuaq, Greenland

"More excuses?" challenged the CEO. "I thought these XLs were going to be eliminated by now. Now you're telling me you can't find them. Have you sent a second team out there?"

"We've sent a second team out there," responded the security agent. "They're in Greenland but apparently they've been stranded for the last couple days trying to find a pilot that will take them to the Northeast corner of Greenland. You have to have a small plane, because the runway is short, but you also need sufficient fuel capacity for a trip that goes out that far. Not everyone wants to go that far, especially now that one of their friends has disappeared. And a lot of them are occupied with the recovery."

"They've found the missing plane," continued the agent. "they're saying it was shot down. That has my second team of agents freaked out. They're worried that these XLs have some kind of ability to shoot them out of the sky. So, I would imagine they're also not trying very hard to get out there."

"Give them a kick in the butt," replied the CEO. "I want those XLs eliminated. I need to put an end to this XL nonsense."

"Will do," replied the agent. "At least the mission in South Africa was successful."

"That's old news," replied the CEO. "I need new good news."

"I'll work on it," replied the security agent.

After leaving the office the agent placed a call to his team waiting in Kangerlussuaq Airport and that was trying to get a flight to Daneborg Station in the North-East Greenland National Park. "Hello," was the answer on the phone.

"What are you guys doing up there?" asked the agent. "I need you to get to the park and complete your mission."

"We're hearing that the plane was shot down and no one here wants to fly that route until they figure out who shot them and why," replied the assassin in Greenland. "Apparently getting shot down in Greenland is a big deal since there isn't a lot of military around here. We're going to have to pay them at least triple their normal rate just to get them to even listen to us."

"Do what you have to do. I'm tired of getting my butt chewed out over this. Take a different route if you have to. I don't care if you have to travel around the world and go over Antarctica to get there, just get there and do the job. When do you think you'll get going?" questioned the security agent.

"They have a crime investigation team on the ground at the wreckage and everyone is waiting to hear what they find out," replied the assassin. "That will take another day or two. No one is going to want to leave the ground and fly anywhere close to the north-east until they know more."

"Just remember, you're not there for a vacation," stressed the agent.

"Anybody who thinks this is a vacation spot is nuts. There is nothing here. I don't know how people live here. You can quickly go crazy from boredom. I think there's a total of a dozen habitable buildings in the entire community, and that includes the airport. You can rent a car and drive around, but it takes hours to get anywhere. You've managed to get us stuck in the armpit of the universe."

"Just get the job done," replied the agent. "Cost is not the concern here. Bribe someone to take you there, even if it means going the long way around and avoiding the area where the other plane was shot down. I'm getting a lot of heat here and we need to get this done."

"Understood," was the response, and the call was disconnected.

The assassin that was on the call relayed the supervising agent's message to the remaining two team members. "We need to get this over with. Not just because our boss is hot but also because I'm freezing my butt off and I want to get back to civilization. I don't want to spend another day in this nothingness. I can't even breathe here. My nostrils freeze together the minute I walk outside."

"Let's go back to the airport and see if there's a pilot we can bribe," suggested a second assassin. "Around here, face-to-face seems to get better results than the phone or anything else."

"Agreed," responded the first assassin. "No need for all three of us to go. I'll go and let you know if I have any luck."

The first assassin went to the desk of the hotel where they were staying and asked for a taxi. The airport was only a couple blocks from the Hotel Tuttu / Reindeer Inn where they were staying. This hotel was a converted former American Army barracks, and it felt like it too. In November weather where the temperature ran between 7 and 17 degrees below zero Centigrade, it was extremely cold. The assassins weren't used to that type of cold. They didn't come prepared with the right kind of clothing and shoes. They were freezing.

Fifteen minutes later he was in a tour bus that doubled as a cab and on his way to the airport. At the airport he went through the ritual of asking around for pilots who had small planes that could take the three of them to Daneborg Station. Initially he received very little interest. But when he started offering double and triple pay more pilots became interested. Eventually he had a couple of pilots that had planes large enough to take the load and small enough to land.

They discussed the need to avoid the area where the last plane was destroyed. They needed to travel directly east until they arrived at the ocean, and then head north to the park. This would require a sufficient amount of fuel capacity to make the longer journey now that they were not taking a direct route. The journey was expected to take about five hours.

They scheduled the departure for immediately after lunch. With that departure time they would arrive late afternoon. They planned to stay the night in Daneborg and then return the following morning on the same plane. They falsely assumed that the assassination of the XLs would be quick and easy.

Chapter Thirty-Two

A Battle

November, 2020 AD, Daneborg, Greenland & Nevada

"We have arrived. Help us find your location," was the message received by the XLs.

It had been a few days since Stephan had received any communications and he was slightly surprised by this new message. In an attempt to be cautious Stephan responded, *"Who are you?"* After asking the question he felt a little stupid. He was worried that these were the bad aliens. But then he realized that the bad aliens already knew where he was located. So, it had to be the good aliens that were sending the message.

"We have come to help with the destruction that some of my people are doing to your planet," was the response.

Stephan sent the image of a map identifying his location. Then he asked, *"How far away are you?"*

"We should arrive in about 15 of your minutes," explained the alien. *"We have been unable to communicate with anyone on your planet. We were surprised that no one seems to understand us. We need you to help us with the communication."*

"Most people on this planet can only receive telepathic messages," explained Stephan. *"They can't respond to them. And they are usually surprised when they receive a message because it's not their normal way of communication. But I have worked out a method of communication with our world's leader and I can help you with that."*

In less than 15 minutes one of the bouncing ball alien vehicles appeared and settled itself close to Daneborg. Just like last time with the other alien ship, a gang plank came down out of the side of the ship. As it lowered to the ground Stephan received the message, *"Come."*

Stephan wasn't afraid this time. He knew what to expect. But he responded with, *"I can't breathe your air for very long."*

"Understood," replied the alien message. *"We will provide a chamber for you."*

As Stephan stepped into the ship, he spotted a small plane landing at the air strip close by. He watched it for a moment, and he could see the pilot and three other individuals getting out of the plane. It was obvious that the three passengers were out of place here in Greenland. They were dressed inappropriately for the weather. Stephan was convinced that they were here for him and the other XLs. Knowing that motivated him to move forward into the ball. He knew that these assassins would have no hesitation about shooting at him, even if he was standing at the door of an alien space craft.

As Stephan walked onto the interior of the ship he noticed it was identical to the last alien ship he had been on. There was no floor, but he knew he could walk out on an invisible hard surface. This time an alien being was waiting for him and directed him toward an area of the ship that looked like everything else, completely transparent. But Stephan could immediately tell that he was somewhere different because breathing was suddenly easier. But then something unexpected happened. Stephan could see the ball's door, the one that Stephan had entered through, was now shutting. And, as if that wasn't enough, he suddenly sensed movement. The ship was taking off. The aliens were taking him with them causing Stephan to ask, *"Why are you taking me with you? I don't want to leave."*

"I thought you were going to help us," was the reply he received. *"How can you help us if you don't come with us?"*

"I thought you came here to stop the destruction of our planet?" challenged Stephan. *"How can I possibly help you with that?"*

"We may need your help," was the only reply Stephan received. He was off travelling in the alien vessel and there was no way to stop what was happening. It was simply beyond his power.

Stephan immediately sent out a message to his XL companions. *"I'm being kidnapped by the aliens. I'm on board their ship in a special chamber so I can breathe. They took off without my knowing about it. They didn't ask. They just took off and when I complained they simply responded by saying they may need me, but they didn't say what they would need me for."*

Frida responded, *"How scary. I have no idea how we can help."*

"You can't," responded Stephan. *"I'm just letting you know in case I lose the ability to communicate with you. This is a little bit scary. They're going off to confront the bad guys from their planet. And I don't know how all that is going to affect me. I don't want to end up in a battle."*

Simultaneously, in another portion of his multiprogramming brain Stephan sent a message to his captors, *"What are we doing? How am I supposed to be able to help? I don't know why you have taken me?"*

The alien response was, *"We need your help. By coming on the ship, you agreed to help us and now we are off to see if we can stop the destruction of your planet."*

"Normally you should ask before you just kidnap someone," responded Stephan.

"You did respond when you came on board," was the confusing alien response. *"We may need you and so you should come with us."*

Stephan immediately realized that there was a major cultural gap here. This was not a conversation about the rights of the individual. The aliens had decided that it was for the greater good that Stephan should come along, and so they simply took him along. It didn't matter that they didn't have a specific use for him. They simply took him with just in case they needed him.

Then the alien disappeared from view. Stephan understood that he had passed through some kind of doorway which blocked visibility. Stephan was now left alone in a room which had no floor, ceiling, or walls. He had no idea how large the room was. He could see the inside of the ship and nothing else. It was like he was floating in the middle of a ball where all he could see was just the inside of the ball. He could feel an invisible solid floor underneath him, so he knew that everything around him was some form of illusion. It was a little unnerving. He wondered if all the activities that must go on in a spaceship could somehow be going on all around him but he couldn't see or hear any of it. He reasoned that there must be a large crew of aliens that were flying this ship. There had to be a military contingent if they were planning on fighting with the bad aliens. There had to be living quarters and offices and workstations, but he saw none of it. It seemed like all the activities that were going on around him were somehow invisible.

The ride on the spaceship was nearly unnoticeable. There weren't the quick jerks up and down that he would feel on an airplane. It was completely smooth, so smooth that initially Stephan didn't realize that he had left the ground. But he did barely sense that there was some directional movement, and he knew he was travelling. The ship was moving at speeds of several thousand miles per hour, but it felt like he was sitting on solid ground.

He knew he was travelling because as they traveled, the ship seemed to slowly disappear around him. He could see everything in every direction. Whereas before he could only see the inside of the space ball, now he couldn't even see the ball at all. He could look up at the sky above, or down at the ground beneath. It was like he was suspended in the middle of nowhere, which at first caused a surge of fear and adrenaline. The fear went away as he became accustomed to this mode of travel.

He estimated that he must be at an altitude of about 40 to 50,000 feet, slightly higher than a commercial airliner would travel. In a matter of about 10 to 15 minutes he had traveled from the northeast end of Greenland to the plains of Nevada. Now he could see the enormous dust cloud created by the mining machinery below him.

The alien craft had dropped to an elevation of about 5,000 feet above the mining operation. Stephan wasn't sure what would happen next. No aliens appeared for him to communicate with. And talking to midair was disconcerting so he resisted doing that. He was awed by the alien technology which allowed him to view the world around him in every direction.

Stephan knew the reason for coming to Nevada was to stop the mining operation, but he had no idea how that was going to occur. The miners on the mining ship didn't seem to take notice of his ship's arrival.

Suddenly and unexpectedly Stephan's ship jerked hard to his left. Stephan didn't feel the jerk. He was looking at the ground at the time and seeing the quick movement of the ship toward the north caused him to sense the jerk. It turned his stomach and gave him a feeling similar to being carsick. This ride on the alien spaceship would make any rollercoaster seem mild. There were no restraints and no protective cart around him. It was just him suspended in midair, or so it seemed.

Looking up he saw the cause of the jerk. Another alien ship, most likely the one that Stephan had encountered in Greenland the first time, had struck them. This seemed strange to Stephan. They didn't get shot at. They were bounced. It looked like two giant balls bouncing against each other.

The ship that Stephan was on reacted to the hit by shifting direction and moving rapidly towards the ground. At first Stephan thought that the ship had been damaged and was about to crash. But then the ship simply bounced off the ground, somehow gaining speed from the bounce, and then struck hard at the other space ball. This sent the bad guys flying off. The bad guys' ship shifted its direction as well and headed towards the ground. Focused on the heat of the battle and not really caring about the humans on the earth, the bad ship hit the ground and annihilated a small Nevada town, pressing it into the ground as if a giant steam roller had run over it. Stephan was shocked at how quickly and easily an entire community of people could be eliminated. The bounce must have killed numerous individuals. The other bad guy's ball returned, flying at Stephan's ship with their own bounce attack.

This time the hit was from the bottom. The bouncing ball smashed into the underside of Stephan's ball jerking it upwards into the sky. The hit easily caused about a 20,000-foot change in altitude. Now it was Stephan's ball's turn to retaliate. His ball charged to the ground, took a bounce, and smashed into the underside of the other ball.

The balls bounced against each other again and again in what seemed like a ridiculous kid's game. The bouncing went back and forth for a long time. It was a confusing yet somehow strangely ethical battle in the way they fought each other. They took turns in their attacks. One ball would hit the other ball, and then it was as if the offending ball would just sit and wait for a retaliatory attack. The two balls both behaved in an identical fashion. They took their hit, and then waited to get hit. It was the strangest type of battle Stephan had ever seen. There was no shooting, only bouncing. Both spaceships seemed to be playing a game rather than fighting a battle.

What bothered Stephan was how ethical the aliens were with each other, but how little they cared about the humans on the ground that may be getting killed with each bounce. The humans seemed to be irrelevant. Their code of ethics was only relevant when it came to interacting with each other, and no one else.

The back and forth bouncing continued for nearly one hour without any apparent change in who was winning and who was losing. From Stephan's perspective, both sides seemed to be having fun. Then suddenly, and unexpectedly, the bad guy's ship stopped moving. It didn't take its turn to bounce against Stephan's ship. Stephan didn't know what the change meant. He couldn't see any damage on the other ship. It just stopped and slowly started drifting to the ground. Over time it became more like a fall because it wasn't an aggressive drive towards the ground as previously. And there was no bounce. The ship just hit the ground hard and stayed there, right on top of west Elko. The ship looked dead and Stephan was convinced that the part of the town that was hit must also be dead.

Stephan had no idea what had just occurred. It seemed like his team won, but he had no idea how. Suddenly his ship moved and he found himself a couple hundred feet above the mining dust cloud. But the cloud was growing smaller and smaller. The mining machine seemed to have stopped in its tracks. Stephan spotted aliens coming out from the dust cloud and standing upright with their hands up in the air in the form of a V. It looked like they were hailing Stephan and his ship, but he knew it couldn't be true. Then strange ropes started to drop down from Stephan's ship. The ropes looped themselves around the hands of each of the aliens as if they were being lassoed and started pulling them up into the air. Stephan realized that these were captured prisoners. These individuals were being arrested. But he had no idea what would happen to them. As the ropes towing the alien hostages came up into the ship everything simply disappeared from view. He concluded that everything that was in the ship was invisible to him. The rope and its captive became invisible as soon as they passed the outer surface of Stephan's alien ship.

After another 15 minutes the dust cloud had settled enough to where the alien mining machine was visible. Not surprisingly it was completely covered with dust. It was enormous, about two miles across and a half mile high. Stephan no longer wondered what had happened to the captives. He knew that he would probably never know their fate. He started to wonder about the materials that had been mined. He decided that they must have been processed and stored on the mineral mining ship. But he wasn't sure where. Everything about these aliens was a complete incomprehensible mystery.

After collecting the captives from the mining ship Stephan's ship returned to hoover over the disabled ship. A similar process of rounding up captives occurred here as well. The bad aliens left their ship, were picked up by ropes, and were deposited somewhere into Stephan's ship.

With the hostages in hand, the aliens attempted to communicate with Stephan. It was so sudden and unexpected that it came as a surprise to Stephan, and he wasn't sure how to react. Everything had been so quiet up to now that when they finally communicated with him he was taken back. Their message was, *"We need to communicate with your leader. Would you open up communication with him?"*

Stephan didn't know how to handle the necessary communication with the president. Sending messages to the president wasn't a problem, but how was he going to be able to get the president's response so he could communicate it with the aliens. Stephan decided that he was going to have to go directly to the president and meet with him there. Stephan sent a message to the aliens showing them where the White House was located and asked them to park the ship over the west lawn. He informed them that he would need to communicate face-to-face with the President and that he would then be able to share the President's message with the aliens.

Then Stephan sent a message to the President informing him that he was coming along with the aliens and that both he and they would need his protection. They would be there in a few minutes.

Chapter Thirty-Three

The President

November, 2020 AD, Washington, DC

Stephan asked the President if he could come out to the ship after it landed. Since the President couldn't respond, Stephan hoped that the President was at the White House and that the interaction with the aliens would not be a problem. He also hoped that the security forces around the President wouldn't create a problem by shooting at the ship.

A few minutes later the alien ball ship was hovering over the White House and was descending toward the West Lawn area as directed by Stephan. The ball didn't settle in on the lawn because it was too large. If it landed, it would wipe out a large portion of central Washington, DC.

The ship was immediately surrounded by Secret Service agents with their weapons pointed at the ship. This seemed ridiculous to Stephan. Did these guys really think they had a chance in a shootout against these aliens? All the aliens had to do was bounce their ball and they would wipe out the White House and everything around it.

The alien ship lowered its gangplank. Stephan informed the aliens, *"I'm going to go out to meet the President and his security team to let them know that the President will not be in danger if he comes on the ship. Can you promise me he will be safe and that you won't try to kidnap him?"*

"We don't know what you mean by kidnap but please proceed," was the alien response.

Stephan didn't feel a great deal of confidence by this response from the aliens. He decided he would let the President know of the dangers and let the President make it his own call whether he wanted to meet the aliens face-to-face or just communicate with them through Stephan.

As he came to the door of the alien spacecraft Stephan left his protective breathing chamber. It was a little confusing because there were no walls and there was no door to walk through. There were no identifying markings showing him where this chamber was located. Stephan wondered how he would find this area again once he returned to the ship.

He walked to the plank. The plank reached out and down onto the lawn. Immediately the weapons of the secret service agents were aimed at him, and he had flashbacks of the attack in Cusco. What if one of these agents was under contract to kill him? Was he putting his life in danger by coming out to meet the President? Then he noticed all the cameras that were pointed at him and at all the surrounding areas. Would anyone be stupid enough to try to kill him with all these cameras pointing at them?

He hesitated for a moment, then he proceeded down the gangplank. He felt nervous and scared, not about seeing the President, but about all the weapons pointed at him as if he was the bad guy here.

He was grateful to see the President walk out of the White House and toward him. That would circumvent his having to explain his presence to a large number of intermediaries who would try to block his contact with the President. As the President walked toward him, he extended and shook his hand saying, "I'm thrilled to finally be meeting you. You're Stephan, correct?"

Stephan in turn responded, "Thank you for meeting with us. I'm thrilled to be here as well even though I'm nervous about my life, especially with so many weapons pointing at me as if I'm some kind of bad guy."

"I completely understand," explained the President who immediately informed his aid that Stephan had been a target of several assassination attempts and that the Secret Service should be looking to protect him rather than aiming weapons at him. The aid immediately informed the leader of the security forces, and the weapons were aimed downwards.

Stephan proceeded to explain the entire history of his interactions with the aliens. He had already confessed to the president that the XLs were the reason for the aliens' arrival to earth. He additionally informed the President about all the early communications with the aliens, and their initial responses. He informed the President about being contacted by the aliens in Greenland, feeling that it was no longer a secret and that the whole world now knew about Greenland. He explained his being kidnapped by the aliens and the battle that had just occurred over Nevada. "The aliens would like to communicate with you. They can only communicate through mental telepathy, and you can only communicate through voice, so I'll need to be the intermediary between the two of you for this conversation. If you would tell me what you would like to say I'll relay the words directly to the aliens, just the way you say them. I think the aliens would like you to come on board their ship, but for now we should stay here because they just might kidnap you too like they did me. These guys are really hard to read."

The President started, "tell the aliens that I am honored to be meeting them and I hope we can have a long and lasting relationship. I hope we can find mutual grounds allowing us to work together."

Stephan simply recorded the President's message and mentally transmitted the message to the aliens. They sent their response and Stephan read it off to him directly the way it was given to him. "There is no basis for a long-term relationship. We do not communicate with foreign life forms. It's too much trouble. They are constantly requesting help from us and we don't give help. And there is nothing that we can learn from you. The only reason we came here now was because of the damage some of our people were doing to your planet. We have eliminated that problem. But we want to see if you are willing to trade with us. The individuals we have captured were mining a resource which is extremely valuable to us. We would be interested in trading for this mineral. Of course, if you disagree to the trade, we will take it anyway. But we would prefer to avoid a conflict if possible."

Stephan and the President looked at each other slightly confused. Was this a threat, or an offer to trade? Stephan added, "I told you these guys are hard to read. I have no idea what all of that really means."

The President responded with, "What are you offering us in return?"

Again, through Stephan the alien said, "I don't know what we have that you would want. We won't give you any type of technology that can be turned into a weapon. And whatever we give we will give to everyone on your planet. There will not be any exclusive trades giving one group of people an advantage over another. I am waiting for you to tell us what is needed by you. For us, to start with, we want to take all the resources that have already been mined. We can use this as our initial trade. When you know what you would like in return, please let me know so we can make the necessary arrangements."

The President saw no loss in giving these aliens the resources that had already been extracted. His response was, "Go ahead and take what has already been mined and please let us know what it is you were mining for. And let us know how much of it you need so we can see if we have the capacity to extract it ourselves, or if we will need your help in the extraction process."

"Agreed," responded the alien. "We will now leave you and pick up the mined materials. Communicate your terms when you have decided what you want from us in return." Then to Stephan the alien said, *"Please come back on board."*

Stephan informed the President that the aliens want him to return onto the ship and asked him if he wanted to meet the aliens. The President declined, stating that he didn't want to become one of their captives, but that he would probably get another opportunity to meet with them in the future. Stephan posed the question to the aliens, *"Would you like to come out here and meet the President?"*

The alien response was expected, *"No."*

Stephan asked the President if there was a better way for the two of them to communicate directly. The President said he had been thinking the same thing and gave him an encrypted satellite phone which communicated directly to the President's private phone number. "This should make it easier for you to update me. The call will be answered by my secretary, and then transferred directly to me wherever I happen to be."

Stephan responded with, "And when you've decided on what you want in trade, let me know so I can communicate it with the aliens."

Stephan bid farewell to the President and hesitantly started to ascend the plank returning to the alien ship. He didn't want to continue being their captive, but he was also uncomfortable staying in Washington under the aim of so many guns. He decided to take his chances by returning to the ship in the hope that they would return him to Greenland. As he entered the ship the plank behind him immediately started to retract. Stephan wondered where his breathable room was located but noticed that it was now possible for him to breathe from anywhere. The aliens explained, *"We have modified your breathing room so that it will travel with you wherever you go in the ship. You no longer need to stay in one place. It will be invisible to you, but it will always be around you."*

Stephan asked, *"Are you returning me to the place where you picked me up?"*

"No," replied the aliens. *"We are bringing you back to our home planet."*

"Why," protested Stephan. *"I thought we weren't of any use to you. I thought you would be returning me to the location where you picked me up."*

"These people aren't of any use to us," explained the alien. *"But you are. You have the ability to multitask and do several things simultaneously, and we want to learn how to do that."*

Stephan continued to protest, thinking of Abigail, *"But I have a life here and I want to continue living it!"*

"You may be able to come back later, but now you have to come with us so we can study you," responded the alien.

This didn't sound too promising. He would leave and his return would be uncertain. He would now become the lab rat for aliens rather than for humans. All his efforts to hide out from the earth scientists had been in vain if he was now going to become a similar lab rat for the aliens. And he would have no other humans to communicate with or work with at this new location. He decided to push the issue. *"How long will I be gone?"* questioned Stephan.

"That is up to our scientists," replied the alien. *"It is for the greater good. Therefore, you are obligated to come with."*

Stephan's private thought was *"Whose greater good? Definitely not mine! Definitely not for earth! These guys are going to turn me into a lab experiment for their own good."*

The alien continued, *"Where are your two friends. There were two more like you. We need them too."*

Stephan wasn't about to turn his friends into lab experiments as well. It was bad enough that he was going to get kidnapped and dragged off many light-years from home. He relayed the alien's request to Frida and Cheng feeling that they had the right to make up their own mind, but he made sure that they knew he didn't think it was a very good idea. It wasn't long before he heard back with the anticipated response that they had no interest in joining the aliens. With this response he was able to respond to the aliens, *"They don't want to go with you. They won't give me their location."*

The alien sounded a little confused in his response, *"That wasn't an option. We want to know where they are so we can learn from them. They can't deny us the right to learn. That's a universal right that every creature has. They must comply."*

"*Learning is good,*" replied Stephan. "*But you can't do it at the expense of someone else's safety.*"

"*You don't understand,*" replied the alien. "*There is nothing optional here. Where are your friends?*"

"*I don't know and wouldn't tell you if I did know,*" replied Stephan. "*I respect their choices more than I respect yours.*"

Apparently, this was a new experience to the alien since he didn't seem to understand how to process the denial. He just expected to get whatever he requested. There was a long pause before the alien was able to respond, "*We need all three of you. Taking only one of you back to our home planet will not be sufficient to show us the difference.*"

Stephan didn't like the sound of that, "*I'm not sure I want to go either because it sounds like you will be doing experiments on me. It sounds like you will be probing and testing me. I would prefer to not have to put up with that.*"

"*Your choosing has been superseded by the better good of the population as a whole and so you are coming with us. We will be putting up an extensive search for your friends. We will find them and bring them back too.*" The alien's comments were matter of fact as if it was obvious that Stephan was going with and there was nothing else to discuss.

Chapter Thirty-Four

The Ship

November, 2020 AD, Nevada

Stephan resigned himself to the fact that he was stuck on the alien ship, at least for now. He felt conflicted. The opportunity to visit an alien world was extremely exciting. But he wanted to do it on his own terms. He didn't want to become a lab rat for them. He didn't want to become a caged animal where he would be stuck in some science facility, and he wouldn't be able to experience the alien world. That wasn't the way he wanted to visit another world. He decided that he didn't want to go with these aliens. He knew he would constantly be on the watch for a chance to escape. But how do you escape from an alien world? Fear started to creep in.

The alien ship Stephan was on was en route to Nevada to pick up the mined materials. The trip was short, only about 15 minutes, but during that time Stephan decided to make the best of his captivity and take a tour of the alien ship. He wanted to test the limits of the movable breathing room that he was inside of. It was difficult to call it a room since there were no visible walls, ceiling, or floor. But then nothing seemed to have floors, walls or ceilings. To Stephan it appeared as though he was entirely on his own, floating in the air.

As the ship traveled it had no perceivable shell. Stephan could see the ground below and the sky above. He could see himself whizzing through the air. But he knew that anyone outside looking up at the ship would see the ball and wouldn't see Stephan at all.

Stephan decided to test the limits of the ship's exterior. He decided to walk in one direction continuously until he bounced against the ship's exterior walls. But he was surprised because he never bounced. At first he simply assumed that the ship was too large and that he would eventually hit a wall. He assumed that it just took longer than he expected. But when he kept walking and walking, never finding the exterior edge, he became confused. Was there an actual wall in this ship? He knew he was moving. He felt the motion. But there was never an end. How was that possible? He knew the ship was of limited size. He had seen the outside of it and there was a definite exterior surface. But in the interior, there seemed to be no walls. It seemed like he would be able to walk forever.

Seeing the futility of his walking to the edge he sent a message to the alien, "*I would like to see more of the ship. How do I do that?*"

"*You picture it in your mind and a door opens so you can go there,*" was the response that he received back.

"*But I don't know what the other places in this ship are. How do I know where I want to go? I don't know what's here,*" responded an exasperated Stephan.

The alien sent Stephan images of the various chambers that he might want to visit. Stephan was sure that they left out the key areas, like the command center and the engine room, but that was okay. He was excited to see anything he could see. He tried it. He envisioned one of the rooms and magically, in midair, a door opened up.

Stephan walked through the door to discover what was on the other side. It was exactly as he had seen in the vision. He had to spend a few minutes analyzing what he was looking at. At first, he wasn't sure what room he had just entered. He assumed it was a bedroom. Along one side of the room was something that looked like a stack of pipes with the open end facing out towards him. Each pipe had a diameter of two feet. They were stacked six high, staggered, so that the total height came to ten feet. The thought of cramming himself into a tube and trying to sleep in that made Stephan shudder. But he was sure these were sleeping chambers. The wall opposite the bed tubes was assumed to be some sort of open bathroom. It had several hoses and tubes hanging from the walls. Stephan was sure he didn't want to know how those were used or what body part they might be attached to. He decided he really didn't want to know.

Having seen enough of this room Stephan pictured a different room in his mind and a door opened up. It was the same door that he had just walked through but this time when he walked through the door, he found himself in a different room, the room he had pictured. He expected to be returned to the lobby area where he had initially found himself when he arrived on the ship for the first time. Instead, he ended up in the room he had envisioned.

This time he found himself in what must be a living area or rest area. He was alone in the room, which didn't surprise him except he wondered where all the aliens were. They had to be in one of these rooms. In this room there were images on all the walls, the ceiling, and the floor. There were scenery pictures from what Stephan guessed must be their home planet. There were also pictures of what must be families and homes.

He found the pictures fascinating. He looked closely at one of the scenery pictures, trying to make sense of what he was seeing. But to his surprise, as he focused on the picture long enough his mind seemingly took him to that location, and it would be as if he was visiting it in person.

The picture Stephan had chosen to look at appeared to be hills, but unlike the hills on earth, these were multicolored and multilayered. There was no vegetation, just the raw mountain. The hills reminded him of one of his grandmother's multilayered cakes, where each layer had a different color and flavor. In his mind's eye he could look in all different directions as if he was actually on location. He could see that the various hills had different hues. One of the hills looked exactly like the Rainbow Mountains in China. But the most interesting was a mountain which had about twelve layers and several of the layers were invisible. It wasn't that he could see through the layer, it's just that it wasn't visible. Stephan asked his alien contact why this mountain had empty layers, sending the alien the image of what he was looking at.

The alien responded, *"Every layer in that mountain is visible to me. I can see from your message which*

*layers are invisible to you and which are not. I think the
reason they are invisible is because you simply do not
have the ability to see them. They are outside your
visible color spectrum and even though they actually
exist, they are not there for you to see."*

Stephan was completely fascinated. He had never
considered the fact that there might be colors that he
could not see. It was a completely foreign concept to
him.

The surface of the alien world was covered with hills,
mountains, rivers, and oceans. The vegetation was
minimal, but what plant life there was looked a lot like
a mangrove swamp. When there was any vegetation, it
engulfed the entire area, going over the tops of
mountains and out into the sea. It seemed to propagate
like a weed.

What Stephan found interesting was that there were
no people or animals on the surface. He questioned the
alien for an explanation, *"Why don't your people live on
the surface? Why have they all migrated underground?"*

The answer came back, *"Living on the surface is
dangerous. Many generations ago our people did live on
the surface, but we were attacked by meteorites which
contained a toxic contaminant. This ended up polluting
our waters. Then, because the water was polluted our
rain was also acidic. It resulted in a plague which killed
off over half the population that was living on the
surface. The remaining population desperately looked
for alternatives, and they found that living in caves kept
them safe. The acidic water that filtered through the
ground somehow became purified and the underground*

water pools were drinkable. From this beginning my people started digging caves deeper and deeper into the planet, and now there is rarely a reason to leave the sanctuary of our underground homes except for things like these expeditions to your planet. And even then, the spaceships depart from an underground chamber, not from the surface of the planet. Since that time living on the surface has become impossible. Today we are quite comfortable living underground. It has become completely normal for us. Living on the surface the way you do is strange and uncomfortable to us. In fact, it can even be considered scary. Our people are afraid of the surface. That's one of the reasons none of our people want to leave the safety of the spacecraft."

Stephan, feeling he had sufficiently explored the anomalies of the alien surface, mentally brought himself back to the alien spacecraft. He was back in the room with all the images of the alien planet. He moved on to the next image in the room. In this case he was looking at a picture of what he thought must be someone's home. Stephan focused on this image and suddenly he was transported to the room in the picture and was able to look around. It was the strangest house he had ever seen. He could never have imagined something so foreign and outlandish. The entire home appeared to be one big cube. Like any cube, there were four sides, a top, and a bottom. But each of the surfaces in this cube functioned as a different room of the house. Every surface was visible to all the other surfaces. But every surface was a floor. People could be found standing or moving around on any of the six surfaces as if it was the ground to them. Aliens on the ceiling were upside down from the aliens on the floor. And aliens on the walls were horizontal to the individuals on the floor or the ceiling.

Looking in the direction that Stephan considered to be the floor, Stephan saw an area that looked like it was used as the living room. There were aliens lounging around on what looked like large pillows and they seemed to be engaged in some kind of game. He wasn't sure what they were doing, but he could see a lot of interaction between the individual aliens.

The surface that Stephan considered to be the ceiling appeared to be the bedroom and bathroom combination. It had the same large tubes that he found in the bedroom here on the spaceship. There were aliens inside several of the tubes who appeared to be asleep. There were also three aliens off to one side of the room cuddling together. At first Stephan couldn't figure out what they were doing so he looked closer. But then he realized that they must be having their version of sex and he was completely embarrassed and quickly looked away. However, the aliens didn't seem to be bothered by the fact that anyone on any of the other five surfaces could be watching them. Apparently, sex was a very normal and open process in this alien world.

One of the walls was interpreted by Stephan to be their version of a garden and kitchen combination. He could see several individuals milling around the plants and working with some implements which he interpreted to be cooking utensils. He was delighted to see that plants existed in this world. However, apparently because of the acid on the surface, the plants had to be grown underground using ground filtered water. Taking a closer look Stephan also saw small, caged animals. The animals in one of the cages looked like a Quokka which were the critters that were unique to Rottnest Island in Western Australia. Another animal looked like the combination of a snake with the head of a chicken. There were more animals, each one stranger than the last.

Another of the walls was interpreted by Stephan to be the alien version of an office, study, or library. It included tables and chairs with individuals sitting around talking about a holographic projection that was in the middle of the table. He initially thought they were watching their version of a movie, but there seemed to be a lot of interaction between the aliens which led Stephan to believe that they must be doing something interactive. Perhaps they were playing a game. But watching the projected image seemed more like a movie. Stephen couldn't be sure what he was observing.

The function of the remaining two walls was so foreign to Stephan that he couldn't even guess what they were used for. They had a variety of machines and equipment which, if they weren't inside the home, might be interpreted as a lab or possibly manufacturing equipment, but Stephan couldn't make sense of what all of it could be used for. One guess he had was that some of this equipment might be used for traveling around in this underground world since he didn't notice any kind of exit door.

Light and heat for this house was provided by a central mini sun-like object which floated dead center of the complex without being attached to anything. There wasn't any visible means for holding it in place. It just hung there as if his house had its own sun.

Transferring mentally back to the alien ship Stephan was able to see more scenery pictures each of which was impressive in different ways. *"This would be an incredible planet to visit and tour,"* thought Stephan to himself. *"But what fun would that be if I could never share it because I could never come home."*

Stephan saw pictures of various plants and vegetation, and several additional animal species. Some of the animals seemed like pets because they were pictured with individual aliens while others seemed like they were being raised for food because they were in cages. None of it was familiar to Stephan. At this point he didn't want to take the time to explore each of these in depth the way he had the first couple images. He assumed he might get another chance in the future to do more exploring. He mentally returned to the alien ship that he was riding on and pulled himself out of the picture.

Next he became fascinated by and attracted to the family pictures. In each family picture there were always three parents and any number of children. It fascinated Stephan that there were never any two parent or one parent families. There were always three parents. He questioned his alien source, *"Do you ever have families that have less than three parents? Don't people die or get divorced?"*

The alien explained, "*I don't understand divorce, but I think I understand your question. When we get married, which may already have occurred in a previous generation of any of us, we don't marry an individual, we marry a line or individual type. So, if one of the individuals in that type dies, we still have plenty of others in that type that we are married to. We are not restricted to a specific individual relationship the way you are. So, we are never in a situation where we don't have three parents.*"

"*Then who do the children belong to, if the parents are so mobile and variable?*" challenged Stephan who was getting more confused than ever.

"*The children belong to and are primarily taken care of by the individual who gave them birth, which is the b-type individual. Of course, the other two parents are active participants, but the b-type is the birthing plantation and that's who retains the initial development of any individual that they gave birth to.*"

"*This is the weirdest thing I've ever heard of,*" thought Stephan to himself. At this point he was too confused to ask any more questions. He assumed more questions would just lead to more confusion. He had to process what he had already learned and make sense of it first.

In the family pictures that Stephan was looking at the parents appeared to be distinguishable by the colors of their apparel. There was always one individual who favored red, one who favored blue, and one who favored yellow. He also noticed patches in the clothing that seemed empty or blank, but Stephan interpreted these to be areas that were in a color that he couldn't see, much the same as he experienced when he was looking at the mountains. Since everything else was so strange, Stephan was surprised to find that the aliens seemed to use the same three primary colors as the people on earth, with the exception of the invisible colors which he couldn't explain.

Stephan concentrated on one of the families, hoping to be transferred into their lives just the way he was previously transferred to the mountains and the house. He wanted to learn more about family life when suddenly one of the aliens stepped into the room. *"Why are you invading my family,"* complained the alien.

Stephan, not realizing that he had overstepped some unknown taboo, responded, *"I'm sorry. I didn't know that was an invasion. I was just trying to learn more about family life on your planet. I won't do it again."*

"Good," was the blunt reply as the alien disappeared back through the same doorway.

Stephan decided he had enough of that room and visioned another of the rooms in the alien spacecraft in his mind. The door opened and stepping through the door he found himself in a room that looked like a recreation or exercise room. This time the room wasn't empty. It was quite large and there were over twenty aliens in the room engaged in some kind of activity. He couldn't tell if it was a game or work or what. They were flailing their arms and legs around in erratic patterns that would make humans cringe in pain. There seemed to be minimal contact between the aliens, but when there was contact it was extreme. It was all or nothing. When they made contact, they would be entangled in ways that seemed obscene. Stephan wasn't sure if he should stay or leave. Initially he thought he was watching a sporting event. But now he started to feel like he was in the middle of some kind of mating ritual. It felt a little embarrassing.

The aliens ignored him as if he wasn't there. They continued moving through their gyrations. Occasionally an additional alien would enter the room and join in on the activity, or one of the aliens would leave. It was hard to tell what triggered the alien exchange. But regardless, the gyration process maintained itself uninterrupted.

After ten minutes of watching, he sent a message to his alien host. He wasn't sure if he had ever met this host. He wondered if it was one of the people, he had encountered face to face. But whoever it was, he sent that alien a message asking if he could see the control room. Rather than receiving a response in the form of an answer, he received an image of the control room. He was delighted that they didn't refuse his request. Taking this new image as an invitation, Stephan appropriately pictured the image and a door opened. Walking through that door he found himself in the control room of the alien spacecraft.

The control room turned out to be as confusing as the rest of the craft had been. It contained 20 aliens all sitting at small desks in a circle facing each other. In the middle was a hologram of various components of the ship and of the external environment. The aliens sat and stared at this central image seeming to do nothing but watch. They also had their own projections at each of their desks. It looked as if these projections were of components of the ship. Stephan could see shifts and changes in the various images and he knew that somehow the aliens were giving instructions which were causing the changes.

This room had no floor, walls, or ceiling, just like the room through which he had first entered the vessel. In this room he was again hanging in midair floating along at high speeds. He was able to see outside the ship in all directions, as if the ship wasn't even there.

This was obviously the control room, but there was very little Stephan would be able to learn. The process that was occurring here was beyond the scope of his understanding. He decided to ask, *"What is going on in here? What are these individuals doing?"*

"Flying the ship," was the blunt and meaningless answer Stephan received. He decided not to pursue the questioning. The aliens didn't seem to show any willingness to teach him anything. He felt they were extremely condescending; that he was a lessor species and not capable of understanding anything.

Stephan wondered if the imaging process that he used for moving from one room to another worked anywhere. He wondered if by imagining the earth below him he could transfer there. So he decided to try. He pictured the land below him, but nothing happened. No door opened for him to pass through. He tried again, this time imaging a building that was whizzing by beneath him. Again, nothing happened. He resigned himself to the fact that the doors only worked when moving between locations that were actually part of the ship.

Watching the aliens at the controls was also a bit disconcerting. Their eyes moved around their head in what appeared to be a random motion. He couldn't tell if they were looking at him or looking at the hologram in the center of the circle, or looking at their own holograms, or at the ground, or the sky. He couldn't make sense of which direction they were focusing their attention.

He watched the aliens operating the control room for a couple more minutes as they arrived at their destination, which was the mining operation in Nevada. Suddenly there was a flurry of activity. The aliens suddenly seemed to become stressed and excited. Looking closer at the mining operation he could see what they were excited about. The mining equipment was back in operation. The large cloud of dust had reappeared. Someone was running the equipment and the aliens on Stephan's ship obviously hadn't anticipated seeing it back in operation.

Chapter Thirty-Five

The Battle Renewed

November, 2020 AD, Nevada

Suddenly the aliens in the control room seemed to be focused up into the sky. Stephan guessed that this must have been their focus since one of the eyes on each of the heads was suddenly looking upwards.

Stephan looked upwards as well, just in time to see two new alien spaceship balls coming directly at his ship. Apparently, the original aliens had returned in a second ship and he was now in the middle of a retaliatory attack. The original group of aliens that had visited earth must have returned and they obviously weren't happy about their mining operation getting shut down. They had returned and resumed the operation.

Stephan's ship made a sudden jerky move attempting to avoid the attack. It was too little too late. The move managed to avoid one of the bouncing balls, but the second ball hit them squarely and directly pushing them roughly toward the ground. This second attacking ball maintained the pressure on Stephan's ball until it had a hard hit on the ground.

Suddenly the control room aliens became even more animated. There wasn't any noise. The communication between them was completely telepathic. But Stephan could tell they were in a panic. Stephan guessed they were scared.

With Stephan's ship pushed to the ground, he suddenly and unexpectedly saw aliens running out of the bottom of his ship. At first, he thought there must be some kind of danger on the ship, like a fire or a pending explosion. He wondered what he would need to do in order to escape the ship. But then he noticed that the escaping aliens were heading towards one of the attacking ships. They weren't passengers from his ship fleeing danger, they were captives fleeing captivity and attempting to return to their own ship.

He wondered how they were able to get out of this ship. Was there a door of some kind on the underside of the ship? Was it a door that he could also use to escape?

The attacking ship landed on the ground and the aliens which had escaped from Stephan's ship were starting to climb on board the enemy ship. Stephan decided that these must have been escaping prisoners. So what about the ship he was on? Were these aliens from this ship going to become captives on the "bad guys" ship? Were they destined to become prisoners? And if so, what would happen to him?

He looked at the aliens in the control room. They were frantically doing something, but he wasn't sure what it was. They must have a plan of some type that they were working towards. They didn't act like they were giving up.

Stephan asked, *"What's going on? Are we in trouble?"* But he didn't receive an answer. He assumed their silence was because they were too busy. He decided to stay in the control room. He assumed it was the pulse of the alien ship. Whatever they did he would simply follow. He didn't know what else to do.

Stephan started concentrating on the activities of the aliens. He watched their movement and what buttons were being pushed. He decided that it may become important for him to know more about this ship's operation. His photographic memory allowed him to watch for and analyze repeated patterns of behavior. He noticed that some behaviors were specifically affecting the movement of the ship. Other behaviors were causing reactions amongst the crew. He memorized the actions and behaviors until he was able to define repeated patterns of movement.

After the escaping aliens had boarded the "bad guys" ship, the ship started to slowly climb into the air in a somewhat threating posture, or maybe it just seemed threating to Stephan who was excessively cautious and nervous about ever escaping safely. As he observed the behavior of the aliens, he noticed them going through the motions of attempting to get the ship that he was on to move, but nothing was happening. He knew they were trying to raise the ship because of his memory of how they had raised the ship in the past. But still nothing happened. He could hear messages being sent between the aliens because they were now being sent out to everyone in the room, but they didn't make any sense. He hadn't learned the language of these aliens and they weren't bothering to translate the messages for his benefit.

Then, as if to add additional complexity to the situation, the United States Air Force had jet fighters appear on the scene. These fighters were circling the area around the mining operation and the location where Stephan's ball ship was stranded. As if to shoo a pestering fly away, one of the attacking alien ships swooshed towards the Air Force fighters at high speed and stopped just short of impact. The fighter couldn't react as quickly as the alien ship and was nearly knocked out of the sky. But like any annoying fly would react, the fighter continued to circle the area and the alien ship repeated its attack twice more. Not receiving the desired response from the Air Force, apparently expecting them to leave the scene, the very next time the alien ship swooshed toward the fighter, it struck and knocked the plane out of the sky. The other fighters immediately responded by firing at the alien ship, but the missiles just seemed to hit the ship and explode with no apparent impact on the alien vessel.

The alien ship seemed to tire of this game and struck a second of the Air Force fighters, also knocking it out of the sky. With that the remaining fighters finally received the message and rapidly departed from the scene.

Stephan knew he had to help. The alien "good guys" were getting beat up and Americans were getting killed. Even though he recently had to flee from the United States and escape to the Center of the Earth for his own safety, his loyalties were still with the U.S., and he knew he had to do something. But he had no idea what to do.

With a new sense of mission and desperation Stephan studied the control room with even more care and caution. He also involved Frida and Cheng, telling them about his dilemma. He stressed his need to help the Americans but didn't know what to do or how to do it.

He sent them images of where he was and explained what was happening. At first there was a silent pause from his companions. This didn't bother Stephan. He simply assumed they were assessing the situation before making any rash recommendations. After a few minutes he received a response from Cheng, *"Frida and I have been discussing your dilemma and we have a few thoughts and questions. It would be valuable for us to learn their language. Perhaps if all three of us worked on their language we might be able to put pieces of it together. Can you send us your photographic memory recordings of their conversations? Next, we think it would be valuable for you to talk to them about going back to their planet. Perhaps, if they didn't see you as hostile, they would be more willing to share with you, which will also help us acquire more information about their language."*

Stephan sent the images as requested. He continued to monitor the activities in the control room with intense interest. Additionally, he attempted to communicate with the aliens, but they ignored him and acted as if he wasn't even there. He wasn't sure if they were ignoring him because they didn't understand him, or if they were ignoring him because they were distracted and busy. He sent out another message to all the aliens in the control room, hoping someone would have the courtesy to respond, "*Can someone please communicate with me and tell me what is going on? Are we in trouble? Do we need to abandon ship?*"

To his surprise and delight one of the aliens responded, "*We are very busy trying to repair the ship. The ship has been damaged and cannot leave the surface of the earth. Our gravity repulsion engine is not working. We have sent out messages to our home planet to try and get support but right now the attackers have overpowered us. They have demanded that we release their prisoners which we have already accomplished. They are stealing your world's resources because they can sell them at a high price when they return to our planet.*"

Stephan asked what later seemed like a foolish question, "*Is there anything I can do to help?*"

"*Of course not,*" was the response. "*You have no idea about what we're doing. You are an inferior species, and our processes mean nothing to you.*"

This infuriated Stephan. He was accustomed to thinking of himself as special because of his superpowers. But to now be called inferior was demeaning and frustrating. He now had a renewed commitment to learn their language and to learn as much as possible about the operation of their spaceship. He continued the conversation, hoping to learn more about their communications. "*How do I get off this ship?*"

"*You are our guest and prisoner and will be brought back to our home planet,*" replied the alien matter-of-factly. Stephan still wasn't sure which alien he was talking to. The way their eyes worked he couldn't tell who was looking at him. He couldn't even tell which side of the alien was front and which was back if it wasn't for the fact that they were sitting. But what confused him even more was that one of the aliens stood up, turned around, and sat back down with his knees bending out in the opposite direction and his eyes flipping around to the other side of his head.

Stephan, trying to drill deeper asked, *"Is there anything I can do to learn more about your home planet so that I am ready for my visit?"*

The alien sounded frustrated but apparently considered it a good idea to give Stephan access to some of their data. The purpose was obviously to keep him busy. *"Yes,"* the alien replied. *"Look here."* The alien sent him a message showing Stephan how to access an enormous system which seemed like a video database containing information on a variety of topics. *"Here is a translator."* The alien showed Stephan how to access this data and how to listen to and read any of the information in it. *"Now we need you to leave and go to this waiting area."* The alien sent Stephan the image of the room where he wanted him to go.

Stephan was already familiar with how to move around the ship by selecting a place to go and then transporting himself there. He immediately made the move. Using Frida and Cheng as an important resource, Stephan sent the information about how to access the translator to them and explained how they could access the enormous database of the aliens. This would allow them to learn information about how the aliens thought and possibly how some of their technology worked. Cheng recommended, *"We should first try to download as much information as possible into our photographic memory. They may cut off access to this information once they realize what we are doing. Let's get images of as much of it as possible before we are cut off."*

"*Agreed,*" responded Frida and Stephan simultaneously. *"Let's each of us record different pieces. We can share information later."* Once he was in the isolated waiting room Stephan started to use the translator to decipher the activities that he had observed in the control room. He replayed and listened to their conversations and watched their corresponding activities. Then he tried to connect their conversations with their activities. Initially it all seemed very confusing. But then he slowly started to recognize patterns of behavior. For example, prior to the ship moving in a specific direction he heard commands that would indicate a direction and he saw the associated activities that would cause the ship to move.

Stephan continued studying his recorded memories of the activities in the control room. This process continued for several hours. But with each passing minute he learned more of their language and the procedures needed to control the movement of the ship. During this entire time the alien ship just sat where it was, motionless.

After a few hours of analysis Frida spoke up, sharing some information she had found, *"These aliens have some interesting cultural anomalies. For example, they see nothing wrong with changing sides. For example, in their recent battle, if someone is captured by their opponent, they immediately become part of the opposing team. Those prisoners that you thought were* escaping were probably individuals that had changed sides which could have included previously captured individuals, but it also could have included a crew of the ship that you are on. It's extremely confusing but apparently there is no sense of loyalty."

Frida continued, "It's also very confusing as to who is in charge. Apparently, there is some higher power that resides on their home world, and which guides all their activities. This higher power has some kind of control over these aliens. It's almost like this higher power is another species entirely. They have no pictures of this individual or collection of individuals. It's just a power that's there and everyone accepts its presence and commands. It's almost as if this power is some kind of god and everyone acquiesces to its will.

"One more thing," she added jokingly, "In my attempt to keep this short explanation long, these aliens don't seem to have a mind and will of their own. They act like some kind of collective. It reminds me of the Borg collective in Star Trek. They have one mind, and they all work together towards that one mind's objectives. Apparently, this god figure gives direction, and they all fall in line in unison. It's really strange for me to try to comprehend how all of this works. But apparently it does work for them. I sure wouldn't like it."

Cheng inserted, "If you were in the collective, I don't think you would know enough to like or dislike it."

"That's probably true," responded Frida. "But I'm not in it and I can tell you that I don't like it."

"So how can we leverage this information to get me free?" challenged Stephan. "They told me I was a prisoner and that they're taking me to their home planet. They were trying to trick me into exposing you guys too because they wanted to take you with as well. Actually, I'd love to see their planet. However, I'm not interested in being forced to go there and then to probably never be able to return to earth. That reality has eliminated my enthusiasm to go anywhere with them."

"I have no idea how to get you free," responded Cheng.

Chapter Thirty-Six

Trial

November, 2020 AD, Nevada, Center Earth

The threesome continued their study of the aliens' language, culture, and ship operations in hopes that they might come across some revelation that would lead them to successfully to help Stephan to escape. In the meantime, Abigail had joined Frida and Cheng in Jericho. Her feelings for Stephan were stronger than she initially realized and the whole drama of him being captured by aliens was a bit too much. She wanted to be closer to the action. Sitting in her hometown of Samaria was no longer acceptable. She arrived in Jericho and immediately went to Frida's workplace to get an update.

Frida saw Abigail coming at a distance and headed towards her in order to meet her. "How are you doing?" Frida asked.

"I am a nervous wreck!" Abigail explained. "I never realized how badly I was concerned about Stephan. I cannot get any work done. I'm sure my imagination is worse than reality. Can you please tell me what is going on with Stephan?"

"I'm afraid it's not good," explained Frida. "He is being held prisoner by the aliens. He is on board their ship. I can place some images of him and his situation into your head if you like. But it isn't nice."

"Please let me see him," she exclaimed. "I just need to see him, even if it's only for a moment."

Frida placed images of Stephan into Abigail's mind and simultaneously sent a message to him telling him that Abigail was with her and was extremely worried about him. He should send her a message assuring her of his safety, even if he wasn't really safe.

Almost immediately Abigail received these messages from Stephan. He tried to reassure her that he was working hard to escape and that she shouldn't worry about him. But things like that were always easier to say than they were to believe. "*I am safe and will be returning to Center Earth soon. I miss you and can't wait till we are together again.*"

Abigail pleaded with Frida, "Can I please stay here with you until this is over, and Stephan is once again safely back here with us?"

"Of course," responded Frida, but in the back of her mind she was slightly disappointed. She enjoyed having the house to herself and Cheng. They had recently become really close and were on the verge of intimacy. She liked where her relationship was going and wanted it to continue to grow. Hopefully Abigail's stay wouldn't be long.

Then, unexpectedly, a pair of local officials came up to Frida and Abigail. "We are arresting you by order of the tribal magistrate." They walked up to each side of Frida, and each took an arm.

"What am I being arrested for?" pleaded Frida.

There was no answer from the officials. Abigail explained, "They don't have to give you a reason. If the tribal magistrate wants you arrested, then you are arrested. The reason doesn't matter." Then, turning to the arresting officials she asked, "Can I go with her? She's not local and will need help going through this process."

"You can come," explained the official in a very bland and authoritarian voice. Then they started leading Frida off towards the center of the village with Abigail tailing behind.

As they arrived at the center of town they encountered a second pair of officials, this time escorting Cheng. Cheng sent Frida the message, *"What is going on here? Did you learn anything?"*

"No idea," exclaimed Frida. Then, turning to Abigail, she asked her the same question that Cheng had asked. And she received the same response she had given.

There were two guards for each of Frida and Cheng. The six of them along with Abigail climbed aboard the transport and took the short trip to the capital of the tribe in Samaria. After arriving they exited the transport and were escorted to the center of town where the official headquarters for the tribe was located. It was the same location where they had visited months earlier. But this time they were no longer the welcome guests that they had been previously when they met with Chaviva.

The entire parade of individuals was escorted into a large chamber which was laid out similar to a traditional throne room. Front and center was a large chair with a back that was higher than everyone else's in the room.

In this chair sat Chaviva. On either side of him were six advisors or counselors: twelve in total. These twelve were positioned in a semi-circle and in what would be the center of the circle there was a small stand.

Frida and Cheng were positioned on the stand and the remainder of the group, including Abigail and the guards, were positioned back away from the central stand. Chaviva made the opening statements, "You were brought here before this council because you are being accused of witchcraft and because it is believed that you are possessed by devils. How do you plead?"

Cheng spoke up in defense, "I need to understand the basis of the accusations. From what I've read about your rules and procedures, there needs to be at least two witnesses and we have a right to see and question these witnesses. Please bring the accusers forward so we can question them."

"This is highly unusual," responded Chaviva. He was completely taken aback by Cheng's abruptness. He had never received this type of resistance to his position of authority in the past. "We haven't received a request like this in a long time. We don't think your request is necessary for us to hold a trial based on the accusations against you. I need to know how you plead."

But Cheng wasn't easily swayed, "I demand that you follow your judicial procedures as outlined in your legal documents. I cannot plead on charges that I do not understand. I need to hear from my accusers what specifically we have done that violates a law. We want to know what law we have supposedly broken. By your code of law, if you can't present legal reasons for our being detained, then we are free to go. Do you have the accusers present as required by your code of law?"

Chaviva stood up and blurted out, "You are not in charge here. We are. You have been accused and we demand to know your plea. Are you guilty or not?"

"I see that your code of law is meaningless dribble since you so freely choose to ignore it," blurted out Cheng. "We don't plead anything since you're going to do what you want anyway regardless of your laws. What difference does it make what we plead? We're not going to play into this nonsense. You accuse us of breaking the law, but in the process of your accusations and this mock trial it is in fact you that are breaking the law and it is you that should be standing here on this stand as the accused."

Chaviva was outraged. His authority had never been challenged like this before. He didn't know exactly what to do. He could hear the room buzzing with whispers and he feared that his authority may be in jeopardy. "We are following procedural tradition, which has existed for many years, and there is no reason to change now."

"Then you are saying that tradition is more important than the legal rights of the accused," this time it was Frida that jumped in now that she saw where Cheng was going with his line of arguments.

"Tradition has become the law," insisted Chaviva.

"That's just fancy wording which means that your will is more important than my rights," challenged Frida. "You're the one that says tradition is more important, and you're also the one who defines what tradition is. That basically makes you all powerful, doesn't it? It basically means that I'm screwed over."

"This is ridiculous," blurted Chaviva. He turned and started to leave the room.

"Your authoritarian behavior is what is ridiculous," insisted Cheng, seeing that he was getting under Chaviva's skin and seizing the opportunity to push even further. "The way you run this mock court is ridiculous. And since you can't document your charges against us through the voice of any accusers, by law we are free to go." By this time Chaviva had left the room, so Cheng continued talking to the remaining members of the council. "Now we not only do not have accusers, but we also don't even have a judge. This entire court proceeding is a sham and I insist on our being allowed to return home."

The lead councilor spoke up, "Yes, you are free to go, but you should realize that you made powerful new enemies today and that won't be very helpful to your cause in the future."

Frida replied, "We're also not being thrown in jail for fabricated charges, so maybe the day isn't so bad after all."

Cheng, Frida, and Abigail left the court and headed to the area where they would find transport back to Jericho. Abigail was in awe and shock at what had just happened. She was conflicted. She felt defensive for Chaviva since he was their religiously appointed leader. But she also saw that the accusations were ridiculous and unfounded. Abigail started the conversation with, "I have never seen Chaviva so angry. I have never seen him storm out of the room like that before. You must have really hit a sore spot with him."

"I just couldn't see pleading guilty or not guilty to charges that didn't make sense to me," explained Cheng. "If I don't understand what they're talking about, how can I plead anything and worse yet, how do I defend against something that doesn't make sense to me? He had been so friendly in the past. It's like we're seeing a completely different side of him. He really sees himself as some kind of superpower in control here."

Abigail was sympathetic, but at the same time she was afraid to say that she understood because she was afraid of also getting caught up in the accusations that Cheng and Frida were getting accused of. She knew there were a lot of listening ears around her at all times and that's probably how Cheng and Frida found themselves in trouble in the first place. Someone must have heard some talk about the outer world or about their ability to communicate with Stephan and whoever was listening in considered it heresy and the work of the devil. She hoped that she wasn't the one who accidentally leaked the information that was now causing their trial.

The three were about to step aboard a transport vehicle back to Jericho when the same four guards that had arrested them previously again appeared and informed them that they were being taken back to the court area. Apparently, something had happened which would affect their trial.

Cheng and Frida found themselves back on the stand in front of Chaviva and the rest of the council. Again Chaviva started the conversation, "You thought you could get away from here quickly but it's not going to be all that easy. I haven't received all the answers that I wanted."

"You left so we left," was Cheng's curt response. He was feeling slightly arrogant at his previous success.

"My departure doesn't give you permission to leave," was Chaviva's response. "Regardless, we have you back here now and your accusers should be arriving any minute."

"Excellent," replied Cheng. "I insist on hearing in detail what we are accused of and I insist that I be allowed to question them. How many are there?"

"Two," was the response.

"Then I want them separated so they can't hear each other's testimony," insisted Cheng.

"We'll take care of that," replied Chaviva, but it was obvious that he didn't like being told what to do.

Cheng continued, "I want Abigail to be with the second accuser so that I am assured that the accusers can't hear each-other's testimony."

"One of my agents will also be there to make sure there is no intimidation or blackmail going on," replied Chaviva suggesting that he didn't trust Cheng any more than Cheng trusted him.

The wait was about fifteen minutes before two individuals arrived at the court room. Cheng and Frida assumed that these must be the accusers, but they had never seen either of these individuals before. Cheng immediately formulated a strategy to challenge their credibility as accusers.

Chaviva asked the accusers to come to the front of the room and outline their specific accusations to which Cheng immediately objected, "We agreed to separate the two accusers first so that we can receive independent testimonies."

Chaviva looked irritated but then asked one of the accusers to leave the room along with one of the arresting agents. Abigail joined them as they left the building. Then Chaviva instructed the remaining accuser, "Explain your accusation."

The first accuser stated that Frida and Cheng, and the third member of their group Stephan, were reported to communicate with each other without saying a word. In his opinion that was satanic behavior. That wasn't normal human behavior. Chaviva turned to Cheng and Frida and asked, "What do you have to say about this accusation?"

Cheng started by saying, "She is correct but that has nothing to do with Satan. Our ability to telepathically communicate is the result of a medical procedure. The three of us were test subjects. In the outer world, a fear arose that our new abilities could potentially replace other forms of communication. The result was the assassination of the only doctor who knew how to perform the procedure. And then, because we feared for our own lives, since we were examples of this medical procedure, we ran away and ended up here. In the outer world assassins tried to kill us several times. Now it looks like the same threats and fears are occurring here. What we have the ability to do is not satanic but is the result of a medical procedure."

One of the councilors spoke up and asked, "Are you saying that this procedure can be performed on any of us with the same result?"

"I would assume so," responded Cheng, "since it was performed three times and all three times it worked. However, as I said, the knowledge of how to do the procedure has now been lost. No one wants to experiment with this procedure because they're afraid of having the same fate as the doctor."

"So, you claim this ability is completely man-made?" persisted the councilor.

"Yes," responded Cheng. "I have a question for the accuser." Then turning to the accuser, he asked, "When did you learn about our abilities? Who told you about them?"

"We haven't met but I overheard Abigail tell a friend about your abilities, and it definitely sounds unnatural and satanic. No one has abilities like that. I don't believe you can get that by surgery. I think you two are evil." The accuser looked physically fearful as if she believed everything, she was telling the court.

Chaviva spoke up, "If no one has any additional questions for the accuser," looking directly at the accuser he said, "please leave and send in your friend."

The first accuser was quickly replaced by the second accuser and Chaviva made the same request, "Explain your accusation."

The second accuser look scared, much more so than the first accuser. He spoke up and said, "I heard that these guys use Satan to communicate with each other."

"Tell me what is satanic about communicating?" asked Cheng.

"You guys don't talk," said the accuser.

"How do you know this?" asked Cheng. "We've never met."

"My friend told me about it, and it didn't seem right."

"So, you haven't seen us do anything Satanic first hand?" challenged Cheng.

The accuser agreed.

"Then you're not a witness to anything Satanic?" repeated Cheng.

"Not directly," explained the accuser. "But it just doesn't seem right."

Cheng turned to Chaviva and demanded, "You have introduced two witnesses, neither one of which has witnessed us do anything. They're both accusing us because of suspicions and gossip. They probably received their information from the same person, or maybe even from each other. Your witnesses are not witnesses because they didn't witness anything. Therefore, you don't have a case against us. You have no business putting us on trial here based on gossip."

Chaviva was so infuriated that he wanted to throw Cheng and Frida in jail just for good measure. But this trial had become such a circus. He knew his reputation was at risk. He had no other choice than to comply with Cheng's request. "I agree. There is no evidence of satanic activities. The accusations are dismissed, and the accused are free to go."

Frida jumped in, addressing Chaviva and attempting to put a positive spin on the situation, "We want to thank everyone who has so warmly welcomed us here. We love it in Jericho and have found it to be a peaceful sanctuary from the cruelty that we were experiencing on the surface world. We look forward to staying here in Center Earth for a long time. We plan to become model citizens that will make you glad you allowed us to stay. This is a beautiful place, and we hope you can learn to tolerate our differences and allow us to become close friends, in spite of our differences."

"We look forward to a long-term relationship," replied Chaviva in an attempt to be politically correct. But he secretly was extremely upset at how this trial turned out. He would be keeping a close eye on these visitors. He didn't want any form of satanic rituals or any other forbidden activities going on in his tribe.

Leaving the court area Cheng sent a mental message to Frida, *"We have the aliens after us, the technology guys wanting to kill us to stop us, and now even these guys in Center Earth have it out for us. Doesn't anybody like us?"*

"Not as long as we're different," was Frida's thoughtful response.

Chapter Thirty-Seven

Planning an Escape

November, 2020 AD, Nevada

Stephan returned to the control room of the alien ship. He felt he had learned all he could by reviewing his memories. He wanted to observe more activities so he could fill in some of the blanks in his understanding. To do this he needed to return to the control room and hoped that the aliens were too busy to bother with him.

Stephan renewed his surveillance of the processes of the control room that the aliens used as their spaceship. He learned a lot from their repetitious activities and from the words they broadcast as commands. He was learning, initially slowly but then more rapidly as he continued to watch. After another couple hours he started to feel reasonably comfortable that he could execute some basic commands on his own.

Stephan also started to listen more closely to the conversations, and he was able to start identifying personalities in the voices. Since everyone looked the same, at least to Stephan, he expected everyone to talk the same too. But that wasn't the case. The various voices that he heard had personalities and different tones in their voices, much the same as humans do in their conversations. He was thrilled to finally be able to identify a characteristic in these aliens that was similar to human behavior.

As he studied the personalities in the voices, he started to notice that there were more voices than there were aliens. He was slowly learning the language and even though he was not able to fully understand their conversations. He was able to pick up a few words here and there, enough to convince himself that the aliens in the control room were receiving commands from other individuals who were not in the control room.

One of the mysterious voices sounded threatening and demanding. Stephan concluded that this voice must be coming from the attacking alien ship. Apparently, it was trying to discourage the aliens on Stephan's ship and get them to come over to the opposing side. This voice kept badgering them and threatening. But the aliens in Stephan's control room seemed to take no notice. They simply continued working on their ship, as if their motions and button pushing actually could fix the ship.

Stephan also noticed another mysterious voice that was being broadcast ship wide. This voice didn't speak out very often, at most every couple hours, but when it did the entire group of aliens seemed to perk up and take notice. Stephan wasn't sure why this voice was so important to the aliens. It must be coming from some higher command, possibly even from the home planet. Stephan was curious how this voice didn't follow a chain of command. It simply spoke to everyone, and everyone listened and reacted simultaneously. Stephan wondered where this voice came from and what made it so important. Up to now these aliens seemed so team oriented. Everyone on the team seemed to have equal status. But this one voice was different somehow. Maybe this was the voice that Cheng had mentioned. Maybe this was the one overpowering person who ruled this culture.

It was getting late into the evening and Stephan was starting to get very tired. But he refused to leave the control room. He still hadn't figured out his escape plan and he wasn't going to sacrifice this opportunity to learn more about the alien's language. He wanted to learn about the operation of the ship. He wanted to learn the alien's areas of weakness. He hoped that at some point he would discover a way out.

It was after midnight when another alien ship appeared. This ship immediately attacked the two vessels that had previously attacked the ship that Stephan was on. Stephan's vessel was still transparent to anyone on the inside of the vessel allowing him to watch all the action.

The battle between the new ship and the two "bad guy'" ships looked like a couple kids playing dodge ball. The ships crashed into each other, knocking each other in a variety of directions. From Stephan's perspective, it still didn't seem like a battle. It still seemed like they were playing a game. But he knew it was much more serious than that.

Stephan's ship's crew attempted to leave the ground and join in the fray, but the ship simply wouldn't budge. His ball just sat there on the ground. It seemed dead.

Stephan again attempted to initiate conversations with the crew. *"Can someone tell me what is happening? Are we in trouble? Will we be destroyed?"*

There was no response. All the aliens seemed to be too busy and too concentrated to waste their time with him. So, Stephan continued to be a silent observer, hoping to learn even more about the aliens.

The battle between the alien balls raged on in the sky above Stephan's ship. The two attacking alien ships would get on either side of the newly arrived ship and would attempt to smash it from both sides. But, just at the last second, the new ship would bolt out of the way and the two "bad guy" ships would crash into each other. Another time the two attacking ships would attempt to push the newest ship to the ground, but again, just as they were about to hit the ground, the newer ship was somehow able to maneuver out of the way and instead the "bad guy" ships ended up crashing into the ground. These types of maneuvers continued for over sixty minutes with the newest ship always getting the upper hand even though it was outnumbered. It was obvious that this latest arrival had a lot more experience in doing battle. Stephan was impressed with the skills of this late arrival. This was obviously a group of well trained and highly experienced fighters.

The battle raged on into a second hour, with the manipulations and gyrations continuing. Neither side seemed to be getting the upper hand. Then suddenly, and completely unexpectedly, the battle stopped, leaving Stephan stunned. What had happened? There didn't seem to be a decisive winner, just a stalemate. Had they given up the battle? Stephan wasn't sure. The newly arrived alien ship came down and parked next to Stephan's stranded ship. It rolled up against his ship so that the two ships were touching. Immediately, as soon as they touched, the second ship became transparent to Stephan, and he could see right through it as if it wasn't there. The two ships had somehow united and become one.

Stephan could see aliens transferring back and forth between the two ships as if there was a crew coming on board to help with the repairs. Stephan wasn't sure what their role was, but it seemed like a reasonable guess.

The touching contact between the two ships had gone on for about 30 minutes when Stephan was inspired with the idea that maybe he could also transfer between the two ships. Maybe he could transfer himself into the control room of the other ship. That would present him with the opportunity to learn more about the aliens and about the operation of these ball space ships. Stephan proceeded to think about the control room of the other ship and suddenly he was there. It had happened so quickly that at first he wasn't sure he had moved. He knew he was there because his location relative to the ground was now different. The control room looked the same, and the aliens looked the same, but he had physically been moved. It was the strangest sensation Stephan had ever felt.

As soon as he arrived in the new control room, he started receiving messages. "*What are you doing here? Are you the earth person that can multiprogram?*" He also intercepted messages between the aliens because they were broadcast to everyone in the room. *"Is it safe for him to be in here? Do we want him observing us?"*

The aliens responded to each other with a variety of interactions, apparently not expecting Stephan to be able to understand their language and their communications. *"I don't like him in here. It makes me feel like I'm being watched." "These earth people are too backwards to understand our technology. They're no threat to us." "If we let him observe us, maybe he'll feel like we are willing to share with him and then maybe it will be easier for him to reveal his secrets to us too." "Leave him be. He'll soon be traveling with us to our home planet, and he'll never be coming back here again. So what threat is he to us?"*

This interaction confirmed to Stephan that he was indeed being kidnapped, never to see earth again. He didn't like what he was hearing. He became all the more determined to make sure he found a way to escape. Stephan decided not to give the aliens any indication that he could understand them. He wanted to maintain his secrecy. Maybe he would learn something more from their conversations.

Suddenly, and unexpectedly, the two "bad guy" balls slammed into the new ship that Stephan was now occupying. With this attack the aliens in the control room returned to their duties and quit worrying about Stephan's presence.

The hits were hard and caused everyone onboard to get a strong jolt. Stephan wasn't sure what had ended the ceasefire, but the battle resumed in full fury. The only difference was that now Stephan was on one of the ships that was doing battle.

Stephan's ship jerked upward, breaking free from the grasp of the other two ships. But it only went up about 100 feet when it suddenly reversed direction and came down hard on top of one of the "bad" ships, slamming it hard into the ground. In an instant Stephan knew that this ship was dead. It had suffered the fate of the ship that Stephan was originally aboard.

This evened the score. There was one ship out of commission from each side, and there was one ship that was still doing battle from each side. Unfortunately, this last maneuver had a price. Three of the aliens in the control room had been brutally thrown together by the impact and they were now lying on the ground, unable to move. They lay completely still.

Stephan was surprised about the aliens getting hurt. He hadn't seen any of them get hurt before. But what surprised him even more was the total lack of interest that the uninjured aliens had for their comrades. They treated it as if nothing had happened. There were three aliens lying on the ground and no one cared. Everyone just went on with their duties as before, occasionally stepping into one of the work locations of one of the fallen aliens in order to assist with their work. It was as if the fallen aliens had gone on break, and no one missed them. They were just gone.

The battle raged on. The two remaining balls kept hitting each other with full force, each knocking the other around, but no one seeming to have the advantage. Stephan noticed that it seemed as if this ship did better when it was fighting against two ships rather than just one.

Stephan walked over to one of the vacant holographic consoles to see what he could observe. He was surprised that he was able to determine what was happening and what had to be done next. He was brutally pushed away several times as one of the aliens barged in front of him in order to start some process on the computer where he was sitting. But Stephan wasn't discouraged. He wanted to learn, and he stayed there as long as possible in spite of obviously being in the way.

Another brutal hit from the "bad guys" caused the ship to again take a sharp surge, throwing most of the members of the crew across the room, their arms flaying in the air. Their uncoordinated motions looked comical. Stephan almost started laughing out loud, but he managed to control himself. He didn't want to draw attention to himself and possibly offend the aliens in the process.

A few jerks later Stephan was starting to get the hang of how the holographic control counsel worked. He had observed how the aliens always reacted the same way to some of the attacks. If the attacker was coming from the top, they would always move horizontally left. If the attacker came at them from the side they would move up or down. The responses were so preprogrammed that Stephan wondered why they even used aliens to make the moves. These repetitive moves could have easily been conducted by a computer.

Stephan decided to risk all and make an adjustment of his own. He wanted to test his knowledge. He wanted to see if he really knew how the controls worked. He decided that rather than do the expected move, he would force the ship to do something unexpected. Instead of dodging the attack, he was going to frontally return the attack. He waited till the "bad" ship was coming straight at them and then Stephan suddenly and quickly grabbed the holographic ball which represented the ship and jammed it towards the oncoming ship in a 45-degree upwards angle. This rammed the other ship so that it was jerked downward hard, and it came crashing down on its companion ship below it which had been grounded.

The aliens in the control room were stunned. They didn't know how to react to the sudden and reckless behavior of their ship. This is not what they were supposed to do.

The "bad" ship that crashed into its' friend limply fell to the side of the ship, hit the ground, rolled slightly, and just stayed in that position. Apparently, Stephan's move had disabled the second attacker. Both of the "bad guy" ships had been disabled.

However, rather than hearing joy and gratitude Stephan heard anger and condescension. *"That was an illegal move. It's not in our list of approved war moves. Who did this? They must be reprimanded. What gives them the right to brutally abuse our rules of engagement?"* There were no "Thank yous!" for Stephan. Instead, he felt threatened.

In spite of the negative responses, Stephan was feeling a new surge of confidence. He was mastering flying the alien ship and he was finally starting to get a reasonable grasp on the language.

The thought hit him that he hadn't communicated with the President in a long time. There had been so much activity, and Stephan was so focused on escaping from the aliens that he had forgotten to update the President. Perhaps it was time to give him an update.

Unfortunately, Stephan still had no clue about how he was going to escape.

Chapter Thirty-Eight

Plan for Action

November, 2020 AD, Washington, DC

"I have no idea what is going on or what to do next," complained the Secretary of Defense to the President of the United States. "We've had our fighters knocked out of the sky by these alien balls. We have no way of communicating with them except through Stephan. And we haven't been able to get ahold of Stephan. We've tried numerous times to call him using the phone that he was given, but apparently the signal cannot penetrate the shell of these balls. We think he is still on one of the balls, but we thought it was the one that was just shrunken down to the size of a basketball. So we don't really know what to do."

"Let's keep trying to get ahold of Stephan," replied the President. "That's really our only option. In the meantime, why don't we send a squadron of fighters to do overflight and see what's going on in the Nevada desert. Don't engage them because that hasn't worked out well for us. Just observe from a distance for now."

"Will do," replied the Sec Def as he stood and started to leave the room. Then he turned around and informed the President, "You heard about the assassination in South Africa and about the plane crash in Greenland?"

"Yes," replied the President. "What do we know about those two incidents?"

"The one in South Africa was definitely financed by the tech company assassins," explained the Sec Def. "There's direct evidence that points to them. But the one in Greenland is a mystery. Those were tech company assassins that were killed in that plane. I'm not sure how they found out about Stephan being in Greenland, and I'm even less sure who shot them down. We have no intelligence that explains any of it."

"Understood," responded the President as he turned away from looking at the Sec Def and looked down at his desk. "Let me know the minute you learn anything." The President didn't want his smile to reveal any of his hidden feelings about the incident.

"Will do," replied the Sec Def as he finally exited the office.

The President started to shuffle the papers on his desk, attempting to determine what the next priority should be. He hated being in the dark. He desperately wanted to know what these aliens were all about. But communication directly with them had proven to be impossible, and Stephan had become nonresponsive. He hoped that this was simply a communication block, and that Stephan was safe. What would he do if extremely frustrated if Stephan was injured and was no longer able to act as translator between the aliens and himself?

Just then a message came in. Stephan gave the President a long memory dump of what had been happening with the aliens. He explained that they were at war with themselves. He described how he had learned the language and had a better understanding of their intentions. He passed all this information to the President as quickly as possible.

The President, in turn, rapidly took notes, doing his best to record all the important key points. He realized the futility of his efforts and that sending the Air Force fighters as observers would gain him very little. But he decided to proceed with this plan anyway.

The President called his secretary on the speaker phone, "I need the cabinet and the Secretary of the Air Force in my cabinet room ASAP. Let me know when they are available."

"I'll get right on it," was the reply.

It took about 45 minutes to get everyone together. As usual, the President entered the cabinet room last, waiting until he was notified that everyone had arrived. He sat down and started the conversation, "I have received a message from Stephan, and he explained the situation to me. As we had guessed, the aliens are fighting each other, and it looks like the 'good guys' have won. At least we think they're the good guys since they put an end to the mining of our Nevada resources." The President went on to explain the battle that had occurred between the aliens. He explained that Stephan had learned a lot about their language and the operation of their ship. There were still a lot of gaps, but at least he was learning.

Then the President challenged, "As I see it, we have a couple of problems here. We have aliens stealing our resources and killing our people with their mining operation. We have aliens that are trying to kidnap

Stephan which is currently our only way of communicating with them. We have people within our own country trying to kill Stephan because of his XL capabilities. And we have other groups of people who have warrants out for his arrest simply because they want to turn him into a lab rat. Stephan wants to escape the ship, but he's worried about what will happen to him if he does. He feels he is in a no-win situation. Fortunately for us, but unfortunately for Stephan, the aliens are leaving us shortly, taking their stolen minerals and ships with them, and leaving us a mess in Nevada." Then, turning the conversation over to his cabinet he challenged them with, "What are your thoughts and suggestions?"

The Secretary of Defense started the conversation, "I sent some fighters into the region to observe close-up what is going on. They should be there in the next 30 minutes. We can see what they observe. My recommendation would be to have Stephan crash the last of these alien ships and then we capture the aliens and interrogate them. That will allow us to recapture the stolen minerals as well."

The Secretary of State chimed in, "That sounds extremely aggressive. I don't think we're up to a fight that we will have a challenging time winning. Wouldn't it be better to try to negotiate a truce before we alienate them completely? I would recommend that we start a conversation with them. We could talk to them about a trade; possibly our minerals for their technologies."

Next it was the Secretary of Education who jumped in, "I lean toward the pacifistic side when it comes to the aliens. If we get them mad, they may come stomping in here with all their guns blazing and we will be destroyed. And they'll still get the resources that they were after. I don't see us winning a battle with them. I only see us loosing.

"But we haven't explored the issues with protecting Stephan. Can we even hope to protect him? We're talking about big money attacking him. Big money has successfully penetrated our military and security forces in the past. Why wouldn't they be able to do it again? And then there are the scientific forces that want to turn him into a lab rat. They already have an outstanding court order which allows them the right to hold Stephan for experimentation and study. How is that any better than being dragged to an alien planet and becoming a lab rat there? I don't see how we have much to offer Stephan. We're destined to lose him."

"But if we lose him, we lose our ability to communicate with these aliens," inserted the President. "I wish we could communicate with him and see if he could work on a negotiated relationship, but apparently our phone signal doesn't get to him. And if he escapes from the aliens, then he'll be able to communicate with us but the aliens will probably not be too eager to talk to him so he loses his negotiation ability. This is a colossal mess. Help me out here," he pleaded with his cabinet. "What can we do?"

The President was amazed. This was the first time since he was elected President that the entire cabinet was silent. He couldn't believe that no one knew what to say.

Chapter Thirty-Nine

More Plans for an Escape

November, 2020 AD, Center Earth

In the meantime, Cheng and Frida were back in Jericho, after their ordeal in the courtroom. Luckily all the drama in Samaria did not slow down the background processing that their minds were doing on the aliens. They continued searching for clues that would help them identify a method for Stephan's escape. They interacted back and forth with Stephan, helping him decipher the language. The work that the three of them were doing together had now started to bear fruit. Stephan was starting to understand the communications that were going on in the ship and he now knew that he could have an impact on the operation of the alien ball.

With three of the four ships no longer in operation, control of the situation had now reverted to Stephan's ship. The atmosphere in the control room became more relaxed. Suddenly and unexpectedly the three aliens that had collapsed to the floor of the alien control room simply disappeared. They were just gone, with no explanation, and no one seemed worried about it. Stephan had no idea if they had died and been disposed of, or if they were now getting medical treatment. They were just gone.

Stephan continued his observations, but he no longer felt lost. He now understood what was happening and as he played back some of his recorded memories he learned even more about the operation of the ship. Observation was no longer important. He had enough memories to study. His learning didn't stop even if the aliens were now engaged in repetitive processes.

The first action of the aliens was to move swiftly to the on-going mining operation and put a stop to it. As they attacked the mining machine, aliens could be seen running in all directions away from the machine. Some came running toward the alien ship that Stephan was on, obviously deciding to change sides in this on-going battle. Others ran away trying to avoid the on-coming ship, possibly not realizing that there was no other rescue ship available and that they would perish in the earth's atmosphere.

The mining machine's motion stopped. Stephan's ship moved close to the machine and landed next to it. Then Stephan could see the transfer of materials from the mining machine on board the alien ball. Apparently, they had no intention of wasting what had already been mined.

With the fleeing of the aliens Stephan was forced back to reality. His original objective had been to escape from the captivity of the aliens. But he had become so distracted by all the battles and with his efforts to learn the alien language and how to fly the alien ship, that he had forgotten his original goal. Now he suddenly became aware once again of his original intention and objective.

Cheng. *"What am I going to do? How do I get back to Center Earth. The pilot that knew how to fly us there is gone and there is no one else who even knows how to get there? I'm not safe anywhere else. I'm not safe here on the surface, and I'm not safe with the aliens."* Then in a childish voice he said, *"I just want to go home!!!"*

Cheng and Frida were still with Abigail and Frida asked her, "Is there any way to get one of those air ships that you have here in Center Earth and use it to fly onto the surface to rescue Stephan?"

Abigail responded, "What's happening? Is Stephan in trouble?"

Cheng and Frida realized that all their conversations with Stephan had left Abigail out of the picture. She had no idea what was going on. Frida responded, "Sit down and we will update you on everything that has happened to Stephan in the last few hours."

She explained the alien battle, the capture of Stephan and the intention to take him back to their home planet. She discussed the fear that Stephan had about being released in Nevada where he would be pursued by various enemies on the surface.

Abigail responded, "My father has connections. I can't make any promises, but I will immediately return to Samaria and talk to him about the problem that Stephan is having. He has trouble telling his daughter no even if he thinks I'm being stupid. The chances are pretty good that he'll think this entire enterprise is stupid. Especially since he doesn't even believe in an outer surface. He thinks our world is all there is. So, it will take some fancy convincing on my part."

"Please do what you can," pled Cheng. "Frida and I shouldn't risk going to the surface because we are also being targeted. Even if we wanted to go, we have no means to get us there now that our pilot has been killed. I guess we didn't think that part through very carefully. Hopefully you will be able to find someone who is willing to take a little risk in order to return Stephan safely to Center Earth."

"I'll leave immediately," responded Abigail.

"Thanks so very much," replied Frida in a pleading voice. "It's hard for us because there are only three of us and we need to fight to support each other."

"It's hard for me too," responded Abigail. "I've become extremely fond of Stephan."

"We can see that," replied Cheng.

Cheng and Frida decided not to share Abigail's efforts with Stephan in case they failed. They didn't want to give him any more disappointments. Instead, they focused on developing an alternative plan which they would possibly need to execute if the first plan with Abigail's father failed.

Chapter Forty

Back Aboard the Ball

November, 2020 AD, Nevada

Stephan observed the extraction of the minerals from the mining machine and watched them being loaded onto the alien vessel. He found the extraction process fascinating. The materials seemed to move from the one location to the other with minimal alien involvement. It just seemed to happen. This process lasted for about three hours. Then, when the extraction was completed, the alien ship raised off the ground and returned back to its cohort ship, the one that was originally grounded and stranded. The two ships once again merged, and a transfer of aliens began with aliens moving from the stranded ship to the recently arrived "good guy" alien ship.

Stephan was under the impression that they were simply going to abandon the downed ship. So he embarked on a plan to escape into the downed ship, wait till the new ship departed, and then find a way to escape from that ship. He visualized the control room of the downed ship and suddenly he was present there.

But Stephan had grossly misjudged the process that the aliens were taking. Instead of abandoning the downed ship, they proceeded to start collapsing it. In a matter of minutes, the ship had shrunk to half its size and Stephan could see that he was in serious danger of getting smashed. He quickly visualized the control room of the operational alien ship that was still viable and suddenly he appeared there, just in time to avoid being crushed. He realized that the alien sensors were probably not checking for human life signs on the compressing ship, they were only checking for alien life signs, and there were none.

The downed ship continued to compress until it was the size of a basketball. Then it was loaded on board the remaining alien vessel where it would be returned to the home planet for repairs.

Stephan now realized that his time to escape from the grasp of the aliens was nearly at an end. It was now or never. If he didn't find a way to escape quickly, he may end up stranded on a foreign world far distant from anyone he knew and loved. This thought was becoming scarier and scarier.

Suddenly and unexpectedly a new problem presented itself. A squadron of U.S. Air Force fighters appeared. Stephan was uncertain of their intentions. He could see that the aliens in the control room were also stressed by their presence. Listening to the alien conversation Stephan heard them say, *"We need to get rid of these human pests. We don't want them watching and interfering with what we are doing. Perhaps a show of strength is necessary. Our last demonstration wasn't enough, or they wouldn't have come back. Let's knock these pests out of the sky."*

The alien ball started to slowly lift up off the ground. Stephan could see that the aliens were moving toward a threatening position. He could see that the Air Force, which was circling the area, wasn't recognizing the threat that was coming at them. Stephan knew he had to do something. In desperation he sent a message to the pilots in the Air Force formation, realizing that his messaging may result in scaring them more than helping them. But he had to try. He broadcast, *"This is Stephan from the XLs. The alien ship that is slowly rising is planning to attack you. You need to flee the area as quickly as possible."*

The Air Force fighters did not respond. It was as if they didn't receive Stephan's message. They continued circling the area where the alien ships had been downed, oblivious to the danger that they were in.

Stephan wondered if his messages weren't getting through the alien ball. He wondered if there was some type of block. He quickly discarded this thought when he realized that he had been communicating with Cheng and Frida. Then he wondered why he hadn't received any phone calls from the President. Perhaps these signals were being blocked by the ship. Looking at his phone he saw the indication that said, "No signal available." This didn't make sense because he knew that the satellite phone should always be receiving a signal. That explained why the President hadn't been in contact with him.

Stephan immediately sent the President the message, *"This is Stephan from the XLs. The alien ship is planning to attack the Air Force fighters. It considers them a threat to their security. They need to flee the area as quickly as possible."*

Stephan couldn't think of anything else that he could do except wait. But the fighters didn't react. Stephan wasn't sure if the President hadn't received the message or if they had simply decided to test the commitment of the aliens. Either way, the alien ship was poised to execute an attack against the American planes.

The alien ship suddenly shot straight up until it was at an altitude that put them even with the fighters. Then, without stopping, as if in one continuous motion, the alien ship flew directly towards the fighters. The alien ship was larger than the combined size of the fighter squadron of jets and was easily capable of taking them all out at once. The alien ship raced directly at the center of the fighter formation.

Stephan was in a panic. He didn't want to see more Americans killed. Just because the aliens saw them as inferior, it was no reason to squash them like annoying mosquitoes. The fighters weren't doing anything threatening. They weren't attacking. They were just observing. They didn't deserve to die.

As the alien craft raced toward the fighters Stephan decided to react. He reached into the holographic console as previously and grabbed the controls of the ball which represented the alien spacecraft. Shortly before impact he jerked the ball downwards driving it into a vertical dive toward the ground.

The aliens in the control room went into a panic. They could see their potential destruction. In their panic they reversed the flight of the alien ball and went back into a vertical climb, directly at the underside of the fighters. They were satisfied for the moment that they had saved their ship. But Stephan wasn't finished. He again grabbed the controls and slammed the alien ship into a decline, reversing its direction and once again aiming the enormous ball on a collision course with the ground.

Once again, the aliens immediately went into a panic, as was indicated by the flurry of activity and the excited comments that Stephan heard them communicate with each other. This time, when they changed the direction of the circular spaceship they moved it off in a horizontal direction. Stephan had no explanation for the lack of understanding, but the aliens didn't seem to connect the alien craft's change in direction to him. Their chatter suggested that they thought the fighters had some type of deflector shield which was diverting their attack. They didn't give Stephan the credit for the diversion. He assumed it was because they didn't think he understood their technology well enough to take control of their ship. If they realized what he was doing they would most likely have evicted him from the control room area. So he decided to not reveal his ability to control the space ship.

Stephan was delighted by their lack of understanding of his abilities. This gave him the edge to keep doing what he was doing. He watched as the alien ball moved away from the fighters and then slowly upwards. He sensed that they weren't done and that they were still planning some kind of sneak attack. He realized he would need to stay alert to their actions. He watched as the ship continued to climb until it was approximately twice as high as the fighters and then it moved slowly over the top of them. Stephan was able to identify their strategy. They had attacked from the side and from underneath with no luck. Now they were going to attempt an attack from above the fighters. Before the alien ship was completely over the top of the Air Force jets, the ball was sent downward in the direction of the fighters obviously hoping to hit the planes from above.

Stephan waited till the ship was close, continuing to support their mistaken idea that some kind of shield was blocking their attack. Then, rather than send the ship downward, this time Stephan reversed the ship and sent it upward, streaking towards the sky.

The aliens were dumbfounded. Now they were convinced that a shield was protecting the fighters and they decided to give up the fight. This was good for the fighters, but it was bad for Stephan because it might mean that the aliens are leaving for their home planet sooner than anticipated. And that's exactly what happened. The alien ship streaked upwards, leaving the earth's atmosphere in a matter of seconds, and bursting out into the openness of space.

Stephan was in a panic and didn't know what to do. He watched as Jupiter blew past them and he began to fear that this might be the last time he saw this solar system. He watched as earth shrunk further and further out into the distance.

Chapter Forty-One

In Space

November, 2020 AD, Washington, DC

"I just received a message from Stephan that the fighters flying around the aliens are in extreme danger." It was the President expressing his concerns to the Secretary of Defense of the United States.

"I'll issue the command to have them pulled back immediately," replied the secretary. "We don't need any more of our fighters knocked out of the sky."

In Washington the use of the term "immediate" didn't mean the same thing that it meant to most other people. By the time the chain-of-command was followed thirty minutes had passed and the alien ship had already left the earth's atmosphere. The squadron leader of the Air Force fighters was connected to the Secretary of Defense to give his report. Since the Secretary had already heard about some of the strange activities of the alien ship, he decided to also connect the President into the call.

Gerhard Plenert

"The alien ship acted like it was attacking us and then just as it was about to strike us it suddenly changed direction. It was as if they were just trying to scare us off," said the squadron leader and commander.

"That doesn't sound right," commented the President. "Why would they knock us out of the sky one time and then only try to scare us the second time?"

"It was strange," replied the commander. "They came at us from the side, then from the bottom, then from the top, as if they were trying to hit us from all angles. But they never made contact."

"This sounds like the work of Stephan," responded the President. "He was saying that he was starting to learn the language of these aliens and starting to learn how the controls of the spaceship functioned. Maybe he learned enough to actually manipulate the movements of the ship. I think we have him to thank if we ever see him again. I'm sure he did this at great risk because if they found him out there would most likely be repercussions. I understand that the ship he was on left the earth's atmosphere and went into space."

"That's correct," responded the commander. "I think he may be gone. There are still the two ships that were grounded. The ones left behind were the ones that were running the mining equipment. The winning ships are the ones that are gone."

The President reversed his previous order and said, "It is my understanding that the grounded ships pose no threat so I think you should stay in the area and continue your surveillance. Let us know the minute you see anything noteworthy."

November, 2020 AD, Near Jupiter

Cheng, who was hearing about Stephan's stress and concern, sent him a possible solution. If Stephan imitated the strange authoritarian voice that seemed to give commands out of nowhere, perhaps he could get the aliens to change their behavior. Perhaps he could imitate this overbearing and commanding voice and get the aliens to return to earth.

"I love it," responded Stephan. "I have absolutely nothing to lose. Besides, these aliens have some kind of mental block which is a weakness that we can exploit. For example, I still don't think they figured out that I diverted their ships away from our Air Force fighters."

Stephan used his memory of the god-like voice and used segments of its previous commands in order to assemble a message. That would be better than him using a voice that might be interpreted as fake. Using the actual voice of the commanding overlord would add a level of authenticity. He considered this a long shot, but then he was desperate enough to try anything.

Stephan's sent out the assembled message in the language of the aliens which commanded, *"Return to the earth and pick up any of the survivors of the enemy ships that want to join our cause."*

At first the aliens in the control room didn't move. Apparently, the command was a surprise to them. It must have been uncharacteristic of the behavior of the authoritarian voice. After a few minutes they started to chatter. From what Stephan could understand, they were surprised but obedient. They slowed the alien craft and then reversed direction, heading it back to earth.

This gave Stephan a little more time to try and discover a plan for escape. The only thing he could come up with was the possibility that if this ship bonded with one of the enemy ships just the way it had previously bonded with their damaged ship then perhaps Stephan would be able to jump from one ship to the other without anyone noticing it. Then it became a matter of Stephan getting off of that ship. But, since it was grounded, there would be a greater opportunity for escape.

Fortunately for Stephan that's exactly what happened. The ship suddenly, and almost instantaneously, returned to earth and parked next to one of the downed "bad guys" spaceships. It pushed up next to the ship and bonded with it so that the entirety of both ships became transparent to Stephan. The two ships seemed to become one. Stephan imagined himself in the control room of the other "bad guy" ship and suddenly he was there. But this time the control room was deserted. It felt as if the entire ship had been abandoned. Stephan was sure that this couldn't be the case. He was sure that just the control room had been emptied because there wasn't anything the aliens could do from there since the ship was disabled.

He imagined himself in the entry hall area where he had entered this ship the first time. He wasn't sure which of these two "bad guy" ships was the one used for his first contact, but he decided that since his "good guy" ship had bonded with this particular "bad guy" ship that it was worth a try. He also assumed that all the ships were probably very similar in layout and that even if this wasn't the same ship, it probably had the same entry hall area.

Once in the hall he discovered that this time he wasn't alone. There were at least a dozen aliens standing around communicating with each other. Stephan wasn't able to listen in on any of their communication because the communication was directly between each other. No one was sending out general messages to everyone.

Stephan went to one of the aliens who appeared to be standing off to the side and alone and asked, "*Is there a way to open the door and let me off this ship?*"

At first the alien didn't respond. Perhaps he was surprised that Stephan had spoken to him. Or perhaps he was taken aback by his assertiveness. After a couple of uncomfortable minutes, the alien responded with, "*I thought you were returning with us.*"

"*That was a mistake,*" replied Stephan. "*I can't come with you this time. Maybe the next time you come I can go with you. But this time I need to return to the earth and to my people.*"

The alien pulled out what appeared to be a small stone, about the size of a baseball, and started poking and sliding his finger on its surface. Apparently, that was some type of control mechanism because suddenly and unexpectedly the outer door started to open, and the gang plank started to extend and lower to the ground outside.

Stephan was so excited at the possibility that he might actually be able to get off the ship that he ran through the door and stepped out on the gang plank before it had completely lowered itself to the ground. It felt wonderful to be out of the ship and in earth's open air. It felt especially wonderful since he had come so close to never setting foot on the earth again.

Stephan ran down the plank and when it was still about three feet off the ground Stephan jumped off and ran. He had spotted a small clump of brush next to a cluster of boulders and decided to hide there. He knew that the aliens could probably find him if they really wanted to, but he hoped that maybe they had forgotten about him. Hopefully they were too busy focusing on the transfer of aliens between ships. Maybe they would be long gone before they realized that they had left him behind.

Stephan crawled into the brush, hoping at the last minute that he hadn't jumped into a nest of rattlesnakes. But, since he felt like he had just escaped something even worse than rattlesnakes, he decided to brave it. Then his phone, the one the President had given him, rang.

November, 2020 AD, Seattle, WA

"I just received news that Stephan has escaped from one of the alien balls." It was the special operations chief delivering the news to the Technosoft CEO. "It was a total surprise because we thought he was on a completely different ship. There must be some way these guys are able to transfer between ships. Anyway, the important thing is that he's on the ground in Nevada."

"Are we going after him? asked the CEO.

"I already sent a team out there."

"You know the whole world is going to be watching," expressed a concerned CEO. "We don't want our pictures splattered all over the world news showing us killing Stephan. We need to make this seem completely anonymous."

"I agree and that's our approach. We're going to go in there with a military helicopter. Our guys are going to be in full military gear. They will do the hit and get out of there before anyone has a chance to know what happened. It will be quick and sweet."

"Beautiful," replied the CEO. "Just make sure nothing leads back to us."

November, 2020 AD, Washington, DC

"I have Stephan on the phone," announced an excited secretary to the President.

"Excellent," was the President's excited response. "Transfer the call in here."

The phone on the President's desk started ringing and he picked up the call with, "Hello, is this Stephan?"

"Yes, it is Mr. President. Apparently, I wasn't able to receive calls while I was on the spaceship but now that I've been able to get off, we can communicate again."

"Where are you?" asked the President. "Are you safe?"

"I think I'm sitting in a rattlesnake den but it's safer than the den I just broke free from," replied Stephan.

"I'll send someone for you immediately," said the President. "We need to get you to somewhere safe."

"I don't know if there is a safe place," responded Stephan. "The guys with the lab coats have the courts on their side and they will try to get ahold of me as soon as they hear you have me, and then there's some group that killed the doctor and they have been trying to gun us down as well. Now I have the aliens who want to dissect me in one of their labs back home. The way I see it, I have three major groups after me and there is no safe place."

"I understand," replied the President. "I can see why you're so apprehensive. I'll have a conversation with my aides about finding you a safe haven. I'm not sure what that would be, but I have a whole team of people that are supposed to know those kinds of things. In the meantime, I'll send a military helicopter out there to try to pick you up. It can't be fun sitting with the rattlesnakes."

The President disconnected the call and immediately placed a call to the Secretary of Defense instructing him to send a rescue team after Stephan and to come up with a safe place to hide him with as few people as possible knowing about his whereabouts. What the President suspected but didn't know for certain was that his own team was informing Technosoft about Stephan and that any team sent out by the military would potentially include someone commissioned to eliminate Stephan.

The president was smart enough to realize that his own staffers couldn't be trusted, not even the Secretary of Defense or the CIA director. Because he had these suspicions, he had privately arranged for the elimination of the assassins that were en route to Greenland. Luckily the second group of assassins was foiled by Stephan getting on the alien spaceship. But in this situation, where urgency was critical, the president was desperate and didn't know what else to do. Stephan needed help now and hopefully he wouldn't regret working with the military. He would conduct his mole hunt later. Now it was important to get Stephan to safety.

Chapter Forty-Two

On the Run

November, 2020 AD, Nevada

Stephan watched the alien action from behind his hiding place. He stayed quiet and hidden. He tried not to move, assuming that movement might attract attention. He was sure a rattlesnake would any minute make its way out from between one of the rocks and bite him in the butt. But so far, he had been safe. He watched the United States Air Force fighter jets continuing to circle the area and he hoped they wouldn't do anything stupidly aggressive now that Stephan wasn't in the control room to divert any alien attacks.

Stephan watched as the "bad guy" alien ship that he had been on and from which he had just escaped, slowly shrunk up and was consumed by the other two alien ships. He assumed that all the aliens that had been on that ship had been transferred, either to join the "good guys" or they were brought into some form of captivity. Both of the two stranded "bad buy" ships were deflated down to the size of basketballs and brought on board the one remaining alien ball. Stephan wondered how four crews along with their ships were now incorporated into the space which had previously only held one crew.

After two hours, which seemed like an eternity to Stephan, the alien ship slowly rose from the ground, acting almost as if it was straining from the load. Then it started circling the area. Stephan suddenly realized that they were looking for him. Apparently, none of the aliens had seen where he went.

Stephan hunkered down into the scrub brush, which was thorny and painful. But he knew he had to avoid being spotted by the aliens. He remained motionless. The alien ship swooped the area in ever increasing circles. Stephan received messages from the aliens, *"Where are you? You need to come on board our ship. It is your duty to return to our planet so we can understand your abilities. Are you alive?"*

Stephan refused to answer, knowing that once he answered the aliens would be able to focus in on him and recapture him. After about 30 minutes of searching, the ship gave up and suddenly it was gone. It rose into the sky so rapidly, with blinding speed, that Stephan couldn't track its movements.

Stephan was overcome with relief, feeling confident that the aliens had given up on him. He also felt a tinge of disappointment at the missed opportunity to travel to a distant world. But what good was there in seeing this other world if there would never be anyone to talk about it.

With that problem out of his way, he could now focus on his next problem. He had no idea what to do next. The alien threat was gone, at least for now, but the other threats to his safety remained. Even though he didn't consider the President a direct and personal threat, Stephan considered the remainder of his staff a threat. Anyone who knew about Stephan's existence had the potential of sharing this knowledge with the people that were hunting him down, either for scientific purposes or to assassinate him.

With still no apparent sign that he was awakening any snakes, Stephan decided to remain in his hiding place a little longer. He communicated with Cheng and Frida about his plight, but they weren't able to offer him any reassurances. They were just delighted that he was still on earth. They had been scared that they had already lost him.

The jet fighters kept circling the area. Stephan wasn't sure why they were still there if the aliens were gone. He assumed it must be because he was still there. After about one hour the current squadron of fighters was replaced by a second, smaller group of just three planes. Shortly after the swap-out of the planes, Stephan could hear a helicopter off in the distance. It was then that his phone from the President rang.

"Hello," answered Stephan.

"This is the President. I am sending you a helicopter. You can come out of your hiding place and wave them down so they can pick you up and bring you to safety."

"Are you sure it's safe?" questioned Stephan. "I don't know who to trust anymore."

"I know what you mean. I tried to get you my most trusted team, our prized Air Force Special Operations squadron is in the helicopter, and they have been instructed to bring you to a safe location within Creech Air Force Base there in Nevada. You will have a detail assigned to guard you. I don't know how I can make you any safer than in the midst of a military compound with an armed guard. What you need to do is to come out of your hiding place and wave down the helicopter so they can find you and pick you up. The planes that are flying overhead have heat sensing equipment and they say they have already located you on the ground, and the helicopter is heading toward the location that they have specified."

Stephan was desperate for another alternative, but there wasn't one. Something just didn't feel right to him. But he couldn't put his finger on exactly what was wrong. It just felt wrong. But he couldn't stay in his hiding place forever. The thought of staying overnight in this location was scary. And now that they had located him with heat sensing equipment, there wasn't much use in hiding anyway. He decided to take the advice of the President and come out to meet the helicopter.

Stephan climbed on top of one of the boulders that he was hiding against, stood on top of it, and waved his arms in the attempt to catch the attention of the helicopter. The helicopter, which was now circling the area, spotted Stephan and changed its direction to move towards his location.

Stephan started to climb off the boulder and headed for an open area sufficiently large for the chopper to land. The chopper was also moving towards the same area so the two could meet up. The fighters that had been flying overhead moved off. Now that the helicopter had arrived, their work was done, and they started to head back to their airport base.

The helicopter parked on the ground and Stephan, being extra cautious, waited till the chopper blade quit moving before working his way to its side. He was still apprehensive, but at the same time desperate. As he started to move towards the open door of the helicopter, at the exact time when he was crossing under the tips of the blades, the body of the helicopter exploded up and out.

Stephan immediately fell to the ground. The blades of the helicopter exploded out and away from the chopper as vertical knives slicing the air in every direction. If Stephan had still been some distance from the helicopter, he would most likely have been sliced by one of these helicopter knives. But luckily, he was within the perimeter of their rotation and was protected from the knives. However, he wasn't as lucky when it came to the explosion of the fuselage which threw shrapnel in all directions. Stephan was hit by several pieces for debris, cutting a large gash into his right arm and burning his lower body with a hot piece of metal.

Stephan narrowly escaped being hit by one of the helicopter doors, which slammed to the ground less than two feet away. The door landed so that the curved interior was toward the ground, which created a small cavern below the door.

Stephan knew immediately that the attack was intended for him. He didn't know who the attackers were. He only knew that they were assuming that he was inside the helicopter. He didn't take time to look for the attacker. He knew he had to find protection in case the attackers came to inspect their handiwork. He spied the door, with its protective cavern caused by its curvature, and started crawling towards it.

As the noise of the explosion quieted and the dust storm it created settled down, the arrival of a second helicopter could be heard in the distance, followed by a spray of bullets. This second helicopter must have been the one that destroyed the helicopter intended for Stephan's rescue. The bullets were obviously intended to make sure there were no survivors. Stephan was motivated to move a little faster, but he didn't want to move so fast that he was noticeable. He finished slipping under the canopy of the door just as he heard the helicopter passing overhead. The spray of bullets continued, and he could see a stream of them coming at him. Fortunately, the door was armor plated and even though the noise was horrific, the bullets never passed through. Stephan was safe from the bullets, even if his burns and cuts from the explosion cursed his body with horrific pain.

Stephan remained motionless, scared, and confused. He was uncertain which group was chasing him. Was it the military that was shooting their own helicopters down? That didn't make sense. Was the President trying to lure him out so he could be eliminated? That didn't make sense either because he could have done it earlier. Which left Stephan with the conclusion that it must be the same people that were trying to eliminate Cheng and Frida earlier in Cusco. It must be the same people that killed the doctor. But how were they able to come up with a sufficient amount of fire power to take down a United States Air Force Security Forces team?

Stephan heard more explosions and shooting. He had no interest in looking outside of his hiding place to see what was happening. He had seen enough to last a lifetime. Stephan started to feel that he had seen the last of his days. He was scared that they would find him. In spite of the horrendous pain, he stayed hunkered down beneath the door and decided to stay there until someone came to him. Then they would either shoot him or pull him out and help him. He had no idea which of these two would occur, but he feared it would be the first.

Chapter Forty-Three

Disaster

November, 2020 AD, Washington,

"Are you kidding me!" barked the President at the news he had just received. "I send my best troops to do a simple recovery mission, and they end up getting destroyed? The person that I had promised to protect has been killed? How is that possible? And it's on American soil. It's not even a foreign operation where there may have been some level of risk. Normally I'm extremely proud of our military and the CIA, but this is an incredible embarrassment and a complete disaster."

The President was yelling at the Secretary of Defense who had just delivered the news. "This must have been an inside job of some kind," continued the President in his tirade. "You must have some kind of leak in your organization. I can't believe that your Special Forces team can no longer be trusted."

The Secretary was annoyed, exasperated, and defensive. "I just lost a team of my best men and you're accusing them of not being trustworthy. That's extremely offensive. We have no idea who this second helicopter belonged to. It looked military and had the weapons systems mounted to make it look military, but it wasn't one of ours. When the Air Force fighters heard the mayday cry coming from our helicopter, they immediately returned to the scene, but it was already too late. Our chopper was already splattered all over the countryside and the attacker was running for it."

The secretary continued his explanation, "Our fighters downed the attackers with a missile and they're still monitoring the area, but they don't see any signs of life at either of the chopper crash sights. They're going to continue monitoring the two areas by circling over them until relief helicopters can get on the scene, but it doesn't look good. I think we lost Stephan and the entire Security Forces crew."

"Who were these guys that attacked?" challenged the President.

"No idea," responded the secretary. "We'll know a lot more once our recovery team gets on the scene."

The President looked down and just shook his head in disgust. "I just can't believe that a promise I made can be broken so easily. Stephan manages to escape from the aliens just to be attacked and killed by idiots from earth. I am so terribly disappointed."

The Secretary was left speechless. He didn't know how to respond to the President's frustration. He could feel it too.

After a pause the President continued, "Let me know what the rescue, response and recovery team finds."

"Will do," responded the Secretary as he exited the Oval Office.

November, 2020 AD, Seattle, WA

"Are you kidding me?" responded the CEO of Technosoft in response to the news from his special operations chief. "They attacked a military helicopter? And they did it while fighters were flying overhead and watching the whole thing? Are these guys' idiots? If this comes back to me, it will be your head!"

The chief knew that when the CEO said "it will be your head" he wasn't using a metaphor. He did his best to cover his backside by saying, "We kept this action as sterile and disconnected as possible. I can't see any way that they would be able to connect this to you or to anyone at Technosoft."

"I hope not," replied the CEO. "And we're sure Stephan has been eliminated?"

"Positive," replied the chief. "They sent a report that everyone on the helicopter has been killed. I received the report just before our helicopter attack team was destroyed. In fact, we hadn't signed off on the conversation when they were attacked, and I heard the explosion. It nearly blew my eardrum out."

"I wish I could trust that report," whined the CEO. "This whole operation of trying to take out Stephan has been a complete disaster. There have been so many misfires that I'm gun shy when I hear a report that the operation has been completed."

"I'll keep my eyes and ears close to what is going on in the Nevada desert, but I'm sure we've finally completed the task," responded the chief. "And I have ears in Washington which will keep me informed from their end, but I'm sure this part of the operation has been completed."

"I sure hope so! Now we can concentrate on finding the other two XLs. We still need to eliminate them as well. And hopefully we make that part a cleaner operation."

November, 2020 AD, Nevada & Center Earth

Stephan received a message from the aliens, which said, *"We decided to leave but we need you to let us know where we can find you so we can pick you up. We will be sending another ship back at a future time to pick you up as soon as you let us know where you are. You are obligated to help us as a translator and to teach us about your abilities to process numerous activities at the same time. Contact us immediately so we can pick you up and bring you to our home world for study."*

"How rude," thought Stephan. *"They don't say it as a request. They don't even say 'please'. They say it as a demand. I can't believe that these guys would expect me to put an end to life as I know it just to become their lab experiment. Their culture definitely doesn't take the individual's interests into consideration. It's all about the will of their higher authority; that god voice that we kept hearing. How arrogant. I wonder what or who is behind that voice?"* Stephan didn't answer the alien's message. As far as he was concerned, he wanted them to think he was dead. That would be preferable to any other option. He had experienced his fill of these aliens.

Just then another message came into Stephan's mind. *"Stephan, are you out there?"* This time it was the pleasant voice of Frida sending Stephan a message, desperate to know if he escaped the aliens.

"Yes, I'm out here," replied Stephan to both Frida and Cheng. *"I successfully escaped from the alien ship and hid behind some brush in the Nevada desert. Then the President sent a helicopter to rescue me, but as I was about to get on the chopper it was destroyed by another helicopter. I suspect it's the same people that killed the doctor and that tried to kill you in Cusco. I barely escaped, but I'm hurt bad. I don't know what to do or who to trust. I'm scared that these killers are going to win. I still hear planes out there and I'm sure they're sending more helicopters. I really don't know what to do. I don't think I can trust anyone."*

"We're going to try to come out there and get you," responded Cheng.

"How are you going to pull that off?" asked Stephan. *"Those guys don't even believe there is an outer world. How are you going to get them to risk one of their flying saucers to come out here to rescue me?"*

"Abigail is pretty insistent," was Frida's response.

Realizing that Abigail was going to be involved, Stephan became extremely worried. *"Please don't,"* insisted Stephan. *"All you're going to do is put yourselves and her in danger too. Center Earth doesn't have the type of firepower that is needed to fend off these military machines. And the aliens may be coming back too. I don't want any of you to be placed at risk.*

Please don't come and put yourselves at risk. There's nothing you can do that will help. Center Earth just doesn't have the military strength."

"We'll just have to see how badly these Center Earth guys want to get involved," replied Cheng. "But, like Frida said, Abigail is extremely insistent and she's pushing her father to mount a rescue mission."

"*They won't even know where to come,*" responded Stephan. "*I won't be able to communicate with them if they did come out. So, their coming out would be a waste of time.*"

"*Cheng and I will have to come too,*" replied Frida.

"*That will give the bad guys the chance to get at all three of us,*" stressed Stephan again. "*You're opening the door for an end to the XLs.*"

"*Doesn't matter,*" replied Frida. "*You're worth it. Besides you just saved the world from becoming an alien mining mess. I think that deserves some attention. And your reward will be Abigail if she has anything to say about it. You wouldn't believe how intense she is about your safety.*"

"*Please don't try this,*" stressed Stephan. He was both excited about being saved while at the same time being scared at the risk associated with the prospect of their coming. He knew they would come, no matter how insistent he was, and he was selfishly glad. He was so tired of running. He just wanted to go home. And this seemed like the only viable option for him to get there. He welcomed and looked forward to their arrival.

Chapter Forty-Four

Saved at Last

November, 2020 AD, Nevada

Stephan had been hiding out under the door of the helicopter for over four hours. He could hear a lot of noise and activity. He heard helicopters arrive at the crash site and he could hear conversations. He knew these people were searching the wreckage for bodies and he somehow felt that it was his body that they were the most interested in. He was too scared to venture out because he didn't trust anyone. He didn't want to risk it. His only plan was to wait until it was dark, hoping that these people would go away, and then he could sneak out and escape. He vaguely remembered a freeway to the south. If he could get to the freeway, he might be able to get a ride to the next city. He would try to blend in and be inconspicuous. But then there were his injuries which would seriously incapacitate his ability to escape.

Stephan hoped that the people that were searching for him would assume he was dead and give up the search when night came. Once he had escaped and was safely away he would then work towards a plan to return to Center Earth and rejoin his friends there. He wasn't sure how he was going to accomplish that last step, but for now, he was focused on the first step in the process, which was to escape from the helicopter door and from the area of the crash site before the searchers found him.

The Nevada desert should have been engulfed in darkness, but it was still bright outside. The recovery team had set up lights surrounding the area. They continued working through the wreckage. Stephan was sure they were looking for him. But luckily, they hadn't worked their way to Stephan's specific location.

Stephan was extremely disappointed. His big escape plan to run away in the dark had been circumvented. His only hope was that they might get tired and quit sometime during the night, thereby still allowing him to escape under the cover of darkness.

Suddenly there was a lot of commotion outside. Stephan wasn't sure what was happening. His questions were answered when he received a message from Cheng, *"We're here at the crash site. Everyone below us is freaking out because they see a flying saucer and they think the aliens are back. But that's OK if it keeps them scared and busy. We need to know exactly where you are so we can pick you up."*

"Are you crazy?" complained Stephan. *"Are they going to start shooting at you?"*

"Nothing like that," replied Cheng. *"They're doing nothing that looks threatening. I think they are too scared to react. I think they're not the guys with the guns. They're a crash site investigation team and they're not weapons ready."*

"*Should I come out?*" questioned Stephan. "*I don't want to get shot at if I come out. I'm under the helicopter door, but they don't know I'm still alive. I think they think I'm dead. What do you suggest?*"

"*They're too busy looking at us and taking pictures so now would be a good time to come out. Run towards our ship and we'll come down quickly so you can get on board.*"

"*I've been burned pretty bad and can't run real fast so the closer you can get to me the easier it would be for me. Are you ready for me to run?*" asked Stephan.

"*Yes,*" replied Cheng. "*Go for it.*"

Stephan slowly crawled out from under the door, attempting to draw as little attention as possible to his presence. Once outside, running for it turned out to be challenging because of the gash in his leg and the burns from the hot shrapnel that hit him during the explosion. It hurt and was hard to run. But he knew this was his only chance to return to Center Earth. He was angry at the risk his friends were taking, but he was grateful that they had taken the risk to save him. Center Earth was now his home. It was now the only place where he felt safe. All the other options seemed way too risky.

Stephan hobbled, more than ran to the area under Center Earth's flying saucer. The saucer timed it perfectly, landing next to Stephan and opening the door to the saucer as it landed allowing him to board immediately as he arrived.

Suddenly, but not unexpectedly, shots started ringing out just as Stephan entered through the door. One of the shots hit him in the shoulder and knocked him down, but luckily, he fell into the saucer. The door started closing as the flying saucer lifted off the ground. The shots kept ringing out and the thin sides of the flying saucer made a poor shield. Unfortunately, many of the bullets came through, striking various pieces of equipment inside the vessel. Frida also received one of these bullets in her leg. But fortunately, even though the bullet wasn't stopped by the skin of the saucer, it had slowed down enough to where the damage to Frida was minimal.

Getting shot at made the escape even more urgent. The pilot of the flying saucer, Abigail's father, rapidly took the ship into a steep ascent and then headed out over the American countryside. The flight was so fast that the US military didn't even have enough time to scramble a response. By the time they were in the air, the saucer was back out over the Atlantic Ocean heading north.

The celebration of the reunion had to wait until the flying saucer was out of range. Once they were over the Atlantic everyone aboard the saucer was able to relax and then it was time for a glorious reunion, with Abigail and Frida wrapping themselves around Stephan in an excited hug. All three of them started shedding tears of joy. Cheng's emotions were also at the surface, and he couldn't stop patting Stephan on the back. The XLs were reunited and safe from aliens, the assassins, and even the President. Hopefully no one would ever be able to find them in Center Earth. No one on the surface knew about Center Earth and no one would be able to find them.

With the reunion celebration completed, Frida, Abigail, and Cheng went to work on Stephan and Abigail's wounds. They would do a better job once they were back at Center Earth and had better medical equipment, but for now, they did the best they could cleaning and bandaging the wounds.

November, 2020 AD, Washington, DC

"You mean he's alive?" questioned the President.

"Apparently he was hiding under the door of the helicopter the whole time," replied the Secretary of Defense. "A flying saucer arrived on the scene, which was the first time we've seen a flying saucer up close. We have no idea where it came from. Was it from the aliens? We really don't know. All we know is that Stephan crawled out from under the door, ran into the saucer, and they flew off. The whole thing is a mystery. The crew on the ground was so busy taking pictures that they never put up much of a fight to try to stop the escape. It has everyone baffled. Here, I have a video of the escape for you to watch." The Secretary handed a disk to the President who plugged it into his computer and watched the replay.

"This video came from the surveillance video of the recovery team," explained the Secretary.

The President perked up near the end of the video and said, "Did they just shoot him? Why were they shooting at him? It looks like they hit him. This looks a lot more like a rescue mission than a kidnapping. It looks like Stephan was trying to escape your rescue and recovery team. And where did the guns come from? Who shot him? I wonder if he is okay. Now we still don't know if he's okay." The president slammed his hand on the desk, looked the Sec Def directly in the eyes, and yelled, "Why were they shooting at him?"

"It was a mistake," replied the Secretary. "The whole thing happened so fast that the troops didn't know how to react. They thought the aliens were going after Stephan and they were shooting at the aliens."

"But they shot Stephan, not the aliens," exclaimed an exasperated President.

"Understood," was the Secretary's reply. "It was a mistake."

"That poor kid," responded the President. "It seems like everyone's out to kill him or kidnap him. He didn't seem to stand a chance."

The meeting ended and the Secretary left the oval office, heading out into the reception area where he used his cell phone to place an immediate call to Seattle. "Hello," was the response at the other end of the line.

"Hello," replied the Secretary. "I just wanted to let you know that Stephan is still alive. Apparently, he was hiding under one of the doors of the helicopter and we have a video of him escaping on board a flying saucer. We have no idea where the flying saucer headed off to or where it came from. One of the guys did get a shot off, but it looks like it just hit him in the shoulder."

"Unbelievable!" exclaimed the CEO. "That guy has more lives than a cat. Thanks for the update and let me know if you learn where he's at."

"Will do," explained the Secretary.

November, 2020 AD, Washington, DC

The president's secretary beeped into the oval office. "Yes?" asked the President.

"Agent Elliott is here and says he has an urgent message for you," responded the secretary.

"Send him in immediately," responded the President. The agent immediately opened the door and entered. "What have you got," questioned the President.

"We just recorded a call that I think you will be extremely interested in." Then the Secret Service agent, who was assigned as a personal agent to the president, working directly for the president and answering only to the president, played back the phone call that was made just a few minutes earlier between the Sec Def and Technsoft's CEO.

"Unbelievable!" exclaimed the president. Then he pushed a button on his desk and instructed his secretary, "Call the Sec Def and tell him I need him in my office immediately."

The Sec Def hadn't left the area, so he was easy to find and was quickly returned to the oval office. He entered the room and asked, "What's up."

The president looked up at him, and then pressed the 'play' button on his computer. The president, the Sec Def, and Agent Elliott listened to the recording of the conversation between the Sec Def and the CEO. Then the president spoke directly to the Sec Def and said, "You have 24 hours to tenure your unconditional resignation from not just your position as Secretary of

Defense, but from all your legal entanglements and areas of influence here in Washington. I want you gone. I can't trust you and I don't want to see you ever again. You betrayed me and I can't work with people I can't trust. And you called this 'A big mistake'. It was defiantly your big mistake."

"You'll get my resignation, but you can't use a recording as evidence in court," responded a defiant Sec Def. He didn't even attempt to defend his actions.

"The courts are the least of your problems," responded the president. "If you don't do what I just ordered you to do, the media will make hash out of you. I don't need to go to court to destroy you. And if I can connect the Technosoft CEO to some of the assassinations that have occurred, like the Doctors, and the helicopter crew, then you'll be connected with that as well. The court of public opinion will hang you before you have a chance to complain to a judge."

"Understood," responded the Sec Def, who then turned and left the office.

The president turned to Agent Elliott and said, "Good job. But don't quit monitoring him just yet. This fight may not be over yet and we may need all the evidence we can collect."

"Yes sir," was the agent's response as he turned and left the oval office, closing the door behind him.

Chapter Forty-Five

Celebration

November, 2021 AD, Center Earth

It was a big day in Jericho. It was two months since the aliens had left the earth and none of the XLs had received any messages from them since their departure. In Jericho, visitors were coming from all corners of the tribal realm. This was the first time in the experience of everyone in the tribe when an event of this type had occurred. It would be a unique and exciting celebration.

The double wedding would be a mixture of Center Earth and outer earth traditions and methods. The wedding gown was red, representing the coming of the Messiah for the Jewish traditions, and the return of Jesus Christ for the Christian traditions. The music was outer world and traditional. The wedding was outdoors, in the central meeting area of the Jericho community. In the front, under the canopy, stood the brides and their grooms.

Stephan and Cheng were sweating profusely. This event was scarier than being taken away by aliens. It might even be scarier than being shot at! But it was necessary. They each loved their ladies and they wanted to demonstrate their long-term commitment. This was what was needed in order to show that commitment. Neither of them minded getting married. It's just that they were stepping into the realm of the unknown, and that's what scared them. The music didn't help. It just emphasized the importance of what was happening.

For Frida and Abigail, it was an exciting and perfect day. They both loved their guys enough that they would do anything for them, but they were delighted by the guys' willingness to take this big step and make this commitment. They weren't nervous like the guys, just excited. It was something that each of them had always dreamed of, and it was happening today.

The wedding ceremony started. The Priesthood leader went through the ritual wording required in a wedding ceremony. But, since there was the mixture of the outer world traditions, he also included the parts where the brides and grooms each said, "I do."

Then, when all the words were said, a glass was laid in front of each of the grooms, and as they were about to crush the glass, a symbol of the completion of the marriage ritual, the three XLs each received a message which said, *"We are coming back for you. We will be there in three days. Be ready. You will be coming to our home planet so we can learn more about you."*

The three XLs looked at each other in shock but said nothing. But they defiantly weren't going to allow the excitement of this moment to be ruined. Cheng and Stephan simultaneously each crushed their respective glasses. The celebration, along with the cake and the dancing kicked into full gear.

ABOUT THE AUTHOR

Dr. Gerhard Plenert has a PhD in Resource Economics and Operations Management, which are fancy words for "a whole lot of math."

He spent 12 years as a university professor and the remainder of his life living and working all over the world in places like Europe, Asia, the Middle East, Latin America, and of course North America.

He has 8 children, and his grandchildren are just starting to get numbered, the last count was 13. He has successfully published over 24 books and close to 200 articles on various business and academic topics. But his love is Jason Bourne and James Bond.

Other Books by the Author

A group of modern-day Templars working as mercenaries are hired by a group of Neo-Nazis to find the Ark of the Covenant. When the Templars learn of the real intent of the Neo-Nazis...to detonate a nuclear device at the Pentagon to celebrate Adolph Hitler's birthday, the Templars unknowingly join forces with the CIA to defuse the catastrophic event. The ensuing suspenseful countdown leads to exotic locations and thought-provoking themes and plots that bring the reader in a tangled web of intrigue and mystery.

Both books are available on Amazon and from fine bookstores everywhere.

www.ingramcontent.com/pod-product-compliance
Lightning Source LLC
Chambersburg PA
CBHW070838260626
47170CB00007B/2422